FOUR
Decades

FOUR
Decades

New and Selected Stories

GORDON WEAVER

University of Missouri Press

COLUMBIA AND LONDON

Copyright © 1997 by
Gordon Weaver
University of Missouri Press, Columbia, Missouri 65201
Printed and bound in the United States of America
All rights reserved
5 4 3 2 1   01 00 99 98 97

Library of Congress Cataloging-in-Publication Data

Weaver, Gordon.
    Four decades : new and selected stories / Gordon Weaver.
       p.   cm.
    Contents : When times sit in—Haskell hooked on the Northern
Cheyenne—Wouldn't I?—Getting serious—Hog's heart—Ah art!
Oh life!—The good man of Stillwater, Oklahoma—Whiskey,
whiskey, gin, gin, gin—The parts of speech—Madness—Return
of the Boyceville flash—Saint Philomena, pray for us.
    ISBN 0-8262-1113-5 (alk. paper)
    1. United States—Social life and customs—20th century—Fiction.
I. Title.
PS3573.E17F68   1997
813'.54—dc21   97-6858
                                                         CIP

∞™ This paper meets the requirements of the
American National Standard for Permanence of Paper
for Printed Library Materials, Z39.48, 1984.

Text Design: Elizabeth K. Young
Cover Design: Kristie Lee
Typesetter: BOOKCOMP
Printer and binder: Thomson-Shore, Inc.
Typefaces: Sabon, Helvetica Neue Condensed Light

For my wife and daughters,

Judy, Kristina, Anna, Jessica,

and for W. D. Wetherell,

one of the very best!

Also by Gordon Weaver

NOVELS

Count a Lonely Cadence

Give Him a Stone

Circling Byzantium

The Eight Corners of the World

STORY COLLECTIONS

The Entombed Man of Thule

Such Waltzing Was Not Easy

Getting Serious

Morality Play

A World Quite Round

Men Who Would Be Good

The Way We Know in Dreams

Contents

FOUR
Decades

At thirty man suspects himself a fool;
Knows it at forty, and reforms his plan;
At fifty chides his infamous delay,
Pushes his prudent purpose to resolve;
In all magnanimity of thought
Resolves; and re-resolves; then dies the same.

—Edward Young, *The Complaint: Night Thoughts*

When Times Sit In

IT WAS CLONTINE, the Red Fox, who first brought the dark specter of Times into Jay Fair's consciousness. The two men had been talking in front of Brown's Shine Parlor and Leather Products, and Jay Fair had started toward his Impala convertible at the curb when Clontine spoke to him of Times. It was not that Jay Fair did not know of Times, but only that this mention forced the image before him and spoiled what had been a cheerful and free outlook on the warm late summer afternoon.

"You cool now, Jay Fair," said Clontine, "but you never know when Times be right behind you, smilin' and grinnin' and just waitin' to sit in and make you low."

Jay Fair stopped and turned around to face the man whose hair color made most of the boys refer to him as Red Fox behind his back. His brow creased in puzzlement, as though the name of Times had caused him an inexplicable chill.

"No, mon, no," Jay Fair said, brushing the cold, dark hint of Times away from some dusky corner of his mind. "Times don't be lookin' for no Jay Fair. Jay Fair be cool always, and his coins be too long for old Times to be sittin' in, mon."

Clontine turned away to go into Brown's as he threw over his shoulder, "Just when you think you at you best, that be when Times get on you and beat you down so low you don't have enough to buy a coke, and you be over in line for turkey-neck at the Baptist Church."

"Aw, mon, no," Jay Fair said, dismissing Times and Clontine both. He held his arm close to his side, spreading out his hand and waggling his palm, saying "Be cool, mon, be cool, don't hurt yourself none."

"I see you, man," Clontine said.

"I gone soak over to Joe Harris's and play me a little number . . . just like I do if Times come too close," Jay Fair fired as a parting shot. But Clontine had disappeared into Brown's and had not heard him.

Jay Fair slid across the hot leather upholstery of the Impala and ensconced himself behind the wheel. No, no mon, Times don't be lookin' for no Jay Fair.

But that image, that picture of Times was somehow too clear in his mind's eye. Incredibly, he shuddered in the heat from a flash he had that Times might be walking up the street even now, hoping to catch him unaware, perhaps slide in beside him in the Impala and go riding about the streets with him.

No, mon, no, damn no! Jay Fair roared away from the curb, instantly relieved. Times had been left somewhere behind, and besides, he was always too cool.

He drove vaguely in the direction of Joe Harris's, but to impress upon himself the very concreteness of his immunity to Times, he made several detours to pass by the corners where he knew some boys would be loitering. He passed them slowly, with his radio playing loudly.

"Hey, man, Jay Fair, you got some tough sounds!" they yelled.

"My man!" they said with a wave.

Jay Fair dipped his head only slightly in their direction. He let his arm hang down over the side of the Impala, and just as he passed closest to a group of his men, he waggled his palm and said, "Be cool, be cool, don't hurt yourself none," in a controlled voice that could barely be heard.

No, mon, no, Times don't be nowheres near Jay Fair. Jay Fair be the man that Times don't get, don't never get. No, Times could not touch, must never touch him. And if Times should ever sit in, if Times should ever grin and smile, and make Jay Fair low, he must never admit it. He must fight Times off and never, never even to himself, admit it. Jay Fair pressed down on the accelerator pedal, and the Impala's tailpipes chuckled for him as he headed toward Joe Harris's in haste to play a number, sure he would hit one.

"My man! Jay Fair!" Joe Harris said happily when he walked in.

"Say, Jay Fair," said another man who was about to begin a game of nine ball.

"Be cool, be cool," Jay Fair answered with his waggling palm.

"What you need, Jay Fair?" Joe Harris asked.

"My coins be shortin' up just a little, so I figure I maybe play a few small numbers, mon."

"Yeah, Jay Fair, play a number and see can we keep old Times off us, huh," Joe Harris said as he walked behind the bar to get a policy slip.

Like a foggy shroud, Jay Fair felt Times near him, frightening him terribly. "Goddamn, mon, ain't nobody ask you to tell me none about Times! Goddamn, if you be jivin' me all the time when I come in here, I go somewheres else for a number and you don't never see no Jay Fair in here!" He slammed his fist down on the bar in front of Joe Harris, almost ready for violence.

"Easy, man, easy, you know I'm okay, you know how I pay off when you win." The man at the pool table looked with curiosity at Jay Fair, who was sorry now that he had shouted. But the reference to Times had struck home like the sound of a coffin being nailed shut, coming so soon after Clontine, and his money was getting just a little short.

He had intended to play only one number, maybe two, but now he panicked just a bit. "I play about three for three," he said. He removed nine dollars from his gold clip and gave them to Joe Harris. Jay Fair had not had a dream for several days, so he picked his numbers at random. He waited impatiently for Joe Harris to fill out the slips, wanting to be back out in the sun with his Impala, for it seemed darker and unfriendly in the pool hall now, almost cold.

"Be cool," he said quietly as he left.

He drove about the streets again, waving to boys that he knew basking in their respectful recognition of him, but he could not shake Times's shade. He passed two men sweeping the gutter on a relief project, and he could imagine Times pointing to them, saying to him: *See there Jay Fair that's what I'm gone do to you. I'm gone sit in and take away all you coins and you be so low when winter come you don't have enough to buy you a coke,* the voice rolling like the fall of cold, black clods of frozen earth.

No, mon, damn Times, damn winter, damn no turkey-neck soup, mon, Jay Fair be cool always, and no Times and no nothin' be sittin' in on him! No, not to him, not to no Jay Fair that don't happen. There be plenty boys for old Times, he don't be needin' no Jay Fair.

And though Jay Fair cruised the streets and waved to his boys, and though he could feel the solidness of his security in the strong whine of the Impala, he could not evade the shadow of Times. Finally, in a desperate attempt to quiet his fear, he drove to his sister's house.

"Jay Fair," she said, "what you gettin' all dressed for?"

"Jay Fair be goin' to Celebrity Night at the Bronzeville and soak a while," he answered. He had put on his finest summer suit, shaved and trimmed his thin moustache.

"You always be so clean," his sister said in admiration.

"Jay Fair be cool always," he said with pride. He had given himself a hair process too, and it lay smooth and bright as soft, black leather. He knotted a gold tie and thought of how far the long knife of Times must be from him now.

Jay Fair, you wig be leapin' and you creases be all clean . . . you got a big tough diamond ring, and you wheels be mean. He laughed. Mon, if old Times creep around, I be specializin' in rhymin' up a few small items on him, and just read old Times off. "Jay Fair!" he sang, "you much too young a man to have so many women!" He grabbed his sister and danced her laughingly around the room.

The band was swinging when he walked into the Bronzeville, but the leader made a special welcome for him with a dip of his horn. Jay Fair said nothing, only waggled his palm in return. He took a table to one side, ordering a drink, but ignoring it to tap out the numbers the band played.

Several women smiled to him from the bar, but he only tacitly recognized them; sometimes with a raised eyebrow of skepticism, sometimes with a wry expression of disbelief and disdain. He was cool always.

Later, when Jay Fair was a little intoxicated, the band leader put the spotlight on him and said to the crowd, after a roll of the trap drum, "I see we have one local celebrity here who I hope will oblige us by doing a number for us." The crowd, most of whom knew him, and knew that he was always cool, stomped and whistled.

"Hey, my man, come on, give us one number!"

"Hey you, you Jay Fair, sing one man!"

Jay Fair smirked only slightly and looked down at his drink. "Naw, mon, naw," he whispered.

"What say, Jay Fair?" the band leader said. "Let's give the man a hand and see will he sing one for us," he called to the crowd. The crowd clapped loudly, then louder, as Jay Fair stood up reluctantly and ambled toward the bandstand. All the way across the floor he waggled both his palms and softly said, "Be cool, be cool."

He started off with "Traveling Man," which got such a hand that he did "Annie Had a Baby" and "Long John" too before he did a small step and hopped lightly off the bandstand and ambled to his table with the spotlight following him, saying "Be cool, be cool" all the way back.

No, old ghost Times don't be no place near the Bronzeville tonight. Times out in the street, prowlin' around all cold and hungry, but Jay Fair be sittin' in at the Bronzeville, too cool, always too cool.

The singing and the applause, and perhaps the few drinks had mellowed him a little; they had really made him feel secure. Never had he felt quite so fine and safe, so immortal. He decided to really do it right, really get a feeling so far away from Times that he might never have to think of it again, ever.

Jay Fair called over to one of the girls at the bar, the lightest and prettiest one in the Bronzeville. "Lee, hey Lee baby, come sit by Jay Fair and have a small nip." She came over quickly, and he had the waitress pour a half-pint of Ancient Age up for two. Then he called over the man who took Polaroid pictures. He put his arm around the girl and they raised their glasses in a toast to whoever might look at the photo someday, and the man snapped them.

Many times in the future, Jay Fair would look at the photo and still not believe in it. Everything in it was so cool. The woman is the lightest and prettiest. His wig is leaping, and the baronial crest on the left breast of his fine summer jacket is distinct. The label on the Ancient Age can be read, and on the hand that holds his glass, Jay Fair's diamond looks big.

But somewhere, either to the left or the right of the picture, Times must have been watching. Just at that very moment, Jay Fair thought, when the man was taking the picture, old Times must have slipped up from somewhere near the bar, silent as an undertaker, and cast the mold of his leer over Jay Fair and his light, pretty woman. Just when he felt the best, when he felt sure that Times was locked out of the Bronzeville like the plague, and out of his life forever, Times must have been smiling on him, ready to sit in.

Times waited. The good safe feeling lasted for a while. The band leader motioned him over, and they went into the men's room and smoked some stuff. When he was quite mellow, Jay Fair went back to the woman and told her that he would look her up sometime.

"Hey, my man, Jay Fair," someone at the bar shouted after him, "you goin' already?"

"Be cool, mon, be cool," Jay Fair said with his hands. There were more friendly words from the bar for him that echoed happily over the dark sidewalk when he was outside, and their warmth aided Jay Fair in feeling that he walked at least a foot above the pavement, despite the slightly sobering effect of the chill night air.

Times was gone, the chance of hitting a number on Joe Harris's wheel, the applause of the crowd for his singing, all gone, and only the dream-walk a foot above the pavement.

He slid behind the wheel of the Impala. No, mon, no, Jay Fair be always cool. Always and always. It was cold, but then summer was nearly over, and damn winter anyhow! Near him, if he had not smoked, and if he were not mellow on the Ancient Age, he would have felt the bony movements of Times. But as Clontine said, Times would sit in only when Jay Fair had forgotten all about him; then Times would be looking for him.

He slapped the Impala into gear, and cramping the wheel hard, he jumped the car into the middle of the street and directly into the path of a Buick coming up behind.

There was an impact that threw him up against the wheel, bumping him up against the windshield, and a tin-sounding crackle and crumple of the rear end of the Impala mashing in. Jay Fair was jarred to his senses, coming down that one foot of air cushion to walk on the pavement like all mortal men, and he perceived the hand and the skull-smile of Times in what had happened.

He tried to talk to the big man from the Buick. "Look, mon, let's be cool in this. You car still move, so you just drive away, and you send me the bill for whatever you be needin', and we don't need no police or nothin' on this."

"No, hell no," the big man said excitedly, "we've got to call an officer and make a report, I have to make a report for my insurance."

Jay Fair pleaded with him, almost crying, but the man seemed completely unconcerned with what this would mean for Jay Fair who owed money on the wrecked Impala and had not bothered with insurance.

"Mon," he said, "I got to get me out of this, I can't be havin' no trouble now."

"Look, I'm not going to argue with you, I'm going to call a squad and you can talk to the police about . . ."

No, the man would not listen, and in his relentless, nonpitying attitude of unconcern, Jay Fair imagined the cruel laughter of Times. Perhaps he thought that Times had come to rest, gleefully, on the big man's shoulder, or maybe he even thought that the big man was Times.

But it was more of a last, die-hard swing of protest against the senseless unfairness of Times that Jay Fair felt as he lashed out with his best punch, a bolo right, catching the man neatly under the chin, sprawling him on the street. The man's wife screamed from inside the Buick.

The big man got up and went into a professional crouch, and Jay Fair forgot the frustration of fighting against Times and reverted to his cool fighting self. Maybe I got me a real dick-head here, he thought, maybe he gone nothin' but lay some strong wood on me.

No, the man had nothing; Jay Fair caught him once, twice, three times, a small combination that he had learned well and practiced hard, and the man sprawled limply in the street again. Come on again, mon, for Jay Fair be rhymin' you up and readin' you off, and layin' some bad, bad wood on you ugly head!

By then there were people from the Bronzeville watching, and a policeman grabbed Jay Fair's arm. He turned and hit the policeman, staggering him. Then he knew it was Times, hearing the voice of falling earth. *I gone take you, Jay Fair, gone take you and bury you so you don't be able to buy you a coke, yeah, gone take you, Jay Fair!* Times closing in on him. Come and get it, you! Come and get you wood from Jay Fair, who be too cool always for you, come and he stick a whole mess of lef' hooks on you! The policeman arched his nightstick high and hit Jay Fair only medium hard, and then straddled him to cuff his hands behind his back.

"Lawyer Shulsky," Jay Fair said into the phone, "this be Jay Fair. You come down here and be gettin' me loose. This don't be too cool, mon, not hittin' on too much. They got me in the slam, mon."

When Lawyer Shulsky, whom Jay Fair had long ago engaged to handle such items, had arrived to go bail for him, he asked to see his client before doing anything.

"I'm gonna have to have some money, Jay, I'm just gonna have to have something. You're in pretty deep, pretty serious this time. This ain't no bastardy action, boy, you're in with the big boys now, assault, drunken driving, resisting apprehension, boy, you're in trouble."

"Mon, I don't be havin' too much," Jay Fair said weakly. "Times got . . . I don't be too long on my coins, mon." No, mon, no, Jay Fair don't be sayin' nothin' about Times, or you be so low you never get up. No, not you, Jay Fair, you be cool always, you find a way, got to be a way.

"I'll tell you what," Lawyer Shulsky said in his cigar wheeze, "you give me that diamond and what money you got, and I'll see what I can get for what's left of the car, and I'll see what I can do about bail. You're gonna have to take care of the lien on the car your own way, and this ain't got nothing to do with whatever you get sued for. If you want help on that, or when you come to trial, I'm gonna have to see some more money, okay?"

"Yeah, mon," Jay Fair said, removing his ring, "just be gettin' me outta the slam."

When the bail was set, Jay Fair was released. He had expected to be cheered by the open streets after the gloom of the lockup, but there was a feeling of overcast to the outside also. Times, mon, Times be anyplace huntin' you, very close now. Without a cent, he waited until it was dark so that he could sneak to his sister's house.

"Jay Fair, I can't be havin' you around here when you don't bring no money into this house. You gonna have to leave your clothes here so I got somethin' if you wanna sleep here," his sister said.

As Times patiently waited for him, he made a final effort to escape from the end that he knew loomed for him, still unwilling to believe that it could happen to him. He took the metal comb and the oil and went to a different neighborhood, where few of the boys knew him, to make enough money for a last show. There was still a chance, he could take a couple of numbers at Joe Harris's; he might be right back there again, straight, cool.

"Hey, mon," Jay Fair said as the stranger walked by. He slouched in front of a tavern with the oil and the comb in a paper sack. "Mon, you wig don't be looking too swell, not too tough. Maybe I could be settin' it leapin' for you with a small process."

"How much you want?"

"Say five and no jive, mon." He could still rhyme up a few small items at will.

"You got a place?"

"No, mon, anywheres you say."

He stayed away from his sister's, for he was in disgrace there. He held on to his money until he had enough to make a payment at the credit clothiers, where he fitted himself with a new front of British-style clothes. One day he set his hair with a process and went to an auto dealer's, where he persuaded the salesman to let him have a Cadillac for a test drive.

He went slowly past Brown's Shine Parlor and Leather Products where he knew the boys would be. For seventy feet he drove slowly, one arm hanging out, palm waggling, saying softly, "Be cool, be cool, don't hurt yourself none."

"Hey, Jay Fair, I see you soakin' in a new short."

"Jay Fair, when you get out of that slam?"

"You clean from head to toe, man, most cool."

He would have liked to stop, but he had to get the Cadillac back to the dealer and explain why he didn't want to buy it just now. Anyway, it steered harder than he was used to with the Impala.

It became harder for him to make any money, for he had worked that neighborhood over pretty well, and he did not dare to work his own neighborhood, for everyone would know then that Times . . . no, that he was low, that his coins were short. But there was a last chance for him, for survival, to be cool, if he could get to Joe Harris's and play a number, if he could get there without having to talk to any of the boys and answer questions, for if they still believed, then he could still believe.

To be safe, he put on his best and cleanest British-style front, the one with a gold tie and vest. He set his hair with a process, using the last of the oil, and walked to Joe Harris's. He had not eaten at all that day, and he could not afford a sandwich if he were to get a number, so he stopped in a grocery store and bought a small box of crackers to eat after he got his number.

"Say, mon, put that in a sack for me, huh?"

"That's nineteen cents."

Nineteen mon, cool, combinations of nineteen. No dream for many, many days; only vague memories of nightmares in which he smothered in total, confining darkness. But nineteen would do, it might be the thing.

He played his number, combinations of nineteen, but he had no real confidence in it. As he walked out of the pool room, he saw the Red Fox, Clontine, trot down the street toward him, calling to him, "My man! My man! My man Jay Fair!"

Damn Red Fox, never be cool, never will be cool, damn Red Fox.

"Hey, my man, you must have been in the slam somewhat long. Hey, where you Cadillac, Jay Fair? I hear you got you a Cadillac now."

"Aw, mon, it be in the garage now, I be havin' the steerin' fixed a little."

"Hey, Jay Fair, what you got in that old sack, man?"

"Be cool, be cool," Jay Fair said, pulling away from him, knowing it was all over, hearing the laughter and seeing the skull-smile, the hard, cruel smile of Times in the brisk air.

"What is it, Jay Fair?" he asked, grabbing the sack and opening it. "Crackers? Hey, crackers!"

"Okay, mon, I know it . . . I say it . . . Times got me, mon." The words came out final, hurting. Jay Fair felt the cold in his bones as Times sat in, felt it in the dead autumn leaves that were strewn over the sidewalk, felt it in the unbelieving, stupid laughter of Clontine the Red Fox, felt it in the first funereal rush of winter-promising air as he turned away to go to the Baptist Church and line up for turkey-neck soup.

Haskell Hooked on the
Northern Cheyenne

March 3d

Fr. Cyprian Hogan, OFM
Cheyenne Mission School
Broadaxe, Montana

Dear Fr. Cyprian:
Enclosed please find my check for five dollars ($5.00) in response to your appeal.

My wife and I appreciate the gift of the little plastic tepee, and send our best wishes to you in your work among the northern Cheyenne. We're both sure the money will be put to good use, and only regret it is not more.

Yours Very Truly,
H. Haskell

March 19th

Fr. Cyprian Hogan, OFM
Cheyenne Mission School
Broadaxe, Montana

Dear Fr. Cyprian:
Enclosed find my check for $5.00 in response to your second appeal in as many weeks.

From the letter of thanks you sent after the first check I feel you've gotten off on an unfounded assumption. We're not fellow Catholics. It was the "Dear Friend in Christ" salutation in your letter—or does that just mean someone who appears to feel the same way about things like charity without belonging to the same club?

My wife attended Bible camp for two summers while in junior high, so you could call us generic Protestants; anyway we're not Catholic. If we did attend a church regularly it would have to be one of the Lutheran varieties. Please don't misunderstand.

I like to call myself a liberal, and we both realize your mission helps the Cheyenne regardless of *their* religious affiliations—I remember your statement in the first appeal to the effect that only a small percentage of the tribe are practicing Catholics.

I only want the record straight. I give because I want to. Again, we send along our moral support. I know nothing about the problems you face, the daily lives of the Indians, but have some general ideas about poverty, bad nutrition, illiteracy, etc. prevailing on our federal reservations.

Yours Very Truly,
H. Haskell

P.S. You might like to know the little plastic tepee's in good hands. We have no children, but I gave it to a neighbor child, who was quite pleased. A miracle, her mother came over to thank me, and she's never done more before this than nod hello as she pulls out in her station wagon. I guess it's not the sort of toy one can buy in the stores here.

April 17th

Fr. Cyprian Hogan, OFM
Cheyenne Mission School
Broadaxe, Montana

Dear Fr. Cyprian:
What is it with you, Father? No, that's wrong. I don't want to offend, vent spleen, etc. But you're imposing, and I've got to express it. My wife warned me not to write—"Just simply ignore it," she said. "Is there a law that says you have to answer all the junk mail you get?" But you owe me a hearing.

In two weeks' time we received two appeals from you for donations to your work among the northern Cheyenne. I sent you $10.00. The canceled checks have already come back from my bank ("He didn't waste any time cashing in," my wife said when she was going over the monthly statement).

I hoped I conveyed good will, a recognition of your need, and I hoped—in vain I see now—you understood my position, that in good will you would not try to take advantage; now I get a third appeal for money. Let me be understood.

I am not wealthy. My salary is *exactly* $26,400 per annum (all right, so I get a little more each June when we work evenings on inventory). If you're interested (I doubt this), I make my living as a technical writer.

I write: technical manuals to accompany industrial air conditioning and heat transference units, explaining operation and maintenance for the layman; the text of advertising brochures used by our sales engineers; short articles on business conditions (marketing prospects, government regulations, technical developments, credit prospects for the near future) for a monthly trade magazine published by my employer.

Ye Gods, if I was rich wouldn't my checks have been larger? Wouldn't I beat the income tax with huge gifts, trust funds to see Indian orphans through graduate school? Wouldn't I sign over the deeds to properties to you, endow a chair in some university to study your problems? You abuse me.

Don't I give enough? My newsboy comes to the door in the evening to demand a contribution for summer camps for kids like himself—I give, not much, but give. College dropouts come around with magazine subscriptions to get trips to Europe. Brownies come in uniform to sell their cookies; I eat them for lunch faithfully. A neighbor (who holds loud parties we are never invited to) comes with a clipboard and informs me everyone is pledging twenty dollars for the ambulance service. I mail a buck to both political parties to keep democracy strong.

I'm not safe on the streets. Little Leaguers jump me on the way out of the bank with tin cans because they want an electric scoreboard. I get a Buddy Poppy each for wife and self. The Salvation Army surrounds me on the asphalt parking lot in the shopping center. At work, the United Fund sends me an IBM card via one of the girls in the steno pool. What is it with these people? I ask. "We've got to live here, don't we?" my wife says. I grin and give.

And now my name's on some religious sucker list. Because I've given you ten you think I'll give a hundred. I call halt. An unsolicited plastic tepee does not obligate me; I know the law. Catholics may be bound by oath or faith or mortal sin to support you. I am not.

How many of those printed formats do you have at the ready? Save it for someone else; I'm not a colored pin on a map, no target in your war to save the Red Man. I'm young, not thirty yet, owe on house and car, support a wife, heavily insured, need to hire a tree surgeon to save the one big elm on my property, suspect our furnace won't make another winter through. Give me a break.

Understand. "And then you go and write him another check," my wife says in disgust, and now pretends to be watching television too intently to hear me when I speak. "I don't want him to misunderstand is all," I say. So, $5 more, to convince you of good will, that I intend no hurt. Take it in the spirit it is given.

Sincerely,
H. Haskell

April 28th

Fr. Cyprian Hogan, OFM
Cheyenne Mission School
Broadaxe, Montana

Dear Fr. Cyprian:

I have received your long letter. You say: the force that carries you out there is the same spirit of charity you appeal to in me. Will it work to let you forgive me too?

What can I say? How kneel, sackcloth and ashes, beat the breast, how *mea culpa* from a thousand miles away via air mail? The whole thing reeks of ignorance and selfishness—all mine. Haskell thinks he understands, complains that your appeals are mass-produced, steals your time by demanding a personal reply.

I showed your letter to my wife. "I wish you'd just drop the whole thing," she said. "I should never have said those things. I didn't understand the way I do now," I said. No avail. "Just leave me out of it," she asks. Forgive her too.

When I started writing this she took the car and went over to my brother's house to visit with his wife. Have you heard anything from my brother? I gave him your address and one of the pamphlets. "What am I supposed to do with this?" he said. "Send him something." At least he folded it and put it in his pocket. "You ever heard about charity at home?" he said. Then we took turns cutting his lawn with his new electric mower.

I plead ignorance in the first place. What did I know about the northern Cheyenne, Father? The story of Thomas, the little boy abandoned in the wrecked car by his parents because they couldn't feed him, that one did me in. Literally, real tears; fortunately I happened to be home alone then too. Sure I knew the Indians had it rough, but never the details. The TB, the drunkenness, infant mortality, what did I know? What I knew I only guessed. Thomas turning blue with the cold in that rusted junker, asking how far down in the milk bottle he could drink, here I was ignorant. Can you forgive?

The same for the history pamphlets. I had ideas, broken treaties, destroying the buffalo herds, but that's all from the movies. My brother read the one about Shivington's massacre of the women and children in the village. "They had that on TV a while back, I think," he said. "This is where it happened," I said, "here, these people I'm telling you about." "I know it happened," he said, "when the program started it said it was based on an actual fact." What does he know?

I tried getting angry, the Bureau of Indian Affairs, the Secretary of the Interior (I don't even know his name), the President, affluent citizens of Montana. No good. It all came out shame in the end.

Then comes selfishness. Watch out here for self-pity.

Sometimes there's nothing to hold on to. I mean, wife, work, responsibilities, installment payments, become a little too much. I get afraid I can't hold it together for long, pieces are going to fall out, and where are we all then? Tangled up, I can't see out: it makes me selfish.

A few minutes ago (my wife still isn't back—she must be staying for the late show. Out the picture window, the last visible porch light blinked off—no parties tonight)—a few minutes ago I promised myself not to talk about my problems. But to apologize I need to be understood.

Believe it, I work hard. If I'm a success, industrial air conditioners are sold, stock dividends are voted (I don't own much yet), but where am I? I go to sleep at night promising to be ready to eat the world the next day, but it's hard to concentrate with the township's teenagers peeling the corner at the end of the block. I must dream. The resolve to be enthusiastic is sapped when the clock radio buzzes—"I suppose it won't do to heat up last night's coffee for you, it's got to be fresh-made," my wife says. How would you feel?

Do priests get up before the sun to pray? Is that me, the swollen face shaving in the bathroom mirror? The glazed eyes mine? My wife sings with the sizzling bacon in the breakfast nook, I stand dumb, looking at the sick elm in our yard. But I *do* get off to work. Do you understand me?

The days are longer now, still light when I come home, and I admit (why should I feel guilty?) to moments of peace after I greet my wife. We sit and watch the wars and speeches on film on the evening news, but who believes in that stuff? I drink a cold martini—okay, sometimes three—we talk about her day ("Did you see the moving van down towards the circle?" "Not when I came home, no. Who's moving out?" "I don't know their name, but there was a van there all day moving them out. It's the ones with the Imperial I told you about she's always driving by in." "So if you don't know their names who cares if they move?" "I didn't say I cared. I just told you.")

"Be a doll and mix one more," I say, "Two olives." All's well. I admit to moments of peace. Is it my fault they don't last?

I work in a cubicle in a large office (air conditioned). From my desk I can look out through glass panels at the busy secretaries in the steno pool, their ears plugged with dictaphones, eyes fixed on proof sheets. I never know their names until one comes around to collect donations for a wedding gift for Marie or Ardenne or Patty. I believe most of them are secret gum chewers.

Engineers and marketing analysts and file clerks pass up and down aisles, say, "Here you go," when they toss a sheaf of paper into my *In* basket. Am I making sense?

I do try though. Excelsior. This Saturday I have decided to dig a small garden next to my garage. I was talking to the neighbor girl (she still has the tepee); she likes flowers, so I'll plant some along with a few vegetables. Back to the land.

Too tired to read it over, I hope what I've written is clear. The check, you'll see, is for ten this time, all I can do for now. Please continue to let me hear of your good work at the mission.

With sincere regard,
H. Haskell

May 29th

Fr. Cyprian Hogan, OFM
Cheyenne Mission School
Broadaxe, Montana

Dear Fr. Cyprian,
I thought I would not hear from you again. Good to know I am not forgotten. Is the little Indian chief doll authentic? I mean, are headdress, decorations on the jacket, etc., the kind the Cheyenne wear—wore once? We've put him on the mantelpiece above the fireplace. My wife thinks he's cute. She calls him Sitting Bull, though I tell her he wasn't a Cheyenne. Or was he?

Not cute though. I've been analyzing the expression on his face. At first I said: Stoic. But that's all in the folded arms. Then: Courageous. But the brown painted eyes are too pale, no steel there. Sad? His back's too stiff. Finally I knew. "He disapproves," I said to my wife. "Who what?" "He condemns." "What are you talking about, Haskell? Did I make that martootie too strong?" (She never uses my first name; nor do I—have you noticed? Hollis: my mother's maiden name—my brother got Jack, because he's the older.)

Unless I can learn to stare him (Sitting Bull) down I'm going to give him away too. "I tell you he doesn't like it," I said to my wife. "All that Indian wisdom in him disapproves." She said, "I think you're getting hooked on the northern Cheyenne, Haskell." Pure fantasy, Father, I assure you.

I wish this check could be more, but insurance all comes due at the same time: automobile, theft, fire, property, hospitalization, life.

Are there any extra pamphlets (describing the work) lying around in your office? I want to give some to friends and people at work.

Hoping to hear from you soon again,
H. Haskell

P.S. My garden progresses. Besides flowers, I planted sweet corn, tomatoes, lettuce, beans—a landmark in this neighborhood. The little girl next door has never seen a tomato growing on a vine before in her life. "My daughter tells me you're planting regular vegetables and stuff here," her father said to me. He had come out in his slippers. "I'm Haskell," says I, hand extended. "I know who you are, I can read the writing on the mail box like anybody else, can't I? What do you want to do a thing like that for, can you tell me that?" "I like fresh corn." "You know this is gonna make my house look like hell too, don't you?" I promised to try and keep it small. "What did you expect him to say?" my wife said. Who could tell? What a world we live in, Father.

P.P.S. Next stop: public library—subject: American Indians.

June 16th

Dear Fr. Cyprian:

Pardon poor penmanship. I should be working, but who are we trying to kid? The wooden trays on my desk runneth over—copy piles up awaiting my initials (HHH—my mother's mother's maiden name was Hart). Through the glass wall around me I can see the steno I'm keeping idle. She is at a loss, buffs her nails, cleans her teeth with her tongue, changes typewriter ribbons, stacks carbons in readiness, switches off to the ladies room, returns too soon, panics, looks to me with terrified eyes, and I shake my head, pontifical as Sitting Bull on my mantel, and she slumps into her chair, defeated. The trouble is I get to thinking.

In the cafeteria a salesman said to me, "What's the use of working when the government takes a fifth of what I make before I even see it?" I swallowed my bread. "Do you know the Indians out in Montana make less a year, on the average, than you probably pay in taxes in a year?" He threw down his sandwich before he blasted me. "Oh for the Christ's sakes (he said it, Father, not me) Haskell, will you get off the goddamned boring damned Indians in Montana!" Dessert, two cupcakes under cellophane, passed in silence. What's the use?

I gave up reading the library books. "Are we doing anything tonight?" my wife asked. "Doing? I'm doing, I'm reading, right?" "If you're sticking your nose in a book all night, sure," and she turned on the television extra loud to get even. "Do you know all about Indians now?" the librarian asked when I returned them. What do I know?

Last Saturday I was weeding and cultivating my sweet corn. Pleasant, hot sun, hands sore and back stiff, but my neighbor was watching me from his garage, pretending to putter with his son's go-kart. At last I waved and he came over. "Great day for outdoor work," says I. "Can I ask you something in a nice way? Can I ask you something simple like one gentleman to another?" Shoot. "Will you get rid of this corn patch? Flowers I have nothing against, but you'll agree I got ninety-four thousand dollars invested in a home, I've got a right to protect it." "I'll share the sweet corn with you. Would you and your wife come to a corn roast? I'm thinking of building a barbecue, would you like to help?" He affirms that he has tried to reason with me, now warns he will go about it in a different manner since I only want trouble. Do I need trouble, Father Hogan?

How is the work going on the dormitory? I looked around at my corn, the small green tomatoes, climbing beans, remembered the Indian children afraid to eat your school's hot lunch because they never have lunch at home, afraid to eat today because tomorrow they'll be hungry again. I checked out a book on bricklaying yesterday. My wife doesn't understand at all.

My supervisor approaches, the steno at his side. He is grim, puzzled. She wrings her hands. Must close.

In haste,
Haskell

July 27th

Fr. Cyprian Hogan, OFM
Cheyenne Mission School
Broadaxe, Montana

Dear Fr. Cyprian:
Telephoned home this afternoon. "Any mail?" I asked my wife. "Where are you calling from?" "Work, where else?" "I thought you weren't supposed to make personal calls." "What mail?" "There's one." "Are you trying to make me angry? One from where?" "Postmarked Montana." "Bring it down, I'll meet you in the parking lot." "I've got better things to do with my time." Name one, I said, but she wouldn't, so I had to wait to get home this evening to write you.

I am honestly excited about the possibilities of the new industry as a means of helping the Cheyenne. My professional opinion of the full-color brochure layouts on the jewelry you're making is no less than good. Good.

If you want I'll show them to the art boys at work and pass their judgment along. How are the orders coming in?

After sound and fury, my wife agrees to telephone all her friends and drum up a big sale for you. "How?" she says. "Have a party, I'll get out of the house, the way they do for pots and pans." Tomorrow she promises to start.

At first I pondered: Indian jewelry? But *what* doesn't matter, I see now. *Why* is all. You start with fifteen employed—how soon can you expand? You make mail order jewelry in order to remake men; I sell air conditioners. The check's only ten again, but I'll nag my wife to come up with an order for the beads that will more than make up for it.

I appreciated the personal note. Was my letter "diffuse"? It was one of those days. That set my wife off again. Am I writing letters on the sly now? I write because I need to write, I feel like writing. Am I going into the charity business? I give because I want to give. She just doesn't understand, does she. All's well now though; I agreed to go visit my brother and his wife with her.

One failure: I tried to ship you some corn and beans I harvested this week (I knew tomatoes would never make it). "Can't take it," said the little man in the blue coat at the post office. "It'd spoil." I might have said: what good's a post office that can't ship food from one man to another? People are starving out there! But he looked tired, and his blue jacket was wrinkled. Will two wrongs make a right?

Your friend,
H. Haskell

P.S. Are summers in Montana such you could use an air conditioner in the school or the new dormitory when it's done? I might be able to start something at the office to get them to contribute one. Isn't it deductible?

August 14th

Dear Father:

No letterhead stationery this time. I'm not at work, but that's all arranged. I couldn't do what I was supposed to. The steno did her best, didn't sic the supervisor on me for some time. "Mr. Haskell," she said, "if you don't give me that stuff then I've got nothing to do and Miss Lubin will be after me for sitting around." No small thing, Miss Lubin is huge and acne-scarred. What could I do. "Maybe later," says I. "Not now." She had to bring my supervisor. His name is Knauer; all my copy has to go through him.

"What is it you think you're doing, Haskell?" "I told him I hadda have that stuff or Miss Lubin gets after me, Mr. Knauer," the steno said. I think she was beginning to enjoy it. "I'll do this," Knauer said. The typewriters slowed down on the other side of the glass; there hadn't been any excitement in the office since personnel hired a mousey girl named Peplinski (her name I knew!) months ago—she was a secret epileptic and threw a fit at her desk, chewed right through some bond paper one afternoon. "I can't do anything," I said.

"Are you ill, Haskell? Are you trying to pull something off on me?" "The Indians need me, Knauer," and I might have gotten snotty with him, but remembered that everyone calls him Weasel Knauer behind his back because of his narrow pointed face, so took pity and kept silence. "He's been talking funny about those Indians," he whispered to the steno, and they backed out afraid. He came back with a janitor to protect him in case I raged. "You can feel free to go home if something's wrong, Haskell," he said. The janitor carried a long-handled broom to subdue me. Am I the violent type? "Just till you feel better. Don't worry about a thing," he said, "I'll contact personnel for you."

"I'm worried about the Indians, Weasel Knauer," I said, but he kept on backing out to make sure the janitor was between us until I left the office. The girls in the steno pool tried not to stare.

My wife won't know about this letter either because she hasn't been here for three days. It could be she calls, or it could be personnel wanting to know if I'm terminating, but I don't answer the phone. I came home like they told me at the office, and I could talk to her, but she didn't quite understand.

"I'm telling you why if you'll listen to me. It was the Indians. I couldn't do what I'm supposed to do there," I said. Said she: "I don't know what's the matter with you, you talk about the Indians all the time. You never say anything except about the Indians all the time. Stay over there. Don't touch me. I don't understand you anymore. I don't want to talk about the Indians anymore." What was there left to say? But I kept on talking, and finally she cried, and she cried, so I stopped for good. So she left. I think she's with my brother and his wife. Her parents live far from here. The phone rings often, and there was someone at the door yesterday and today. I thought I recognized the broken muffler on my brother's Oldsmobile.

Why don't you write? Are you still waiting for that jewelry order I promised? Give up, Father. Nobody wants Indian-style jewelry, not my wife, not anybody. She broke her promise about holding that party to sell it. "I'd be ashamed to show cheap jewelry like that to my friends." I tried to tell her how it was to help the Cheyenne, but who understands? I think they have all the jewelry they need.

I've thought better of it too, Father. Sending out plastic tepees and Indian dolls, cheap jewelry, that's not the way, not for me anyhow. I gave Sitting

Bull to the neighbor girl, but her mother brought it back. "Keep your trashy presents to yourself!" she screamed when I opened the door. I was afraid she'd have an attack of some kind. When her husband came home that night he stood in his yard and glared at my cornfield with his hands on his hips. My tomatoes are rotting on the vines. I started with a bushel basket full at the other end of the block to give them away, but when the woman (maybe it was a maid?) peeked through her curtains to see who it was she waved me off. The word must be out on Haskell.

No, the way is things like the mission school, and the free hot lunches for children who don't get them at home, and finding Thomas abandoned in the auto wreck. That's the way. Build that dormitory and staff the school with teachers so you can have classes more than half a day. What kind of a world is this?

The doorbell's ringing. Maybe you've written, but I haven't gone out to see the mail. There won't be any money in this letter because my wife took the checkbook with her. I might as well answer the door, I've got to go out to mail this (if I can find a stamp). Money's not the way anyhow.

September 5th

Dear Father:

Here's proof I no longer ignore the mail, though now all my letters are delayed a day or two because of my change of address. I've been with my brother and his family for the past few days. My wife is now with her parents, and while I'm grateful to my brother for taking me in, I will be glad to leave (he is glad our mother didn't live to see this, etc.). My sister-in-law won't stay alone in the same room with me, and their children are with her parents until I go. Can I blame them? Accept, I say to myself, they don't want to understand.

From your letter, Father Hogan, I'd almost think you didn't understand either. I'm satisfied to think that's just a problem caused by my "diffuse" expression. I comment briefly; there's much to do before I can be on my way.

Agreed, the world's as it is because we're like we are. Now concede we can change it by changing ourselves. Proof? Look in the mirror. I'm argument enough for me.

Friends, clergyman, psychiatrists? Come on now! Do I need friends with a brother like mine? I went to church last Sunday—my brother's high Episcopal these days—it's the closest one. "Excuse me, Reverend," I said (my brother says he's called Father, like you). "Would you read this little prayer and appeal for the northern Cheyenne at the end of your sermon for me today? I've got my telephone number right there if anyone wants to call in a pledge." I still have the mark on my arm where my brother grabbed me when he pulled me away to a pew. "Can't I even let you out of the house?" he said. You're the only clergy I know, and I've been consulting, not your letters, but your example. I don't see doctors because I don't have money (that's all my wife's: house, car, our small savings)—what do I need money for? I know the language of psychiatrists. They don't want to change the world.

Here I am then. We can talk all this over in detail later if you want. I wish I could say exactly when, but there are papers to be signed, arrangements— I hope for the best. Who knows, with luck I might arrive at the mission shortly after this letter.

You'll see, I'll be of use. I'll mix cement, lay bricks, teach school. I'll scour the mountains for abandoned children. I can learn. I haven't told you before this because I feared you wouldn't understand. But you'll see. It may take longer than I think. I have so little money I may have to hitchhike all the way to Montana. What does time matter when you've found your way at last, Father?

My brother shouts from downstairs that dinner is ready. The flesh must be fed. I'll close:

H. Haskell, Your Friend in Christ.

Wouldn't I?

THE COMPOUND LEADER took the reports from the prisoner squad and platoon leaders like Lou; they wore special white canvas armbands that said *Squad Leader* or *Platoon Leader* under the big black *S* all the prisoners wore. Then the compound leader read some announcements from his clipboard, checking them off one by one with a mechanical pencil. He had Lou fall out the last thing before he read off fatigue detail assignments. "Hey you, big Baxter," he said, and looked up from the clipboard to find Lou's face.

"Here, sergeant," Lou said.

"Okay old Baxter, you fall yourself out to the billets and get in class A uniform. You're going to trial today. They'll be an escort from your company come to pick you up." In Lou's squad, where none of the MP personnel standing near the compound leader could hear them, some men made a few cracks.

"Say hello to my brother in Leavenworth for me, big old Baxter."

"I got money says Baxter don't get more than five years nor less than one. Cover me."

"Baxter don't want no court-martials, he's got it too good in jail."

"And I want to thank you kindly too," Lou called out back to the compound leader, then double-timed it back to his barracks. He meant it too. Over in Funston and Forsythe the barracks were all the T-types put up during the Second World War, flimsy, hot in summer, and cold in winter, but the Fort Riley stockade was on the main post, the old part that went back to the cavalry days, so the prisoners' barracks and the admin buildings inside the fence were all old horse barns, built of stone with thick walls that kept the heat out no matter how bad it got out in the open compound under that August sun. It was a perfect cool, moist sleeping temperature inside all the time.

He changed from fatigues to suntans, but didn't bother to change his boots for brogans. He didn't know if he was supposed to wear his armband on his suntans or not, so folded it and put it in his hip pocket just in case. He stretched out on his bunk for a snooze; he was tired. The thing was he felt just mostly always tired these days. And the stockade was about as comfortable a place as any to rest up if only they'd let a man alone and didn't send him out on fatigue details six days every week.

22

Old big Baxter liked it in jail, someone said. Didn't he? He liked it in this jail all right, so long as he had to be in some jail at all. The town clink in Whipple, Tennessee, now that place purely smelled. They had one big drunk tank there, and if the turnkey emptied the slop bucket during a weekend it was an accident. He didn't miss Whipple, Tennessee, not one bit, because every time he thought Whipple he thought the smell of that drunk tank's slop bucket.

Compared to the detention and disciplinary compound at Eta Jima, Japan, this stockade was a regular hotel. Eta Jima was just tent flys inside a barbed-wire fence, but it rained every day the week Lou was there under investigation for murdering a Japanese and besides, his mouth had been full of stitches then. He was dreaming and fingering the scars around his mouth one minute, and then he must have dozed off, because the gate runner was shaking him awake the next.

"Big man Baxter," the runner said, "there's a skinny, no-assed man out by the sallyport with a gun to take you away."

"Ain't there?" Lou said.

"There is. Court-martialed today, the man said, huh Lou? They gonna give you the time today, right? How much time you figure you're subject to get, old big Baxter?"

"I'll inform you straight," Lou said. "Three months I'll pull. I can do three months standing on my head under water. Six months I'm not about to pull."

"Would you ex-scape, Louie?"

"Wouldn't I?" He walked across the compound to the sallyport with the runner following him like his pet hound. He was let through the first gate. Inside he looked around for his escort to see if it was maybe one of his friends from the motor pool, but the escort must have been standing back in the shadows of the guardshack. "Good morning to you, Corporal Pollard," he said to the MP who came over to shake him down. Lou took off his garrison cap and showed him it was empty inside, nothing stuck away in the lining.

"Frisking you is like frisking a small mountain, Baxter," Pollard said. "I never knew you were a Pfc."

"You must not of been here when I came in. I had it sewed on all my suntans and my OD's, but I never put it on my fatigues. I won't be one long no way." Pollard patted his armpits, crotch, and the bottoms of his trousers where they bloused over his boot tops.

"Well good luck to you anyhow, Baxter. Say, would you mind telling me where you got all those marks on your lips if it's not too personal? I always wanted to ask you that."

"I was in a hatchet battle," Lou said, "and everybody had a hatchet but me." When Pollard was opening the padlock on the outer sallyport gate, Lou saw his escort come out of the guardshack shadows. He didn't recognize him. He was a kid maybe five and a half feet tall, eighteen or nineteen, a private, his suntan uniform not fitting any too well. He wore a scuffed helmet liner that looked too big, and he wore army-issue eyeglasses, plain steel frames and bows. His pistol belt was so loose the holster hung too far down on his leg, like some bony little four-eyed cowboy.

Lou was about to say hello to the escort when the Sergeant of the Guard came up behind the kid and yanked the .45 out of the open holster. "Damnit, soldier," the Sergeant of the Guard said, "when you push a prisoner, always push him loaded." He spun the kid around and grabbed the clip out of his hand. He jammed it into the handle and cocked the action to feed a round into the chamber. "There now," said the Sergeant of the Guard. "Now you can push him anywheres you need to go," and he dropped the .45 back into its holster.

Now Lou was close enough to read his name tag. *Yingst* the name tag said—now what kind of a name was a *Yingst?* The sergeant went back into the guardshack. "I do hope we're not going to hoof it all the way to Funston, Yingst," he said. "It's one hot day."

"The jeep's up the hill," Yingst said, but didn't move, so Lou started up the stone steps to the main post street, and the kid just naturally fell in behind about a dozen paces back. Then the compound gate runner took it into his head to cup his hands at his mouth and yell out a wisecrack.

"Boot him one square in his little fanny, Louie! Take that gun away from him an' make him ask you polite for it back, you big Baxter!" Neither Lou nor the kid Yingst said anything.

The jeep driver was C. T. Sneed, a good friend. He winked at Lou, and Lou flipped C. T. Sneed a mock salute. He waited for Yingst to catch up. "After you, son," he said.

"Are you trying to be funny or something?" Yingst said. He had one wild, cocked eye, and every couple of seconds he squinted and worked his forehead like his GI glasses didn't help him to see so very good. "The prisoner rides up front next to the driver and the guard gets in back. I know that well enough." Lou looked at C. T. Sneed, who grinned and shrugged like he didn't know this Yingst kid either.

"I certainly got no objections to riding next to old C. T. Sneed, and that's fact," Lou said, and climbed in, but Yingst didn't smile. The metal was scorching hot where Lou touched the jeep.

"Just don't think you're funny," Private Yingst said, and got into the jump seat, climbing over the mounted spare tire. C. T. Sneed started the engine. Lou turned around to speak to the kid and jumped himself when the kid half jumped out of the seat. "Don't get funny," he said again.

"That boy in there that hollered that to us," Lou said, watching this Yingst closely, "he's just a big-mouthed boy likes to yell at people. That's why he's on the inside. I was just wanting to say he's just a boy talks a lot," Lou said, because he'd seen from the first Yingst was afraid of him, and he didn't like that feeling behind him.

"I didn't worry about it if that's what you think," Yingst said, and Lou liked that even less, because it was a pure lie.

"You think maybe old Louie Baxter'd like some good company chow before he goes to see the man for trial?" C. T. Sneed said.

"Wouldn't he?" Lou said, and made himself forget the kid in the jump seat. Sneed put the jeep in gear and drove them to the company area in Camp Funston.

They got to the big consolidated headquarters mess right in the middle of the meal. The word was out that he was coming, all his friends from the motor pool waiting for him. "I saved you the seat of honor, Louie, that is if our friend here don't have objection." Lou looked back at Yingst.

"Just go on," he said. "I know he's supposed to eat lunch first."

Lou went in and his friends hollered out to him. Tired as he felt, he gave them a big smile and shook hands all around the table where they'd saved a seat for him, but to tell the truth he'd a lot rather been still snoozing back on his cot in the stockade. "Aren't you eating?" he asked Yingst when the kid didn't take a tray off the rack and fall in behind him in the chow line.

"I can't very well sit down and eat and be your guard at the same time, can I?" Lou set his tray on the steam table and stepped over to talk to him. "You stay right where you are," Yingst said.

"I just want to talk private with you."

"Talk from there. I hear you. Don't come so close to me. I'm your guard, remember?" and the Yingst kid smiled.

"Well you don't have to take it so serious, son. I'm not subject to run off on you—"

"Not while I'm guarding you you're not, that's for sure."

"—well. Just relax, son. I'm only interested in getting some of these good vittles." The menu was Swiss steaks that day. The cook serving on the line forked Lou out a big one and dropped it on his tray with a wink.

"You're looking awfully good in your war suit today, Mr. Baxter," the mess sergeant said to him.

"Probably it's the last day I'll wear it for a while," Lou said. Yingst followed him right to his table and leaned back against the windowsill while he ate. When he was finished his motor pool friends all shook hands with him and wished him luck at the court-martial. Even the first sergeant stopped by at his table when he came in for coffee and wished him good luck, too. "I'm ready to go if you are, son," Lou said.

"Don't call me son. I don't like it."

"Any way you say." And they went off to the JAG building for the trial, the kid Yingst ten or a dozen paces back. The afternoon sun turned on like an oven, and there wasn't a stir in the air except for one little dust-devil that scootered down the shoulder of the road toward Lou and on past him to Yingst. Lou looked back over his shoulder and laughed, but Yingst didn't join in; he just walked along with the heel of his hand resting on the butt of the .45 like some kid playing at cowboy. "You know you don't *have* to *not* talk to me," Lou said. "I just *might* appreciate some talk."

"I didn't hear anyone talking to me before now," this Yingst said. Still he didn't change the expression on his face, but later, outside the courtroom while the court-martial board was getting seated, he did talk a little.

"You were in Korea, weren't you?" Yingst said.

"Wasn't I? You know that, friend."

"I know that from that patch you have on your right shoulder. That's the Forty-fifth Division. The thunderbird."

"That's the one. General P. D. Ginder commanding. Was you there too?"

"You must think you're being funny again. I've only been in the army seven months."

"I figured you were new in the company. I never seen you around before today."

"I've been in the company five months almost. I was in basic training in the Eighty-seventh and then they shipped me to headquarters because I had typing in high school."

"I never seen you I guess," Lou said.

"I've been here, but I don't have a regular job, like in the motor pool or supply. I take care of the dayroom and sometimes I help the mail clerk, or the first sergeant gives me a special job to do like this one guarding you. First I was in the motor pool, but McLennon kicked me out for smashing a three-quarter when I was learning to drive. I never learned to drive. He never gave me a fair chance. He just kicked me out, so now I fiddle around the dayroom all day."

"I don't get to the dayroom much, I'll admit. Old McLennon's a good enough motor sergeant. I think he was in the Fifth RCT in Korea, same as old Sneed, same as the CO, too. McLennon's a good old boy but I grant you he's tempered sometimes."

"I've seen you around the company though, you and those guys like Sneed at chow from the motor pool, your friends. You're the one who socked Lieutenant Loeffler, aren't you?"

"Ain't I? You know I am. I didn't hit him though, I just threatened to, which is just as good for court-martialing as if I did. You know old Loeffler too, do you? I don't mind him so much, really. He's not but a snot ROTC motor officer, but he's okay I guess."

"You're one of the first guys in the company I've talked to in five months," Yingst said. "I don't know anybody in this company." Lou unfolded his arms and looked at the kid and was about to say something, but his defense counsel, a colored first lieutenant from quartermaster, came out of the courtroom and told the escort to bring his prisoner in.

It was a quick trial. Lieutenant Loeffler was the only witness called. He told the straight truth, word for word, of what took place. He was good enough to say that he thought Pfc Baxter would never have threatened him if he hadn't been intoxicated at the time, and also that Pfc Baxter was a very efficient vehicle driver, an asset to the motor pool. The colored lieutenant didn't call any character witnesses, but he did read a list of Lou's decorations from Korea, forgetting that he got two Purple Hearts and not just one. This was a mistake. It caused the prosecution officer to mention Lou's general court-martial for murder while a member of the Eighth Army in Japan.

"He oughtn't to mention that, sir, I was found not guilty on that," he whispered to his defense counsel.

"We'd better not make a fuss," the Negro said. He was very nervous at his first court-martial. Also the prosecution read off Lou's page in the company punishment book: two restrictions, one with extra duty, for being disorderly in the barracks at night. Lou, his counsel, and his escort went outside in the hall again while the board deliberated his guilt. The lieutenant excused himself and went across the street to the Service Club to get a Coca-Cola.

"What was that about murdering?" Yingst asked him as soon as the officer was gone.

"That's a long story."

"I have time."

"The army thought I killed a Jap, but it was a friend of mine did it. Both of us was not guilty on that."

"Was it really the other guy who did it?"

"Damn straight it was! What'd you ask for if you won't believe me? I got other things to worry about right now. Let me alone." By rights he should have been worried about what the board was doing, but nothing seemed so important except that tired feeling running all through him. Hot as it was, he'd as soon gone to sleep right there with that ugly Yingst kid watching him.

"How'd you get those scars on your mouth?"

"Will you let me alone?" Actually, it *was* his buddy old Forbes who killed the Jap. Lou told him to. The Jap was some uncle or something, kin to the little cho-san he and Forbes came to see that night. Small as he was, he *could* fight. Forbes was fumbling around in the bedroom of the house there at Eta Jima looking for something to club the Jap with. Lou wrestled him to the floor, but the Jap rolled on top of him and all of a sudden, like some damn animal, bit right into Lou's mouth with his teeth. With the little Jap there holding on, with his teeth meeting right through Lou's lips, Forbes came over with the gun at last. He whacked the Jap alongside his head, but he didn't loosen his teeth. "Shoot him!" Lou yelled as best he could like that. Forbes put the muzzle into the Jap's ear and shot him. Together they pried his jaws loose.

"What's wrong, are you ashamed of where you got the scars?" Yingst said.

"Would you believe me if I told you a man's teeth did it?"

"No."

"All right then."

"Say for a minute you really didn't do the murder and your friend did. If you were in his place, would you have done it?"

"Wouldn't I?" Lou said. The lieutenant came back and said he thought they had a good chance. The court's law officer called them back in. Lou was found guilty of all charges and specifications, sentenced to reduction in grade from private first class to private, forfeiture of two-thirds of all pay and allowances for a period of six months, and six months' confinement to the post stockade.

"We'll appeal it. There's an automatic review of sentence by the next higher command," the lieutenant assured him. "Don't take it so hard, Baxter."

"The whole thing makes me tired, sir," Lou said. Yingst was given a carbon copy of the court's findings and told to escort the prisoner to his company to await the decision of the reviewing authority. They didn't speak on the walk to the company. At the orderly room the first sergeant told them to go over to Lou's old barracks and relax until the review was phoned in.

"They just might cut the stockade time off, Baxter," the first sergeant said. But that was only like wishing him good luck. The best, the very best Lou could hope for was maybe a reduction of the sentence to three months, and this seemed like too much effort.

It was clean-linen day in the barracks. The bunk springs were bare, the striped mattress ticks rolled up at the head of each cot. The T-type barracks were hotter inside than out; Lou took off his necktie and opened his khaki shirt.

"You get on that side," Yingst said, pointing. "I'll stay on this side so I can watch you."

"I'll tell you something, young man," Lou said. "This morning I swore I'd run off if they gave me six months . . ."

"Is that right?"

"Yes it's right. But just now I couldn't care less if it was six years at Leavenworth. I'm laying down to rest on old Sneed's bunk here and I'll thank you to let me be."

"Go ahead," Yingst said, and it couldn't have been more than a minute and Lou was asleep. He didn't remember anything but the ending of a dream about a widow woman in Whipple, Tennessee, he'd loved for a while once. His eyes just opened up when he woke, and there was this Yingst kid propped up on a bunk across the aisle with his legs crossed, his face all screwed up, taking a bead on him with the .45.

"What the hell you doing?" Lou said. He didn't move his hands from behind his head. He'd sweated through his shirt, and his neck felt wet.

"He's awake," the kid said, and lowered the pistol to his side. It clanked against the metal springs.

"I hope you remember the man jacked one into the chamber there at the stockade." He eased his hands out and laid them open in his lap.

"I have to practice, don't I? I never fired familiarization on the .45. Just the M-I and carbine. I'd have to know how to aim it if you got up and started running, wouldn't I?" Lou kept his hands in sight. He listened for sounds in the company street, but it seemed empty. Wouldn't old C. T. Sneed be dropping in to talk if he could? Wouldn't they keep Sneed on standby to take Lou back to the stockade when the review came down? He wondered how long he'd been asleep.

"You know why the army developed the .45?" Yingst asked. He had the pistol in front of him again, but not pointed at Lou.

"No word on the review yet?" Lou said.

"Because they couldn't stop the rebels in the Philippines with a .38. They'd keep coming no matter how many times they were shot with a .38. These were the fanatics that fought us in the Spanish-American War. They developed the .45 and it stopped them. I used to read about guns all the time when I was in high school."

"Can I get up and get a drink of water?" Lou asked.

"I prefer you stay right there." Yingst pointed the pistol at him again.

"All right. All right whatever you say."

"Even somebody as big as you are, you couldn't take a .45 and still stand up. I've seen them fired on the range. The kick throws your arm up over your head. If you were coming at me and I shot you with a .45 right where you are now, you'd be knocked against the wall."

"Well I'm not about to be coming at you, see?"

"Did you ever kill anyone, Baxter?"

"I told you my friend killed that Jap, not me."

"No, I believe you about that. In Korea I mean. Any North Koreans."

"I don't know. I shot at some but I don't know certain I killed them."

"I could shoot you right now, Baxter. I could just shoot you and say you were coming for me. No one could say different. I heard if a guard kills a prisoner they promote him one stripe and take and transfer him then. Is that the truth?"

"Why would you want to kill me? I never even knew you before this."

"I could do it. Nobody could prove you weren't getting away."

"Now why should you do that?" Lou said. He listened to the company street, but there wasn't anyone out there. He was probably near twice as old as this Yingst, and very tired of being in jails and in the army; he was tired of men picking fistfights with him just because he was the biggest man in sight. He wanted a drink of water. Yingst kept the pistol on him, squinting his eyes behind those G.I. glasses. He thought of Forbes and C. T. Sneed and of a widow woman he'd loved once for a while in Whipple, Tennessee. He thought of the smell of that drunk tank in the Whipple town clink, and he was tired and scared.

He raised up a little on the bunk. This Yingst kid wouldn't shoot him. "You wouldn't just here and now shoot me, would you?" Lou said.

"Wouldn't I?" Yingst said.

Getting Serious

WHEN CAPTAIN GUY ROLAND of the Army Air Corps came home from the war, he drove his Lincoln Zephyr coupe right up to the edge of the bluff above Silver Lake, and blew the horn again and again to tell the world he was back. He leaned on it, long blasts that echoed out over Silver Lake, rolled through the pine trees, stopped us all where we stood, like an air-raid siren.

"What the goddamn hell!" my father said.

My mother ceased priming the kitchen pump with lake water, the pitcher in one hand, the other resting on the pump handle. "I think the Roland boy is back," she said, turning to see through the screened window.

"Where are you going?" my father said to me.

"I want to see."

"Let him go," my mother said.

"Far be it from me to insist on a damn thing," I heard my father say before the screen door slapped shut behind me.

Captain Guy Roland honked the horn of his Lincoln Zephyr, and his parents closed the bar and restaurant of the Silvercryst Resort and came outside. People came out of the bar and restaurant carrying glasses and bottles. Somebody gave him a bottle of beer he waved and pointed with while he dug things out of his duffel with his free hand. Everyone shook hands with everyone else.

The sun came through the swaying tops of the tall Norway pines, dappling us where we stood on the bluff above the lake. A light breeze rose off the water, stirring the surface of Silver Lake to glisten in the sun like chips of diamond or glass, lighting Captain Guy Roland's return. Mrs. Peaches Roland kissed her son on his cheek, his ear, his neck, keeping her cigarette away from his face. She carried a frosted Collins glass in her other hand. She said, "Baby, baby," to her son and kissed him again. I could see lipstick she left on his neck and jaw. He shook hands with everyone while his mother kissed him.

Mr. Roland shook hands with his son, shook hands with all the people who had come from the bar and dining room, then stepped back to some shade and smiled, squinting at it all, twirling the melting ice in the bottom of the glass he carried with him from the bar. Captain Guy Roland shook my hand.

"Our summer house is right next door to your resort," I said. I think he said that was keen, or swell, something like that, and then he was being kissed again by his mother and shaking hands with more people. The sun dappled us, the breeze swayed the tops of the Norway pines, shook the varicolored heads of the zinnias and marigolds and hollyhocks Mrs. Peaches Roland cultivated in tiered rock gardens on the slope below the bluff. The wind on Silver Lake shot the sun back up to us like the scraps of tinfoil I saved to aid the war effort.

Captain Guy Roland gave his mother a ring in a wooden box. The ring was silver, set with pale stones, the box a dark, reddish wood, lined with purple silk. "That comes from Manila," he said. "Diamonds go there for a fraction what they're worth."

"Baby," Mrs. Peaches Roland said, kissing him with cigarette smoke coming out of her mouth. She carried the open box around for everyone to see, tried to make it sparkle by turning it to the light, clutching the box and her leather cigarette case and her empty Collins glass in her frail hands.

He gave his father a short Japanese sword. There were braided cords with tassels tied to the lacquered scabbard, and Guy showed us how the haft opened to reveal a piece of sheer rice-paper, spidery calligraphy. "You commit harakiri with it," he said. Prayers to your ancestors were written on the rice-paper to get you to heaven after you stabbed yourself.

"Wicked," Mr. Roland said when he unsheathed the sword and put the ball of his thumb on its edge. The cigarette in his mouth made him squint and cough while he handled his son's gift.

"You hang that up over the fireplace," Guy said. He gave me a Japanese army forage cap and a wad of occupation money that also came from the Philippines. "In Manila you could buy a hot time with that," he told me. I stayed there and watched until Mr. and Mrs. Roland opened up the bar again and everyone went back inside the Silvercryst Resort.

These are not *living* details for me. Rather, after thirty years, it is a kind of tableau, a group of people frozen in my memory like statues, like a memorial to the people, the place, the world war. I can look at it whenever I wish, but it does not *live* for me.

We are set in place on the lawn next to the huge Lincoln Zephyr, outside the Silvercryst Resort bar and restaurant, dappled by the sun that penetrates the top of the pine trees. We are frozen in place by the edge of the bluff above Silver Lake. On the slope descending to the beach, Mrs. Peaches Roland's bright flowers bloom. The water slaps at the dock and the moored boats, laps the sandy shore, lights our pageant with reflected sun that blares brilliant as an air-raid siren. I am part of it, this picture, yet outside it. It is my vision of the time and place of my beginning, but after thirty years it is no more than that.

Captain Guy Roland is the center of this picture. His hat, bent in a fifty-mission crush, is cocked back on his head, his blond pompadour ruffled as if by design. His captain's bars gleam, his pilot's wings a duller silver. On the left breast of his officer's dress-uniform jacket are the muted plots of color of his campaign ribbons and citations; the flat gold bars of his combat service track his sleeve. His uniform trousers, a faintest suggestion of pink, are sharply creased; the toes of his cordovan shoes glisten, spit-shined to the hardness of mirrors. *You can get diamonds for a fraction of what they're worth,* he says, and *You hang that over the fireplace,* and *You can buy a hot time in Manila with that.*

My world, in this time of my beginning, is no more or less than my vision of it, and this picture is my vision, this time and place these people.

"Look," I said to my father when I came back to our summer home, "it's invasion money."

"That and a nickel gets you a cup of coffee," he said.

"He was a *pilot,* I think," I said.

"I flew a Spad at Fort Sill, Oklahoma," my father said. "You didn't know that, did you."

"You flew back and forth to Texas because you couldn't get whiskey in Oklahoma," my mother said.

"Another precinct heard from," he said.

"You should see that sword!"

"Any luck, some night in his cups the son of a bitch'll cut his throat with it and bleed to death," my father said.

"*Will* you stop!" My mother said.

"Not unless I'm asked nicely."

"He gave her a ring from Manila," I said.

"Know why they call her *Peaches?*" he said. "Ripe for the picking."

"Do you care at all what you say to him?" my mother said. My father did not answer her.

"In Manila you can spend this just like real money," I said.

"Get that nasty thing off your head," my mother said. "God only knows where it's been before now."

"And He ain't telling," my father said.

After their divorce, my father moved to Minneapolis and remarried. He wrote me regular letters I answered whenever I could not resist my mother's urging. He was, after all, she would say, still my father, even if he had abandoned us both. In my letters I told him yes, I was working hard and doing well in school, I was behaving myself, I was a help not a hindrance to my mother, I was enjoying my summer on Silver Lake. It was not lying, just something I had to say to please both my parents.

I remember it as my summer spent hanging about, lurking in some shade of pine tree off to one corner of the beach, smoking cigarettes, watching, savoring my boredom and bitter envy.

In 1950 Guy Roland drove a custom Ford convertible. It was the summer I affected T-shirts, my cigarettes rolled in one sleeve—hidden in the top of my sock when I had to go home to eat or sleep—wore Levi's slung low on my hips, black shoes with spade toes, my hair long on the sides and back, short on top. It was the summer season I gave over to hating myself for my boredom and resentment, detesting anything that chanced to come to my attention—except Guy Roland.

His father still ran the Silvercryst Resort, was still to be seen on the restaurant veranda, drink in hand, talking real estate with people who came to buy parcels of the lake frontage he had to sell. He was an immaculate man, his hair a spun white meringue, crisp shirts and casual slacks creased like knife blades. He wore two-tone brown-and-white shoes. He often stood on the bluff above the lake, jingling the change in his pocket, squinting against the glare of the sun off the water, as if counting the heads of vacationers who paid for beach privileges along with the cabins he rented. When he noticed me, he squinted a little harder, as if that was the closest to a smile of recognition he could muster. I would nod or shrug or blow cigarette smoke defiantly, flip butts into his wife's flower beds on the slope.

Mrs. Peaches Roland still came out late mornings to tend her zinnias and hollyhocks and daisies. Still light and colorful as the flowers she loved, she wore garden-party hats, the broad brims waving slowly in the lake breezes, tied under her chin with swaths of filmy gauze. She carried her cigarettes and lighter in the patch pockets of her pastel smocks, one hand free to carry a trowel. Eyes shaded by opaque aviator's sunglasses, she teetered as she stepped among the blossoms on platform shoes with open toes. The flaming reds of her lips, fingernails, and toenails always matched. When I slouched close enough, I heard the popular songs she hummed to herself, caught the wall of scent that surrounded her like a sweet cloud.

Guy Roland came and went all summer. I remember it as his perfect summer, the season I would have signed away my future to share the smallest part of—one week, a day, an afternoon.

Like the summer he came and went. He always had friends. From where I brooded, some shaded corner of the resort I do not recall, I heard the crunch of the Ford's whitewalls on the gravel parking lot. The convertible's radio carried through the pines, played all the way up so they could hear it through the wind whipping them as they drove—from wherever to wherever. He pulled his car right up on the grass and pine needles at the edge of the bluff, always honked the horn in some rhythm as his friends climbed out without opening the doors. *Watch the paint, watch the paint!* he would say. He and his friends would laugh.

He drove barefoot. He and his friends were barefooted, wearing swimming suits, carrying bath towels and beach blankets, a big portable radio, cigarettes, and bottles of suntan lotion, sunglasses, unbuttoned shirts with tails that hung down over their swimsuits.

The girls were always beautiful—long legs, skin tan-gold, hair pulled up off graceful necks, pouty lips, full breasts bound in halters or swim-tops. Some of the men wore sweatshirts with the sleeves cut off raggedly, faded Greek letters on their chests. His friends started down the slope to the beach while Guy went to the bar for their beer.

I put myself in his way whenever I could do it without awkwardness. If he saw me, he would nod or wink, or say hello, and I would nod, smile, wave my cigarette at him, make that do for the day.

"So what's the program plan?" Mr. Roland would say if he could catch Guy before he got away from the bar with paper cups and the cooler of beer.

"Busy, Popper, busy," Guy said to his father. "Hello there, Miss Peaches!" he would shout to his mother among the flowers as he passed her on the way to his friends. His mother waved, blew a kiss to his back as he disappeared down the slope. I followed no sooner than I had to.

Guy Roland and his friends spread their blankets on the sand, extended the radio's antenna to bring in the music of Chicago and Milwaukee, popped caps off bottles of beer, rubbed lotion into each other's shoulders. The beautiful tan-gold girls untied their halters, lay down on their stomachs to brown the whole of their broad glazed backs. I could get near enough to smell the tang of the oil. Guy Roland sat up on one elbow, squinting at the harsh sunlight reflected off Silver Lake. The breeze flipped his blond hair. He smoked cigarettes and drank beer, kept time to the radio music with one foot, the vision of a man in his perfect summer, a perfect life awaiting him in the distances not quite visible beyond the far shore of the lake.

They lay, soaking in the sun, seldom touching, never swimming, paying no attention to the children who dabbled in the shallows, the boats that docked and left—never noticing me, squatting at the base of the slope, souring my mouth with cigarettes, almost content with nothing more than my vision of them—static, impervious, unconcerned. It is a picture, but I am never in this one.

Guy Roland came and went, from Memorial Day through Labor Day, this summer I call the season of my rage at myself for being what I was without even the right to claim that I had made myself what I had become. His father ran the Silvercryst Resort and sold what remained of the lake frontage that he owned. Peaches Roland babied her flowers late mornings, drank away afternoons and evenings in the resort bar. What I hated most was my conviction that nothing would ever change.

"Where have you been so long?" my mother asked me when I returned.

"Nowhere. Down by the beach."

"I smell cigarette smoke."

"Cut it out," I said.

"You've been smoking!" she said. "What would your father say if I wrote him and told him you smoke?"

"Come on, cut it out."

"I give up," my mother said to me. "You don't listen to me. When are you going to be serious about anything?"

"I'm serious," I said. I was.

The truce had been signed for two years by the time I came back from Korea. I was hospitalized a long time in Japan, a long time in Fitzsimmons Hospital in Denver, and a long time in out-patient rehabilitation at Fort Sheridan, Illinois, while I tried out my rebuilt knee in what they called *real-life situations*. They rebuilt my knee with steel and wires and plastic, and it worked fine. I only used a cane because I was afraid it might give way at any moment. They said that was psychological. I thought I could hear my rebuilt knee make a clicking noise when I walked, but that was psychological too. My mother was very nervous about it.

"You're being silly," I told her. "It's the strongest part of my body. It's like a spot weld, the last thing that's going to break."

"I'm sorry," she said, "I can't help worrying." She had not changed while I was away. She looked just a little older. She was really upset only when we happened to talk about my father who had died suddenly in Minneapolis just before I came back from Japan.

"It's nice," I said. "Seriously, nothing's any different." She had not changed, except to look, naturally, a little older, and of course my father was dead, but he had gone out of my life years before.

It was night, so I picked my way slowly with my cane across the patches of moonlight breaking through the pine trees. I stopped to rest on the bluff, watched the moonlight ripple on the surface of Silver Lake. The lake stretched out below me, shimmering with the moon-haze that drifted over the pines above and behind me. Dock lights defined the far shore, and I could hear the same lapping of the water against the beach, the wind swish in the tops of the pines, the rustle of insects in the grass and ferns at my feet. I could hear the music of the jukebox in the bar of the Silvercryst Resort.

I knew what I would not find. Mr. Roland was also dead, my mother told me, a suicide. He shot himself about the time I was in Denver. She did not know the story. Business, perhaps, or his wife. He drove out on a dirt road, put the barrel of a pistol in his mouth, killed himself. Maybe it was his wife.

Peaches Roland had begun to need long stays at a downstate sanitarium, drying out. Now, my mother said, her mind was gone and she was committed forever to the sanitarium. "You ought to see how he's let her rock garden go," my mother said. Guy owned and operated the Silvercryst Resort, but he was no businessman, my mother said.

I expected at least a small crowd on a Friday night before Labor Day weekend, but the bar was empty except for Guy and a woman. The jukebox glowed, played loudly, and the fluorescents lit the back bar softly, but there were only the two of them, sitting on stools at the end of the bar as if they were customers, the bartender on a short break.

I smiled, put my weight on my cane, held my hand out to him. Guy Roland stared at me for a moment—the woman with him did not raise her head until we were introduced—then squinted, recognized me, smiled, took my hand.

"You don't have to wear your war suit," Guy said. "I'll serve you even if you're not of age. Hell, we're old folks, you and me."

"I'm old enough," I said, "just. I haven't had much chance to buy something that fits."

"Meet Sue," he said. The woman smiled at me as if I were going to take her picture. She was a good-looking woman. "This is my old buddy what's-his-name," Guy said to her, and "Sue is a personal guest here. I stress *personal*," he said, "because I hear rumors she favors men in uniform." She laughed and lowered her face to her drink—she drank bottled beer, liked to peel the labels off the bottles, pile the scraps on the bar. I said hello, and she laughed but never, I think, spoke to me all the time I sat talking with Guy.

She was fine-looking. I imagined her one of the girls who came and went with Guy through the summers before I went away. I could see her as one of those girls on the beach, gold-tan skin glossed with lotion, unfastening her swimsuit top to get the sun evenly across her back while she napped away the season's afternoons on a blanket, the portable radio playing music from Chicago and Milwaukee.

She was old enough to have been one of those girls, paled now because she spent her time indoors, wearing dangle earrings and chain bracelets that slid and rattled on her bare white arms as she picked at the label on her beer bottle. In the lulls of the lake breeze coming through the screened windows facing the bluff her heavy scent reminded me of Mrs. Peaches Roland drying out forever in a downstate sanitarium.

"Drinks on the house!" Guy said. "You name it, you got it," he said, "just so I can get to it without moving, that is." Sue laughed and tinkled her bracelets. Guy stretched across the bar, pulled up a bottle, splashed a refill in his glass—he did not bother with ice and water or soda. He spoke clearly, weaved a little when he tried to stand or walk, but did not stumble or stagger. When Sue wanted another bottle of beer to tear at, she got up and went behind the bar for it herself. She looked fine walking, too, jewelry glinting and ringing, her skin very white under the fluorescents. Guy grunted, stretched far enough to find me a shot glass.

"I'm not used to taking it straight," I said, but he paid no attention.

"Happy happy," he said, and we all drank. He closed his eyes when he drank as if he needed to concentrate to get the full taste of it, touched his lips lightly with his forefinger after he swallowed, sighed like a man falling into a long deep sleep. "So what the hell's with that walking stick?" he said. I told Guy and Sue about the mortar shell that fell near me. "You're crapping me," he said.

He leaned close to me, squinted, as if the campaign ribbons I wore contained fine print. "Real?" he said. "This is a *real* Purple Heart?" he said, pointing.

"That's the Syngman Rhee Citation. This one's the Purple Heart."

"You got to be crapping, buddy," Guy said. He made me pull up my trouser leg, show him the swollen, pink-stitched seams. I told him how it was rebuilt with steel and wire and plastic, that I imagined at times I could hear it click when I walked.

When he stopped laughing he said, "Six bits in the PX and you go off and get yourself the *real* thing!" Then he told me how he spent his war at Pensacola, Florida, some kind of air-corps liaison with the navy's flight-training school. The work called for a captain, so they made him a captain. When Sue laughed, she was laughing to herself. His campaign ribbons had all come from the Pensacola Naval Air Station PX, bought the day he got his separation papers.

"Why the hell not? My folks got a bang out of it."

"You bought those souvenirs at the PX too?" I tried to see into the darkened dining room, see if a Japanese sword hung over the natural-stone fireplace.

"I could get all that crap I wanted from the swabbies passing through flight school. You forget that was a *big* war, son," he said.

We talked, and we drank from Guy's bottle, and when I was feeling the whiskey, I told him my father was dead. When he only nodded, I said, "I was sorry as hell to hear about your father."

"That's a whole long story itself," is all he said, drinking, pressing his finger to his lips to dry them. Sue kept the jukebox playing, reaching into his pocket for quarters whenever it stopped.

"I'm sorry about your mother."

"She just needed a rest," he said. "You can understand a person needing a rest. Like yourself," he said. And: "So what the hell you figuring on now?"

"Home and sleep it off. If I can keep from going over the bluff with this cane." Sue thought that was funny, laughed with us.

"Smartass," Guy Roland said, "I mean your damn life."

"College, I think," I said, and told him what the GI Bill plus my permanent disability pension came to every month. He squinted at college, like it was a book he tried to recall reading, then smiled as if remembering it was amusing, but not serious. He had tried college, a couple of those winters that hit so quickly after Labor Day, upstate in Wisconsin.

"Don't break your fanny on my property," he called to me as I went out the door, keeping my cane out carefully in front of me—I believed my knee was going to collapse somewhere in the dark.

"Hey," I said, looking back at them from the doorway, "Where's everybody? Is this Labor Day weekend or not?"

"He must think this is a business or something!" he whooped. "Close the screen doors, you'll let mosquitoes in," he said, and got up to stretch for his bottle again.

My mother waited up for me. "What did you find to do all night?" she asked.

"Talking with Guy." I did not kiss her, did not want her to talk about the dangers of drinking so much when I could so easily fall and really hurt myself. "It's like a tomb at Silvercryst," I said to be saying something as I went toward the porch where I always slept at Silver Lake.

"He'll finish the ruin his father started," she said. "He takes no care at all."

"It's sad," I said, but my mother had no sympathy to spare for Guy Roland and his parents. I lay on my bed on the sleeping porch, waiting for the spinning whiskey to slow so I could sleep. When I could clear my mind I stayed awake a while to plan my life. I felt very good about it, as if my life was something I just discovered that I owned, mine to do with as I wished. I was pleased to discover that I was so mature.

I went to college and I got married. I studied nothing in particular in college, but I was graduated. The girl I married came from a very good Winnetka family. I learned the construction business from my father-in-law. I did not marry the boss's daughter and take over his business; I worked very hard, and the business was better for my work. First I lived in a fine home in Winnetka, near my wife's parents. After my children were born, I built a wonderful new home for us out in Skokie, where we lived close to wealthy Chicago doctors and lawyers and a few men who, like myself, were very serious about what they did for a living.

We built luxury condominium developments that sold as fast as we built them, and I had first a son, then a daughter, and a special wing on our wonderful home in Skokie, where my mother lived with us the last two and a half years of her life. I had no trouble at all in my life, and even my marriage was as good as most marriages—most of the time.

When my mother died, in the late spring of 1965, I used that as an excuse to go up to Silver Lake. "We can all go," I told my wife. "The kids would love it. You might even like it. Mix pleasure with business."

"That's your story," she said.

"I can't sell it out without being there," I said. "Those country real-estate boys will rob me blind."

"I'm *not* packing us all up and hauling all the way up there," she said.

"I have to go," I told my wife. "I can't handle it long distance."

"You do what you think you have to."

"I always have," I told her. "That's why I'm so good at it. Or didn't you notice?"

My wife and I never talked about our failing marriage, because it was too serious and depressing a topic and because, I suppose, we thought our failure would heal itself if we left it undisturbed long enough.

A lake, something in nature, does not change. The water level goes up or down a little from year to year, but as I stood on the bluff above Silver Lake, the moon still shimmered coldly on the surface, the breeze shushed in the tops of the pines above and behind me, the far shore was steady with dock lights. I did not see the fading paint on the summer home in the dark that first night, did not notice the pine needles banked up against the house by the winter, the remains of our pier heaved and broken by the winter ice, but inside, the walls held the musty damp of the closed winter that I remembered from opening the house each season after Memorial Day, years ago. Inside, everything was in place, clammy to the touch after several years undisturbed, but whole and unworn. The music still came through the air from the Silvercryst Resort, higher and stronger than ever, drowning out the lapping of the water at the beach below the bluff.

The resort was very crowded—the bar, the dining room, the new wing that held a second small bar and a sandwich shop and a souvenir counter. The music was a man in a tuxedo jacket and bow tie, playing a piano-bar. He had a machine he worked with a foot treadle. When people shouted requests from the dining room or the bar, or a woman at the piano-bar bent close to his ear to whisper a request, he riffled the keyboard, smiled, nodded that he knew the song. With his foot treadle he flashed a slide of the lyrics on a white screen mounted on the far wall. The projector was built into the piano-bar. The projector light also illuminated a nameplate on the piano-bar that said *Little Freddie Kay.*

The bartender was a man my age. The crowd kept him busy, but not too busy to take the drinks he was offered when someone ordered a round. He was a thin man with very black hair, long sideburns, a black mustache, a goatee so black it looked pasted on his chin. He wore a white shirt with ruffles, a red satin vest, frilly red garters on his sleeves to keep his cuffs out of the wet. He wore a colonel's string tie, trying for a western or 1890s idea in his costume. "Where's the boss?" I asked him. I had to speak loudly to be heard—Little Freddie Kay worked the projector treadle, and the crowd sang along with him. "On the Road to Mandalay." "K-K-K-Katy." "Down by the Riverside."

"Me myself and I," he said, grinning at me. He had very small and deep-set eyes, as black as his goatee, always lively, as if lit indirectly, like his back bar.

"Guy Roland?"

He grinned again. "He'll be along."

"You own this place now?"

"Since many moons back," he said, and went away from me in a hurry because they were calling for another round at the far end of the bar, insisting he have a drink with them.

"You a friend of Guy's?" the new owner of the Silvercryst Resort stopped later to say. When he grinned, his white teeth were very white against the black of his mustache and goatee. I wanted to reach out and pull his goatee off, but his white pointed teeth were like a dog's when the dog snarls.

"I used to know him a long time back."

"Now Guy is a man can drink drink for drink with you," the new owner of the Silvercryst Resort said, "but he only puddle-jumps now," he said, and shook his head and changed his grin to a sad grin. Little Freddie Kay sang "Waltzing Matilda" and "Roll Me Over in the Clover," and the crowd roared along with him. I waited, wondering why I was not with my family in my wonderful home in Skokie, and thought about my father who left me when I was fourteen, my mother who had only recently died. From time to time I tried to see through the reflections in the thermal panes of the big picture window, see the opposite shore, but could not make anything out clearly. Little Freddie Kay and the crowd sang "There'll Be a Hot Time in the Old Town Tonight."

When Guy Roland came in they were all singing "Row, Row, Row Your Boat." I remembered his drinking, but he was only a puddle-jumper now. He sat among all the singers who were singing "Danny Boy" now, sat in the middle of the singers and big drinkers, as quiet as if he were absolutely alone in the room. He did not call out or wave for the bartender. He sat on his stool looking straight ahead at nothing, somewhere in the reflecting glass of the picture window that was supposed to frame the view of Silver Lake. He stared like a man who sees only what he is thinking about.

When the new owner of the Silvercryst Resort chanced to look his way, Guy raised one finger, made a dry kissing motion with his lips to order the beer he drank now that he was only a puddle-jumper. I waited before going over to speak to him, to get two things firm and clear for myself. One was that I could never again truly imagine the past. The other was that I would have no difficulty imagining the future.

I could no longer imagine Captain Guy Roland of the Army Air Corps returning from the world war. I remembered it clearly, had it as I would have a snapshot in an album, and I was in that picture, but it was just something I remembered. I could no longer imagine Guy Roland coming and going, coming and going in his custom convertible through the long summers of my own ripening season. I remember his sporty car, and the tan-gold skin of the girls, his friends with their cutoff Greek-letter sweatshirts, the smell of suntan lotion in the lake breeze, music on a portable radio, but it is just another picture.

There were many fine-looking women in the new Silvercryst Resort bar, types of the woman Sue who tore labels off bottles all one night in that same room, ten years before, but I could not imagine Guy Roland anywhere before that moment, watching him drink his beer slowly while Little Freddie Kay led the hoarse crowd in "Oh! Susannah."

What I got very clear for myself, watching him from my end of the bar before I went over and spoke, was that time and change are facts of life for all of us. Time and change are what we are talking about when we talk about the future, about what we want for ourselves in life. These are the facts of life.

He would have, I saw, the spun white meringue hair of his father—already the blond was shot with silvery streaks that caught highlights. He wore his hair longer, in the new fashion, slicked with dressing to hold it all in hard and perfect order. His face had thickened to hint of jowls and double chin—Guy would grow heavier with the years. His cheeks, the tip of his nose, were lightly flushed—the years, doubtless, when he had matched every drink. Years of cautious puddle-jumping would not bring back the fairness of his prime. His blue eyes were still bright, like the eyes of a child after weeping, but ten years clung to him like a sad chronicle laid down in sedimentary stone.

"It's my turn to buy a round," I said. He recognized me at once.

"I'm double damned," Guy Roland said. His handshake was still solid, his voice unbroken; it was like hearing a recording that holds its fidelity after years of storage. "Your money's no good here," he said, taking out a clip of bills.

"This puddle-jumper," the new owner said, "I seen the day he'd drink you drink for drink, make you beg mercy."

"A real authentic shit," Guy Roland said when he left us.

"Why'd you sell out?" I asked. He had an easy laugh that had been used too often and too easily to ever be able to mean anything is ever funny any more.

He said, "Six of one, half a dozen of the other. I took enough out that I'll never have to work a day in my life. My old man always told me I had no head for business," he said. "All I needed was a few seasons to prove it." I looked to the door, to be sure there was a path I could maneuver with my stiff knee—in case I wanted to get away in a hurry. "The sauce," he said, tipping his glass to show me the beer in the bottom. "I was bombed for years. The amazing thing is I lightened up once I cut this place loose. I go three, four weeks at a crack without touching hard stuff. Keep an eye on yourself," Guy said, squinting, laughing, nodding at my drink; "a man can end up like Miss Peaches before he knows he's halfway there."

"I'll stay alert," I said, meaning it.

He told me Mrs. Peaches Roland was still alive, still lived in the downstate sanitarium. I told him my mother was dead, that I had come up from Chicago to see about selling the summer home. "Sell, sell," Guy Roland told me. "All the lake frontage's gone. You can turn it over in a minute. Get smart. Get free of it while the getting's good."

I told him I would, deciding I would not. I told him I was married, about my wife and son and daughter in our wonderful home in Skokie, Illinois, about constructing condominiums that sold faster than my father-in-law and I could build them. He stared off at nothing as I talked, licked his lips, savored the beer he drank three or four weeks at a time before he jumped into another puddle of the hard stuff. He did not tell me he was not married, that he did nothing, because he did not have to. I could read him as clearly as if his life were projected for me on the screen by Little Freddie Kay, between the lines of song lyrics.

Before I left, I asked him, "Guy, do you remember that girl Sue?"

"The which?"

"Sue something. She used to hang in here with you. Years ago."

"Sue," he said, trying to see something in the empty air in front of his eyes. "Double damn me if I do," he said. Why should his memory have been any better than mine?

Another ten years passed, and things were very different. When my father-in-law died, there were problems with our construction business—he left less in it than I thought he would. The construction business went bad for everyone, and almost nobody could afford to buy condominiums. Then I could not get money from banks to build them any more. Still it was not so bad until my wife divorced me and took almost everything that was left. Then I was no longer in the construction business.

I did not live in the wonderful home in Skokie, and I did not see my former wife or my son or my daughter any more. I had to drive up to Silver Lake in the dead of winter to sell the summer home because I needed the money badly, in a hurry, because I had almost nothing left. Guy Roland had put me in touch with a real-estate agent named Harley Eagan who, Guy wrote, handled most of the lake frontage that was bought and sold on Silver Lake these days.

I was almost snowblind for a moment, my eyes running tears from the bitter wind, when I got inside the Silvercryst bar. I stomped my feet free of snow, brought the sting of feeling back into my toes, coughing on the sudden warm air. When I took off my coat it was like taking off the cold winter air, like the season had changed back suddenly to late spring. Harley Eagan and Guy and the new owner of Silvercryst and another man I did not know were waiting for me. I thought at first they had opened the resort especially for me.

"Check his ID card, members only," the fourth man said.

"Welcomewelcomewelcome!" the new owner said.

"There's my man!" said the man who was Harley Eagan the real-estate agent. I knew his voice from the telephone. "Give the man a glass," he said. "He's about to dry up and die from exposure."

"No havee membership card, no drinkie drinkie here," said the man I did not know.

"Lighten up, Major," Guy Roland said. "This man's a war hero. I saw the scars myself." It was some kind of club. I dried my eyes on my handkerchief and, shaking, drank whiskey with them to start warmth inside me. They were a club of sorts, meeting daily through the long winter at the resort bar to drink themselves through the long off-season. I think they were close to madness, together like that all winter long.

"I'll be wanting to see those scars," the major said. I never got his name. He was a retired army major, and they called him Major, and almost never listened to him or answered when he spoke. He wore his pepper-salt hair crewcut, and he drank more than any of the rest of them.

"Stuff a bar rag in his mouth," Guy Roland said to the new owner of the Silvercryst Resort.

"Shut your face, Major," the new owner said. "Don't mind the major. The major's a good man. He'll drink you under the table with your little tootsies turned up to the sky." The new owner had not changed in the dead gray light of winter that came in the frosted windows, the stark black of his hair and mustache and goatee was more obviously dyed than I remembered. He had put off his vest and colonel's tie because he had no clientele in winter. His small eyes were still lively, and his pale hands never shook when he poured drinks or lit a cigarette with a lighter that flamed up high and made everyone laugh each time he lit it. "Flamethrower," he said, turning his head away and lighting it again. "Hey, Major, flamethrower!"

"A little pleasure mixed in won't hurt our business, mister," Harley Eagan said when I tried to talk to him about his selling the summer home quickly for me. "Put the next one on my chit, pal," he told the new owner. He reminded me of my ex-father-in-law, who was dead. My dead ex-father-in-law was not an alcoholic, but like Harley Eagan he smelled of aftershave and cologne and the lozenges that a successful alcoholic sucks to cover the drink on his breath. He dressed carefully, tweed jacket and vest, heavy gold cuff links and tie tack, thick digital wristwatch, big Masonic ring. He wore an old-fashioned hairpiece—when I got close I could see the delicate net pasted to his forehead, the artificial brown of the hairpiece marked off sharply from the washy gray of the hair above his ears, at the back of his head.

"I *need* to sell," I told him.

"Get too eager, mister, you'll take a beating. I know."

"Pay heed," the new owner said. "You're talking to the richest booze-hound in this and three counties. And a charter member of the Silver Lake Drunks, Incorporated," he said of Harley Eagan.

"You see me in what I'd call my element," Guy Roland said. Past fifty now, he was different, yet the very same. He was exactly as I would have imagined him, if I had bothered, over the years. His hair was now exactly his father's spun white. He wore it sculptor-cut over his ears, sprayed to hold a sweep low across his brow. He had gained a lot of weight, but covered it

with a loose peasant smock—like his mother, Peaches Roland, used to wear
to tend her flowers. He wore a bead choker, denim trousers, tan moccasins.

"How's your mother doing?"

"She goes on like time itself," he said.

"I thought you only jumped from puddle to puddle," I said.

"This is the puddle. Get it?" the new owner said.

"I'd go insane if I tried to dry out," Guy said.

"This puddle's so deep we grow gills just to keep breathing," the new
owner said.

"I confess I never shed blood for our flag," the major was saying.

"Winters I lie low," Harley Eagan said, tapping his temple with his
forefinger, as if there was a delicate mechanism there he might set right with
the proper nudge. "It's spring I get hustling. I turn over lake property like a
one-armed paperhanger. I'd be afraid to tell the tax man the commissions I
rake in, mister," he said.

"Jesus wept," I said to nobody there.

"So," Guy Roland said, "how's it feel to get up in your old stomping
grounds again?"

Through the frosted thermal windows the sky crept lower and darker
with the snow it promised. I tried to see through to the lake, but had to
imagine the sweep of the blowing snow over the ice, vehicle tracks, a few
ice-fishing shanties, the exact line of the opposite shore hidden under the
snow cover, the stark trees. The dining room was closed off, the piano-bar
draped with a cloth—what happened to Little Freddie Kay? I wondered.

"I'll be damned if I'll try to stay sober through a winter here," Guy said.

"I could sell cheese boxes sitting on postage stamps if it had some lake
frontage, come spring, mister," Harley Eagan said.

"Military life requires a special breed of man to stick it out," the major
was saying.

"What if I next year locked myself in here alone and reduced the inventory
all by my lonesome," the new owner of Silvercryst Resort said. "What'll
you booze-hounds do for laughs then? Major, you'll go completely nuts,
won't you!"

Jesus wept, I thought. I thought about all the people I had known in
my life who were dead, and I thought of my ex-wife and my son and my
daughter who were gone from me, and how when I saw them they would
be so different, so changed they would be like new people I did not know.
The people who were gone from me were like all the people who were dead.

I thought about all the summer homes on Silver Lake, closed up for
winter, dark, empty, how the frozen lake was like the flat expanse of a
cemetery, given up to cold and wind and snow. It was getting dark outside

already. The four of them—five counting myself—were like last survivors, mourners huddling for the last warmth of the last fire, praying on our stools for the hope of springs and summers we have almost forgotten, that we remember only in the way feverish dreams are remembered. I closed my eyes, tried to forget everything about everything I ever knew. I must have said something, because Guy Roland heard me.

"Don't take life so serious," he told me. "It ain't even permanent." I opened my eyes, breathed very deeply, shook my head to be sure it was not the whiskey making me talk.

"Oh, it's serious," I said.

"No, it's not," he said, finishing his drink, setting the glass on the bar for a refill.

"I know better," I said.

"No, you don't," he said. He held up his fresh drink, squinted to see through the whiskey to the window, out the window into the winter dark.

I said, "Even if it's not, it used to be." He drank, puckered his lips, shook his head as he held the drink in his mouth, rolled it on his tongue. No. It was not. "At least for me it was, once," I said. He looked out the window, drank again, shook his head. No, not even for me. "Then what are we even talking about it for?" I said. He shrugged.

I left as quickly as I could. I settled the picture of them together there, half-mad, and I was in it, and not in it, and then I left. Thinking, I sat a long while in my car, letting the engine warm, the heater going. I thought about it all the way back to Chicago on the superhighway made treacherous by swirling snow and patches of ice. I could wait for spring to sell the summer home, a better market.

I thought about all the dead and living people I knew, and about the living people like Guy Roland, who were dead, and about all the living people who had gone from me, like the dead. I thought about all the living people I knew who were all going to die, when they died, or before they died.

I drove slowly so I would not worry about the road. I did not play the radio, tried not to read the green and silver signboards with the names of all the small Wisconsin towns, so I could think about all this, and about myself.

I tried to decide if I was living or dead. If I was living, would I wait to die to be dead, or if I was already dead, when had it happened? How long had I lived? These are serious questions. I do not ask them lightly, and I continue to work on the answers.

Hog's Heart

Nor mouth had, no nor mind, expressed
What heart heard of, ghost guessed

—Gerard Manley Hopkins

IT IS EVERYTHING and it is nothing. Hog says, "Different times it's different feeling. Sometimes I feel like that it might could just be a feeling. Sometimes I feel it is happening right then."

"Goddamnit, Hog," says Dr. Odie Anderson. Hog, perched on the edge of the examination table, cannot be more precise. He feels ridiculous, feet suspended above the floor like a child's, wearing a flimsy paper hospital gown that, like a dress, barely covers his scarred knees. Though the air-conditioning sighs incessantly, he exudes a light sweat, pasting the gown to his skin, thighs and buttocks cemented to the table's chill metal surface. "Is it pains?" the doctor says. "Is it chest pain? Is it pain in your arm or shoulder? Is it pain you feel in your neck or your jaw?"

Hog says, "It might could be I just imagine it sometimes." Dr. Odie Anderson, team physician, sits in his swivel chair, lab coat thrown open, collar unbuttoned, necktie askew, feet up and crossed on his littered desk. Hog sees the holes in the soles of the doctor's shoes. Odie Anderson's head lolls slightly, canted. His eyes, bulging and glossy, like a man with arrested goiter, roll. He licks his lips, moistens the rim of scraggly beard around his open mouth.

"Damn," says Dr. Anderson, "is it choking? Your breath hard to get? Sick to your stomach a lot?" To avoid looking at him, Hog turns his head to the window before opening his eyes. The rectangle of searing morning light dizzies him. He grips the edge of the table with both hands, tries not to hear the doctor, feels the trickle of sweat droplets course downward from the tonsure of hair above his jug ears, from the folds of flesh at his throat, the sausage rolls of fat at the back of his neck, from his armpits. He represses malarial shudders as the air conditioner blows on his bare back where the paper gown gaps.

"You want me to send you to Jackson to the hospital? Want all kinds of tests, swallowing radioactivity so they can take movies of your veins?" Almost touching the windowpane, magnolia leaves shine in the brilliant light as if greased. One visible blossom looks molded of dull white wax that will surely melt and run if the sun's rays reach it. A swath of lawn shimmers in the heat like green fire. The length of sidewalk Hog can see is empty. The cobbled street beyond is empty, stones buckled and broken.

"Not now," Hog says. "I got a season starting. I might could maybe go come spring if I can get off recruiting a while."

"Well now," Dr. Anderson is saying, "you *are* fat as a damn house, Hog, and your blood pressure *is* high. You might could be a classic case, except you don't smoke, and last I heard your daddy's still kicking up there to Hot Coffee."

"Daddy's fine. He's a little bitty man, though. I come by my size favoring Mama's people." A pulp-cutter's truck, stacked high with pine logs, and a flatbed truck, stumps chained to the bed, pass on their way up to the Masonite plant at Laurel.

"Get dressed, Hog," the doctor says. "I can't find nothing wrong in there. Hell, you strong as stump whiskey and mean as a yard dog!" Hog buttons his shirt, zips his fly evading Dr. Anderson's leering cackle.

Sometimes it is everything. It is the sticky, brittle feel of sweat drying on his skin, the drafty breath of the air conditioner that makes him shudder in spasms, raises goose bumps on his forearms. It is the late August morning's heat and humidity hovering like a cloud outside, waiting to drop on him, clutch him. It is the baked streets and sidewalks, the withering campus and lawns, everyone in Hattiesburg driven indoors until dusk brings relief from the glaring sun of south Mississippi.

"Say hey to Nyline and the chaps for me," says Odie Anderson.

It is his wife and four sons, it is the steaming campus, the athletic dormitory and stadium, the office where his senior assistants wait to review game films, the approach of the season opener at home against Alabama, this fourth year of his five-year contract, two-a-day workouts and recruiting trips across the Deep South and a pending NCAA investigation. It is all things now and up to now—his folks up at Hot Coffee, paying his dues coaching high school and junior college, his professional career cut short by injury in Canada, all things seeming to have come together to shape his conviction that he will soon die from heart failure.

"We going to whip up on Bama, Hog?"

"We die trying," says Hog. They laugh. It is nothing.

Hog decides he is not dying, not about to, not subject to be dying. It is something that is probably nothing, and because he cannot define or express it, it is a terror there is no point in fearing. Hog decides it is himself, Hog Hammond, alive in Hattiesburg, Mississippi, in the blistering heat of late August, knowing he is alive, no more than naturally wondering about death.

Fraternity and sorority pep-club banners limply drape the stadium walls. BEAT BAMA. ROLL BACK THE TIDE. GO SOUTHERN. WE BACK HOG'S BOYS. The stadium walls throw heat into Hog's face. Pines and magnolias and live oaks droop in the humidity. The mockingbirds are silent. The painted letters on the banners swim before his eyes, air pressing him like a leaden mist. He begins to consciously reach, pull for each breath, lurches sweating, wheezing, into the shade of the stadium entrance to his office.

Inside, the dimness makes him light-blind, the coolness is a clammy shock, his heaving echoes off tile and paneling. Hog finds himself, eyes adjusting, before the Gallery of Greats, a wall-length display of photos and newspaper clippings, trophies and pennants, locked behind nonreflecting glass. This pantheon of Mississippi Southern's finest athletes, record-setters, semi–All Americans, is a vanity he cannot resist.

His breathing slows and softens, sweat drying in his clothes, on his skin, as he steps closer. There he is, the great Hog Hammond in the prime of his prowess and renown. Three pictures of Hog: a senior nineteen years ago, posed in half-crouch, helmet off to show his bullet head, cropped hair, arms raised shoulder-high, fingers curled like talons, vicious animal snarl on his glistening face; Hog, nineteen years ago, down in his three-point stance, right arm lifting to whip the shiver-pad into the throat of an imaginary offensive guard; Hog, snapped in action, the legendary Alabama game nineteen years ago, charging full-tilt, only steps away from brutally dumping the confused Alabama quarterback for a loss. Hog is motion, purpose, power; the Alabama quarterback is static, timid, doomed.

The newspaper clippings are curled at the edges, yellowing. *Southern Shocks Ole Miss. Southern Stalemates Mighty Tide. The Hog Signs for Canada Pros.*

Athletic Director Tub Moorman is upon him, comes up behind him silently, like an assassin with a garrote, the only warning the quick stink of the dead cigar he chews, laced with the candy odor of his talc and hair oil. Hog feels a catch in his throat, a twinge in his sternum, salivates.

"Best not live on old-timey laurels, Hog," says Athletic Director Tub Moorman. A column of nausea rises from the pit of Hog's belly to his chest, tip swaying into his gullet like a cottonmouth's head. He tenses to hold his windpipe open. "Best look to *this* season," Tub Moorman says. Hog, pinned against the cool glass of the Gallery of Greats, gags, covers with a cough.

"I'm directly this minute subject to review game films," he is able to say. Tub Moorman does not seem to hear. He is a butterball, head round as a wash pot, dirt-gray hair slicked with reeking tonic, florid face gleaming with aftershave. He dresses like a New Orleans pimp, white shoes, chartreuse slacks, loud blazer, gaudy jewel in his wide tie, gold digital watch, oversize diamond on his fat pinky, glossy manicured nails. His sour breath cuts through his lotions. He limps slightly from chronic gout.

"This year four," Tub Moorman says. "Year one we don't much care do you win. Play what you find when you come aboard. Year two, year three, your business to scout the ridges and hollows for talent. Year four, we looking to see do you *pro*duce, see do we want to keep you in the family after year five. This is year four. Root hog or die, hear?" The athletic director speaks, laughs, without removing his unlit cigar from his mouth. Hog can see the slimy butt of the cigar, Tub Moorman's tongue and stained teeth.

Hog is able to say, "I'm feeling a touch puny today," before he must clamp his lips.

"You know we mighty high on you, Hog," Tub Moorman says. "You one of us and all." He flicks his lizard's eyes at the Gallery's pictures and clippings. "You a great one. You hadn't got injured so soon in Canada, you might could of been famous as a professional. We fixing to build this program up great, Hog. Fixing to find the man can do it if you ain't him."

"I'm subject to give it all I got," Hog gasps, bile in his mouth.

"Fact is," says the athletic director, "you got to beat Alabama or Ole Miss or Georgia Tech or Florida, somebody famous, or we got to be finding us the man will."

"I might could. I got me a nigger place-kicker can be the difference."

Tub Moorman's laugh is a gurgling, like the flush of a sewer. "We ain't particular," he says, "but the NCAA is. Best not let no investigators find out your Cuba nigger got a forged transcript, son. Best forget old-timey days, be up and doing *now*." Hog hurries to the nearest toilet, the athletic director's stench clings to him, chest-thick with sickness, throat charged with acid, head swimming. Retching into the closest commode, Hog blows and bellows like a teased bull, clears the residue of Tub Moorman's smell from his nostrils.

On the portable screen Alabama routs Ole Miss before a record homecoming crowd at Oxford. Slivers of the sunlight penetrate the room at the edges of the blackout curtains, casting an eery light on the acoustical ceiling. The projector chatters, the air conditioner chugs. Only Sonny McCartney, Hog's coordinator, takes notes, writing a crabbed hand into manila folders, calling for freeze-frames and reruns. Sonny McCartney reminds Hog frequently that national ranking is only a matter of planning, implementation of strategy, time.

Wally Everett, offensive assistant, mans the projector. Once a fleet wide receiver for the Tarheels of North Carolina, he wears a prim, superior expression on his patrician face. Because he wears a jacket and necktie in even the warmest weather, he is sometimes mistaken for a professor. Believing there is no excuse for vulgar or obscene language, on or off the playing field, he is a frequent speaker at Fellowship of Christian Athletes banquets. He sits up straight in his chair, knees crossed, like a woman, hands, when not operating the projector's levers and buttons, folded in his lap.

The defensive assistant, Thumper Lee, slouches in a chair at the back of the room. He played a rugged noseguard for a small Baptist college in Oklahoma, looks like an aging ex-athlete should, unkempt, strong, moody, unintellectual. He shifts his weight in his chair, stamps his feet often as Alabama's three-deep-at-every-position squad shreds the Rebels on the screen. He snorts, says, "I seen two county fairs and a train, but I ain't never seen nothing like them! Them sumbitches *good,* Hog!"

"The problem," says Sonny McCartney, "is to decide what we can do best against them."

"They execute to perfection," says Wally Everett.

Wally rewinds the film for one more showing. Sonny rereads his notes. Thumper Lee spits a stream of juice from his Red Man cud into the wastebasket. The room is darker with the projector bulb off, the air conditioner louder in the greater silence. Hog holds tightly to the arms of his chair. He feels as if, at the very center of his heart, a hole, a spot of nothingness, forms. He braces himself. The hole at the center of his heart doubles in size, doubles again; his vital, central substance is disappearing, vanishing without a trace. He tries to hear the movement of his blood, but there is only the perpetual churning of the air conditioner, the click and snap of the projector being readied.

"Hog," says Thumper Lee, pausing to rise an inch off his chair, break wind with a hard vibrato, "Hog, they going to eat our lunch come opening day."

"Every offense has a defense," Sonny McCartney says.

"There is little argument with basic execution," Wally says.

It will grow, Hog believes, this void in his chest, until he remains, sitting, a hollow shell with useless arms, legs, head. He will crumple, fall to the carpeted floor, dead.

"Alabama don't know we got Fulgencio Carabajal," Sonny says.

"Neither does the NC double-A," Wally says. "Yet. But they will if we let just one person close enough to speak to him."

"Is that tutoring learning him any English yet?" Thumper Lee asks.

"Again?" says Wally, finger on the projector's start-button.

"Ain't this a shame?" says Thumper, "Our best offense a nigger from Cuba don't talk no English."

"*I* did not forge his transcript," Wally says.

"He *can* kick," says Sonny, and, "Hog?"

Hog, dying, rises from his chair. "You-all discuss this without me," he says, finds he can take a step toward the door. Another. "I got to get me some fresh air, I am feeling puny, boys," says Hog, reaches the doors, opens it, leaves, walking slowly, carefully, like a man made of blown glass, no core left to him at all, no heart.

There is no reason Hog should wake in the still-dark hours of early morning, no stomach upset or troubling dream. At first he is merely awake, Nyline beside him. Then his eyes focus, show him the lighter darkness, false dawn at the bedroom windows, and then he sees the ceiling, walls, furniture, the glow of the night-light from the master bedroom's full bath, the light blanket covering him and his wife, Nyline in silhouette, the back of her head studded with curlers. He hears the gentle growl of her snoring. He hears the high sighing of cooled air cycling through the house on which the mortgage runs past the year 2022.

He lies very still in the king-size bed, shuts out what he can see and hear, the rich smell of Nyline's Shalimar perfume, closes himself away, then knows what has awakened him from deep sleep. Now Hog hears, measures the rhythms, recognizes the subtle reduction in pace, tempo, intensity of his heartbeat. His heart is slowing, and this has awakened him, so that he can die knowing he is dying. The beat is still regular, but there comes a minuscule hesitation, a near-catch, a stutter before the muffled thump of each beat. He lies very still, holds his breath, the better to hear and feel. Then he inches his left hand free of the cover, moves it into position to press the declining pulse in his right wrist.

His heart will run down like a flywheel yielding up its motion to the darkness of the master bedroom. He is dying here and now, at the moment of false dawn that shows him the shafts of pine trunks in his yard, the wrinkled texture of his new lawn of Bermuda grass. He will lie there and be discovered by Nyline when she wakes to the electric buzz of the alarm on her bedside table.

"Nyline," Hog whispers. "Nyline." His voice surprises him; how long can a man speak, live, on the momentum of his last heartbeats? "Nyline." She groans, turns to him, puts out a hand, eyes shut, groping. Her arm comes across his chest, takes hold of his shoulder. She nuzzles his jaw, kisses him in her half-sleep, presses her head into his throat, her curlers stabbing the soft flesh.

Hog says, "Nyline, I love you. I thank you for marrying me, when my people is just redneck pulp-cutters and you're from fine high-type Biloxi people. It is always a wonder to me why you married me when I was just a football player, and you was runner-up Miss Gulf Coast and all. There's mortgage life insurance on the house, Nyline, so you'll have the house all paid for."

"Big sweet thing," his wife mumbles into his collarbone.

"No, Nyline," he says. "I do love you and thank you for giving me our boys. I am dying, Nyline, and it is just as good I do now, because we won't be beating Alabama or Ole Miss nor nobody big-timey, and the NCAA will likely soon get me for giving a scholarship to a Cuba nigger has to have a interpreter to play football, and we will lose this house and everything, except I am dying and you will get it because of insurance."

"Lovey, you want me to be sweet for you?" Nyline says, kisses his hairy chest, strokes his face and the slick bald crown of his head.

"No," Hog says. "Listen, Nyline. Tell me can you hear my heart going." She mutters as he turns her head gently, places her ear against his breast, then resumes her light snoring.

Dying, Hog lifts her away to her side of the bed, throws back the cover, rises, pads out of the master bedroom. Dying, he walks down the hall to the bedrooms where his four sons sleep.

He can stand at the end of the hall, look into both bedrooms, see them sleeping, two in each room, and he stands, looking upon the future of his name and line, stands thinking of his wife and sons, how he loves them, in his wonderful new home with a mortgage that runs beyond the year 2022, thinking it is cruel to die when he can see the future sleeping in the two bedrooms.

It is the coming of true dawn, flaring in the windows of his sons' side-by-side bedrooms, that grants him a reprieve. True dawn comes, lights the trees and grass and shrubbery on his lawn, stirs a mockingbird to its first notes high in a pine tree, primes his flickering heart to a renewed rhythm. He feels it kick into vigor like a refueled engine, then goes to the hall bathroom, sits, grateful, weeping, on the edge of the bathtub, staring at his blank-white toes and toenails, lavender-tinged white feet, his heart resuming speed and strength for another day.

Nyline and his sons are somewhere outside with Daddy and Brother-boy, seeing the new machinery shed or feeding Brother-boy's catfish. Hog's mama serves him a big square of cornbread and a glass of cold buttermilk.

The golden cornbread, straight from the oven, radiates heat like a small sun. Hog bites, chews, swallows, breaks into a sweat as he chills his mouth with buttermilk. Not hungry, he gives himself over to the duty of eating for her. He sweats more freely with the effort, feels a liquid warmth emerge in his belly, grow. Hog feigns gusto, moans, smacks his lips, slurps for her. A viscous heat squirts into his chest.

"No more," he says as she reaches toward the pan with a knife to cut him another helping. "Oh, please, Mama, no," says Hog. He tries to smile.

"I want to know what is the matter with my biggest boy," she says. "You say you are feeling some puny, but I know my boy, Euliss. I think you are troubled in your spirit, son."

"I have worries, Mama," he tells her. "We got to play Alabama. I am just troubled with my work."

"Is it you and Nyline? Is it your family, Euliss, something with my grandbabies?"

"We all fine, Mama. Truly." He averts his eyes. She does not look right, his old mama, in this modern kitchen, chrome and formica and plastic-covered chairs, double oven set in the polished brick wall, blender built into the countertop, bronze-tone refrigerator big as two football lockers, automatic ice-cube maker, frostless, Masonite veneer on the cupboards; Hog remembers her cooking at an iron woodstove, chopping wood for it as skillfully as she took the head off a chicken while he clung to her long skirts, sucking a sugartit. He remembers her buying fifty-pound blocks of ice from the nigger wagon driver from Laurel, taking his tongs and carrying it into the house herself (because she would not allow a nigger in her kitchen) until Hog was old enough to fetch and carry for her, his daddy out in the woods cutting pulp timber dawn to dusk.

Hog covers his eyes with his hand to hide the start of tears, hurt and joy mixing in him like a boiling pot, that his mama has this fine kitchen in this fine new brick home built by his daddy and Brother-boy on a loan secured by Hog's signature and Hog's life insurance, that his mama is old and will not ever again be like he remembers her, that she will not live forever.

"I do believe my boy is troubled in his soul," Mama says.

"Not my soul, Mama." Hog comes by his size from Mama's daddy, a pulp-cutter who died before Hog was born; Hog remembers her telling him how her daddy had lost four and a half fingers from his two hands, cutting pulpwood for Masonite in Laurel all his life until a tree fell on him and killed him. Hog looks at her fingers, at his own.

"Are you right with Jesus, Euliss?" she says. She leans across the table, hands clenched in prayer now. "I pray to Jesus," says Mama, "for my boy Euliss. I pray for him each day and at meeting particular." A dam bursts somewhere on the margins of Hog's interior, a deluge of tepidness rushing to drown his heart.

"We go to church regular in Hattiesburg, Mama," he is able to say before the spill deprives him of words and will.

"Pray with me, Euliss," she says. "Oh, pray Jesus ease your trouble, drive doubt and Satan out! Oh, I am praying to You, Jesus, praying up my biggest boy to You!" Her locked hands shake, as if she tries to lift a weight too great for her wiry arms, her eyes squeezed shut to see only Blessed Jesus, lips puckered as though she drew the Holy Spirit into her lungs. Hog cannot look. It is his old mama, who attends the Primitive Baptist Church of Hot Coffee, where she wrestles Satan until she falls, frothing, weeping, to the floor before the tiny congregation, where she washes the feet of elders. "Jesus, Jesus, speak to my boy Euliss," she prays in the fine modern kitchen of the modern brick ranch house built on land won by two generations of scrub cattle drivers and pulpwood cutters.

Hog's heart moves like a wellhouse pump lifting a thick, hot sweetness into his mouth. This death is sweet, filling, filled with Mama's love, all he feels of his memories of her, Daddy, Brother-boy. "JesuspleaseJesusplease," she chants.

"Mama," says Hog, getting up, voice breaking on his lips like a bubble of honey, "I got to go find Daddy and Nyline and Brother-boy and those chaps. We got to be leaving back to Hattiesburg. Time flying, Mama." He leaves the kitchen, the waters of her love receding in his wake.

Hog and his daddy admire the glossy Angus at the salt lick, the cattle clustering in the narrow shade of the old mule-driven mill where Hog helped his daddy crush cane for syrup. Hog sees the Angus melded with the scrubby mavericks he ran in the woods with razorbacks for his daddy, hears the squeak and crunch of the mill turning, snap of cane stalks. "Now see this, Euliss," says his daddy, a small man who has aged by shriveling, drying, hardening. "Don't it beat all for raising a shoat in a nigger-rigged crib?" his hardness glowing redly in the terrible sunshine, burnished with pride over the new cement floor of his pigpen. Hog, gasping, clucks appreciation for him. "Wait and see Brother-boy feed them fish!" his daddy says.

"Daddy," Hog says, "how come Mama's so much for churching and you never setting foot in it, even for revivals?" Hog's daddy blows his nose between thumb and forefinger, expertly flicks snot into the grass near the row of humming beehives that Hog, wreathed in smoke, veiled, helped rob in his youth.

"I never held to it," his daddy says, stopped by Hog's heavy hand on his shoulder.

"Why not? You didn't never believe in God? Ain't you never been so scared of dying or even of living so's you wanted to pray like Mama?" He hears his own voice muffled, as if cushioned by water.

"I never faulted her for it, Euliss," says his daddy. "And no man dast fault me for not. Son, most of us don't get hardly no show in life. Now, not you, but me and Brother-boy and your mama. Life wearies a man. Them as needs Jesusing to die quiet in bed or wherever, I say fine, like for Mama. Me nor mine never got no show, excepting you, naturally, Euliss, a famous player and coach and all. I guess I can die withouten I screech to Jesus."

"Daddy," says Hog. Blood fills his chest, a rich lake about his heart, pressing his lungs. "Daddy, was I a good boy?"

"Now, Euliss." His daddy embraces him, sinewy arms, the spread fingers of his rough hands clasping Hog's heaving sides. "Euliss, don't you know I have bragged on you since you was a chap?"

"Are you proud of me still?" His daddy laughs, releases him, steps back.

"Oh, you was a pistol, son, for that football from the start. I recollect you not ten years old going out to lift the new calf day by day to build muscles for football playing!"

"Daddy." He feels a pleasant cleft in his breast widen, a tide of blood.

"Recollect the time I *told* you not to be blocking yourself into the gallery post for football practice? I had to frail you with a stick. Oh, son, you was a pure pistol for that footballin! Your daddy been bragging on you since, Euliss!"

"Find Brother-boy. Want to see them fish," Hog chokes, this death almost desirable to him. He moves away, suffocating in the fluid of his emotions.

"Brother," says Hog, "Brother-boy, are you resentful you stayed and lived your life here? Ain't you never wanted a wife and chaps of your own? Do you resent I went away to school for football and to Canada for my own life while you just stayed working for Daddy?" Brother-boy looks like Hog remembers himself half a dozen years ago, less bald, less overweight. From a large cardboard drum, he scoops meal, sows it on the dark green surface of the artificial pond. The catfish he farms swim to the top, thrash, feeding, rile the pond into bubbles and spray. "Was I a good brother to you? Is it enough I signed a note so's you can start a fish farm and all this cattle and stock of Daddy's?"

Brother-boy, sowing the meal in wide arcs over the pond, says, "I never grudged you all the fine things you got, Euliss. You been a special person, famous playing football in college and Canada and now a famous coach." His brother's voice dims, lost in the liquid whip of the pond's surface, the frenzied feeding of the catfish. "I am a happy enough man, Euliss," says Brother-boy. "I have things I do. Mama and Daddy need me. They getting old, Euliss. I don't need me no wife nor chaps, and I got a famous big brother was a famous player once and now a coach, and your sons are my nephews." Hog remembers Brother-boy, a baby wearing a shift, a chap following after him at chores, coming to see him play for Jones Agricultural Institute & Junior College in Laurel, for Mississippi Southern, once coming by train and bus all the way up to Calgary to see Hog's career end in injury. "It is not my nature to resent nor grudge nobody nothing," says his brother. "It is my way to accept what is."

Hog lurches away, seeking an anchor for his heart, tossed in a wave of sweet blood, wishing he could die here and now if he must die. But knowing his death is yet to come is like a dry wind that evaporates the splash of love and memory within him, turning this nectar stale, then sour.

Seeking an overview of the last full drill in pads, Hog takes to a stubby knoll, shaded by a live oak tree, its long snaking limbs supported by cables fastened to the tree's black trunk. From here, the practice field falls into neat divisions of labor.

At the far end of the field, parallel to the highway to Laurel and Hot Coffee, chimeric behind the rising heat waves, Fulgencio Carabajal place-kicks ball after ball through jerry-built wooden goalposts, the first-string center snapping, third-team quarterback holding, two redshirts to shag balls for the Cuban, who takes a break every dozen or so balls to talk with his interpreter. Hog watches Fulgencio's soccer-style approach, hears the hollow strike of the side of his shoe on the ball, the pock of this sound a counterpoint to the beating of Hog's heart. He tries to follow the ball up between the uprights, loses it in the face of the sun that washes out the green of the dry grass.

Closest to Hog's shady knoll, the first- and second-team quarterbacks alternate short spot-passes with long, lazy bombs to a self-renewing line of receivers who wait their turns casually, hands on hips. Catching balls in long fly patterns, receivers trot up to the base of Hog's knoll, cradling the ball loosely, showboating for him. He does not allow them to think he notices. The slap of ball in hands comes as if deliberately timed to the throb of his heart, adding its emphasis to the twist of its constrictions.

At the field's center, Sonny McCartney coordinates, wears a gambler's green eyeshade, clipboard and ballpoint in hand. Sonny moves from offense to defense in the shimmer of the heat like a man wading against a current. Hog squints to find Thumper Lee, on his knees to demonstrate firing off the snap to his noseguard, his jersey as sweated as any player's. Wally Everett, as immobile as Hog, stands among his offensive players, stopping the drill frequently with his whistle, calling them close for short lectures, as unperturbed by the temperature and humidity as if he worked with chalk on blackboard in an air-conditioned classroom.

Hog's heart picks up its pace, the intensity of each convulsion increasing to a thud, a bang. Now he cannot distinguish the echo of his accelerating heartbeat from the smack of pads down on the practice field, the slap of ball on sweaty palm, thumping of the tackling dummy, crash of shoulders against the blocking sled, squealing springs, the hollow pock of Fulgencio Carabajal's kicking.

Hog closes his eyes to die, digs with his cleats for a firmer stance on the knoll, prepared to topple into the dusty grass. He tenses, wonders why this raucous slamming of his heart does not shake him, why he does not explode into shards of flesh and bone. And wonders why he is not dead, still holding against his chest's vibrations, when he hears Sonny McCartney blow the final whistle to end the drill. Hog's heart subsides with the blood's song in his ears, like the fade of Sonny's whistle in the super-heated air of late afternoon.

It is light. Light falling upon Hog, his wife still sleeping as he rises. Special, harder and brighter light while fixing himself a quick breakfast in the kitchen, chrome trim catching and displaying early morning's show of light to him while Nyline is dressing, his sons stirring in their bedrooms toward this new day. Light, the morning sky clear as creek water, climbing sun electric-white, overwhelming Hog's sense of trees, houses, streets, driving slowly through Hattiesburg to the stadium. And light, lighting his consciousness, pinning his attention in the gloom of the squad's locker room, the last staff strategy session, his talk to his players before they emerge into the light of the stadium.

Hog tells them, "It is not just football or playing a game. It is like life. It is mental toughness. Or you might call it confidence. I do not know if you-all are as good as Alabama. Newspapers and TV say you are not, they will whip our butts. If it is true, they is nothing any of us or you-all can do. We all have to face that. It is Alabama we are playing today. Maybe it is like you-all have to go out and play them knowing you will not have any show. It might could be I am saying mental toughness is just having it in you to do it even knowing they will whip up on your butt. I don't know no more to say." He leads them out into the light.

He sees, hears, registers it all, but all is suffused with this light, a dependency of light. The game flows like impure motes in perfect light. The game is exact, concrete, but still dominated by, a function of this light. The opening game against Alabama is a play of small shadows within the mounting intensity of light.

At the edge of the chalked boundary, Hog notes the legendary figure of the opposing coach across the field, tall, chain-smoking cigarettes, houndstooth-checked hat, coatless in the dense heat Hog does not feel. This light has no temperature for Hog, a light beyond heat or cold.

"They eating our damn lunch, Hog!" Thumper Lee screams in his ear when Alabama, starting on their twenty after Fulgencio Carabajal sends the kickoff into the end zone bleachers, drives in classic ground-game fashion for the first touchdown. The snap is mishandled, the kick wide.

"I declare we can run wide on them, Hog," says Wally Everett as Southern moves the ball in uneven spurts to the Crimson Tide thirty-seven, where, stalled by a broken play, Fulgencio Carabajal effortlessly kicks the three-pointer. "I have seen teams field-goaled to death," Wally says.

Late in the second quarter, Southern trails only 13–9 after Fulgencio splits the uprights from fifty-six yards out. "We *got* the momentum, Hog," says Sonny McCartney, earphones clamped on to maintain contact with the press-box spotters. "We can run wide, and pray Fulgencio don't break a leg."

Thumper Lee, dancing, hugging the necks of his tackles, spits, screams, "I seen a train and two fairs, but I ain't never seen *this* day before!"

"Notice the Bear's acting nervous over there?" Wally says, points to the excited assistants clustering in quick conference around the houndstooth hat across the field.

Says Hog, "You can't never tell nothing about how it's going to be."

His death comes as light, all light, clarity, comprehensive and pervasive. There is nothing Hog does not see, hear, know. Everything is here, in this light, and not here. It is a moment obliterating moments, time or place.

He knows a great legend is unfolding on the playing field, an upset of the Crimson Tide. Hog knows he has come to this wonder, this time and place, by clear chronology, sequence of accident and design, peopled since the beginning with his many selves and those who have marked him and made him who and what he is in this instant of his death. Light draws him in, draws everything together in him, Hog, the context of his death.

Dr. Odie Anderson sits on a campstool behind the players' bench, feet up on the bench, scratching his beard with both hands, rolling his bulged eyes at the scoreboard. Athletic Director Tub Moorman's face is wine-red with excitement, his unlit cigar chewed to pulp. Thumper Lee drools tobacco juice when he shouts out encouragement to his stiffening defense. Wally Everett smirks as he counsels his quarterback. Sonny McCartney relays information from his spotters in the press box, where Nyline and the four sons of Hog watch the game through binoculars, drinking complimentary Coca-Colas. On the bench next to his chattering interpreter, Fulgencio Carabajal waits indifferently for his next field-goal attempt. In the new modern kitchen in Hot Coffee, Hog's people, Mama, Daddy, Brother-boy listen to the radio broadcast, proud and praying. Only a little farther, folded into his memory, are the many Hogs that make him Hog: a boy in Hot Coffee lifting new calves to build muscle, football find at the Jones Agricultural Institute & Junior College, bona fide gridiron legendary Little All-American on this field, sure-fire prospect with Calgary's Stampeders in the Canadian Football League, career cut short by knee and ankle injuries, high-school coach, defensive assistant, coordinator, Hog here and now, head coach at Mississippi Southern University, all these simultaneous in the marvel of his death's light.

Dying, Hog looks into the glare of the sun, finds his death is not pain or sweetness, finds totality and transcendence, dies as they rush to where he lies on the turf, dying, accepting this light that is the heart of him joining all light, Hog and not-Hog, past knowing and feeling or need and desire to say it is only light, dies hearing Fulgencio Carabajal say, *"Muerte?"* gone into such light as makes light and darkness one.

Ah Art! Oh Life!

OSKAR WATCHED PROFESSOR BERNTSSON paint. The Professor's wife watched Oskar. Oskar tried not to show he knew she watched him. The Professor looked only at his canvas on the easel, and at his image in the large mirror propped against the wall; he glanced quickly at the reflection of himself, perched on the high stool, painting, back at the canvas, a portrait of himself painting a self-portrait. Oskar, seated on the sofa, tried to draw the Professor in the big sketchbook. The Professor's wife sat in the overstuffed chair in the far corner of the room, wrapped in an afghan.

Oskar could see everything: the walls hung with paintings, the Professor on his stool, the image of him in the mirror, the incomplete image in oils on the canvas, Mrs. Berntsson bound in her afghan in the overstuffed chair. He waited and tried to draw, confused by trying to look at so many things at once, knowing Mrs. Berntsson would speak whenever the Professor did.

"How are we coming at it?" the Professor said.

"Me or you?" Oskar said. The Professor laughed, put down his brush and rod and palette, wiped his hands on a color-spotted rag. "Yours is neat," Oskar said. "Mine stinks." The Professor laughed again, took the sketchbook from him. "I can't do it like it should look," Oskar said.

"Are you drawing what you see or what you think it should look like?" Oskar knew what Mrs. Berntsson would say when she spoke.

"He's such a lovely boy," she said. "He is such a sweet little boy. He is the prettiest boy."

"Yes, Karin, he is a fine boy," the Professor said. Oskar concentrated on the sketchbook, the thick soft-lead pencil in his fingers. Professor Berntsson said, "The light's going, we'll call it quits maybe, eat some lunch."

"Why can't we just turn on the lights when it gets afternoon?" He knew what Mrs. Berntsson would say when the Professor fell asleep after lunch.

"Oh no, that's not the same light at all." He waved his hand at the light flooding the room from the big windows, explained again how by the time lunch was over the sun would have moved enough to change the light, reduce it to an indirect glow that was not good enough to work in. "Look here," he said to Oskar, "here's something to learn. What you see is not all lines you have to draw. There's color, heh?" He pointed to his incomplete self-portrait on the canvas. "And *tone*. Light and dark when you're drawing

62

in pencil. What do you think the lines you want to draw always are made of? You see?"

"I guess," Oskar said, and tried to see, but could not.

He talked about light when he showed Oskar his paintings. "Do you like to look at pictures?" Oskar said he guessed he did. "Maybe you could be a critic here, huh?"

"Papa's testing you," Hank Berntsson said.

"Hjalmar," his father said, "you go on out and find yourself an honest job, me and this boy are talking about art."

"Papa thinks everyone's an artist," Hank Berntsson said. There was a catch in his speech, as if he were going to stutter, but did not quite.

"Behave yourself, love," his Aunt Kristina said, and kissed Oskar good-bye. She kissed Hank Berntsson and said, "Luck, darling."

"We're already late, Kris," Elsa Berntsson said, and Gene Berntsson said he enjoyed these sentimental partings as much as anyone, but they were going to be late.

"Go, go," their father said. "Here we're interested in more important things." Hank and Elsa and Gene Berntsson kissed their mother good-bye, and they all left with Oskar's Aunt Kristina. Mrs. Berntsson smiled at them, but said nothing.

"What are you looking at when you look?" the Professor said to him. "Do you see just pictures of people and trees and grass?"

"I guess," Oskar said. "I mean it's a picture of a lady. I see it," he said, looking harder to see if there was something more hidden in the picture's colors and tones, a face, figure, shape.

"No," Professor Berntsson said. "Look at the *light*. Always. What I do best, what I do here, is catching the light the special way it is, always. Everything we see is in the light, huh? That's how we see it. See?"

The apartment's walls were covered with his paintings, all but the kitchen and the bathroom. And he had more, unframed canvases stacked on edge in the back of each closet, laid flat on high storage shelves. The Professor blew dust from them, held them up for Oskar to see, made him stand back for correct perspective.

"Did you paint all these? Is it every single picture you ever made?"

The Professor laughed.

"Hundreds more I gave away, and people have bought many. Many. My work is in museums, and schools, here, back in the old country. So many I couldn't count if I tried."

"Neat," Oskar said. "My aunt said you were real famous. She said you were in the Swedish Academy and you were a professor a real long time."

"Kris is very nice," he said, and "I studied at the Swedish Academy. You know what that is? I am not a member. I retired from the Art Institute here probably before you were born. Us Swedes," he said, "we got to stick together, huh?" and laughed.

There were many pictures of Swedish peasants in full costume, gathered for festivals, dancing in circles outdoors, wearing garlands of wildflowers, dancing indoors before huge fireplaces. "Look," he said, "how here it's dusk. Night is coming. See the sky, the air, all filled with the darkness coming? They dance to celebrate a harvest, the end of summer. Here, the light from the fire, see it jumps up there in the rafters to make shadow. See the woman's face red from the fire? It's winter, so they have a party inside with a warm fire."

There were many paintings of small ponds and pools, reedy banks of rivers and lakes, always in the early morning, mists and fogs over the still water. Young women, nude, bathed in the chilly mornings. "Is it just a naked girl there? What, because you can see her hair? I'm sorry, but you don't look correctly."

"No," Oskar said. "I mean I wasn't just looking because she hasn't got her clothes on."

"The special light I get there. Can't you feel how cold the water is? That's the way light comes just after the dawn. Even Zorn didn't do it better."

There were portraits, very old peasant men and women, only their faces, very close-up. They wore caps and bonnets, kerchiefs knotted under their chins, deeply lined faces, lips drawn back over toothless gums. Oskar could not tell if they smiled or were in pain. "Compare the two now. See the sun hitting her right in the face? Of course it's the sun, where else is all that light from? She squints. Here, what time of day is it?"

"Later?" Oskar said.

"Sure. The light is very different. I didn't paint these to make photographs of people."

"Are they real people?"

"Sure. You're right, there's character in a portrait, you can see the whole of the old country here, you're right. That's us there, you and me, your Aunt Kris, where the Swedes all come from, huh? But the technical problem is light, always."

"What's *technical* mean?"

"Means everything," Professor Berntsson said.

They ate lunch from a low coffee table pulled close to Mrs. Berntsson's chair. Oskar knelt on the carpet to eat his sandwich, drink a glass of milk, pretending not to stare at the Professor feeding his wife, poking cereal into her mouth, catching dribbles on her lip with the spoon, wiping her chin with a damp towel. "Open wide, Karin. Ah. Isn't that good? Good for you. You got to eat nice. What a good girl!" Mrs. Berntsson opened her mouth, closed, swallowed, flicking her eyes from her husband to Oskar to the spoon lifting toward her mouth.

Oskar carried the dishes to the kitchen, moved the coffee table back to the sofa while the Professor carried his wife to the bathroom. He sat at one end of the sofa, waited. He listened to the sounds from the bathroom, the Professor's voice, running tap, toilet flushing. He waited, looked at the paintings on the walls, at the glistening paint drying to a glaze on the canvas on the easel, at his own reflection, sitting, waiting, in the mirror propped beyond the easel. "Now, Karin," the Professor said as he lowered her carefully into her chair, tucked the afghan about her, "we'll relax a little," and, to Oskar, "Let's see how we did today."

He prepared himself to talk, keep him awake as long as possible. Beside him on the sofa, Professor Berntsson slumped, hands open and still in his lap, head tilted a bit forward. He blinked frequently, heavy-lidded. So close to him, Oskar saw how very old he was.

The backs of his hands were mottled with liver spots, crosshatched with raised, purple veins. A long tuft of stiff white hair sprouted in the depth of his ear. His mouth sagged beneath his snowy mustache. A last beam of direct light from the windows bounced off the slickness of the Professor's bald crown. His body looked smaller and rounder, softer, arms and legs spindly, thin ankles exposed below his trouser cuffs. Oskar did not look at Mrs. Berntsson, but said something, anything, quickly.

"Pretty neat, I think."

"What's?" the Professor started, looked up sharply.

"What you painted today."

"Ah. Maybe." He leaned forward, raised his rimless spectacles to look at the drying canvas. "Too soon to say," he said, and, "Sometime I'll show you how many studies I drew for this. Sketches."

Oskar looked at the unfinished self-portrait, then at the Professor beside him. They were identical and very different. "I really think it's nifty so far."

"You don't see the problems." The Professor sat back, sighed. His head canted to one side. His breathing was suddenly shallower and faster, a wheezing.

"How old are you?" Oskar said quickly.

"What? Such a question."

"I'm ten. My brother Lars is thirteen already. I can't tell how old old people are. You're older than my Aunt Kristina and my mom and my dad I know. My Aunt Anna's older than my mom, and my mom's older than my

Aunt Kristina, and my dad's the same age almost as my mom, but I forget exactly how old. My Uncle Knute was older than Aunt Anna but he got killed in a war a long time ago."

"I don't believe Kris mentioned your uncle," he said.

"My Aunt Anna's the oldest one of my aunts. Lars said he didn't care which one we went to, so I picked my Aunt Kristina."

"You don't say."

"I think she's real pretty."

The Professor laughed a tired laugh. "Do you hear that, Karin?" he said to his wife. Oskar looked at her, saw she watched them.

"How old?" Oskar said. "Really."

"You don't give up. How can I keep my vanity? Can you keep a secret?" Oskar nodded. "Eighty-two." He smiled at Oskar. "See, visit me, you learn something every time."

Oskar forgot to think of something more to say. There was the number eighty-two, but it did not mean anything he could understand. He knew he was ten, his brother Lars thirteen. After that he did not know any ages, his mother and father, his aunts, Hank and Elsa and Gene Berntsson, his dead Uncle Knute who was the oldest somehow, but there were no numbers between himself and his brother and the Professor.

The Professor began to snore. Oskar thought to wake him, ask him quickly and loudly how old his children were, the ages for all the people, but when he turned to him Professor Berntsson was deeply asleep, and Mrs. Berntsson was staring at him, and now she would begin to speak to him alone.

At her vanity, his Aunt Kristina hurried with her makeup; she said they would be miles late. "How's come Mrs. Berntsson's so funny?" Oskar said.

"Funny funny or funny strange?" she said, and, "I think she's the cutest little thing. She's like a little Dresden doll."

Oskar said, "Sometimes she doesn't say anything for a long time, and then she says how nice I am and everything, and then she talked real different when the Professor took a nap after lunch."

"Really?" She leaned close to the vanity's mirror to curl her lashes and apply eyeliner, tweeze a hair from one brow, draw in a thin arc. Her bracelets clattered when she moved her hands. Her rings winked in the sunlight from the bedroom windows. Her dangling earrings jumped as she stroked her long hair.

"I don't like it so much being with all old people all the time," he said.

"Come on," she said, smiled at him in the vanity mirror. "Is your Auntie Krissie old? Hank and Gene and Elsa aren't old, are they? Am I old?" She smiled hard at him in the mirror.

"I think you're pretty."

"Flattery will get you most anything in life, Os," his Aunt Kristina said. The scent of her perfume came into the air when she took the stopper from the vial, dabbed it at her ears, throat, the insides of her wrists, and the heavy sweetness mingling with the smoke from her cigarette burning in an ashtray among the clutter of bottles, brushes, combs, powder boxes. She squinted against the smoke as she took a last puff, a last sip from the coffee cup beside the ashtray.

"I wish I could just stay here all day until you come home from work."

"You can't, Os. Be a sweetheart. Go comb your hair again, I want you to look swell for the Berntssons."

To stay, he said, "Do you think my mom and dad will call today and I can go home tomorrow instead of with the Berntssons?"

"There's always a chance for anything," his Aunt Kristina said. A photograph of his aunt sat on the vanity; he could tell it was her, but it did not look a lot like her. She had photographs and snapshots everywhere in her bedroom, on the walls, the dresser, the bedside tables. They were all of herself.

"You sure were pretty," he said. She looked away from the mirror, lipstick in one hand, Kleenex to blot her lips in the other. He pointed at the portrait on the vanity.

"Oh. Well, thank you kindly, sir," she said, and, "That was a million years ago," and closed her lips on the tissue.

She was posed before a flowing swath of drapery, lighted from below and behind her, so that the fabric looked like swirling smoke, and cast an intense halo about the hair piled carelessly on top of her head. The frills of the boa that lay below her bare shoulders seemed electrified by the light, to waver and dance. She held the boa in place loosely at her bosom with the fingers of one hand. Her painted nails and swollen lips gleamed blackly in contrast to the soft, dull whiteness of her skin. Her large eyes were wide, moist, not seeming to look at the camera, at anything. "I had that taken to oblige a gentleman friend," she said.

"Was he the gangster?" Oskar said. When she turned fully away from the mirror to look at him, he said, "My dad said once you almost got married with a gangster. Lars believed him, but I didn't," he said because his aunt was not smiling at all.

"He wasn't a *gangster,*" she said. "Your old man spouts off when he doesn't know beans, which is only part of the headache he's caused your mama. Serves her right for marrying another squarehead Swede."

"Wasn't he really a gangster?"

"You're too young to understand," his Aunt Kristina said, and, "He happened to know some people who were is all. He introduced me once to

Capone. He was a businessman. Your old man should be told to keep his trap shut."

"My dad said he got shot."

"Let's change the subject, Oskar."

"Didn't he get shot by gangsters?"

"My Christ," she said, and now she laughed and smiled hard at him. "Do you pull this twenty questions on everyone or just Aunt Krissie? I'm sorry, Os. Next time you see him, ask your old man if getting shot by a gangster makes you one. That should hold his water."

"Were you married with him?"

She stood up, looked at herself carefully in the mirror, smoothed her dress. "The subject was discussed," she said, "but even the best-laid plans can blow up on you."

"Hank Berntsson got shot in the war."

"He got shot *at*. That's why he's so nervous, I told you."

"My Uncle Knute got killed in the war," Oskar said.

She looked at him for a moment before she spoke. "You've got your wars mixed up, Os," she said. "Hank was in this one. My Christ," and she laughed, "I was still wearing bloomers when Knute went off. *Tempus* do *fugit,*" she said.

"You're getting married with Hank Berntsson," Oskar said. She turned from the mirror to him, smiling, took his face in her hands, bent toward him.

"Every maiden's hope and prayer," his Aunt Kristina said.

"I wish I could just stay here," Oskar said. He began to cry without wanting to.

"Oh, Ossie," his aunt said, "please, sweet doll-boy, don't blubber. Auntie Krissie can't stand to see you turn on the waterworks, please!" She put her head next to his, hugged him.

"My mom said when two people can't get along any more they have to have a divorce. We had to go away to Aunt Anna and you. I wish I could be with my mom and dad and Lars." He began to cry so hard he could not talk. She hugged him tightly, rocked him in her arms.

"Please," she said, "won't you help your auntie? See, I *need* you to help me. I need you to make a real swell impression for me. Won't you be a love and make the Professor and Gene and Elsa just fall in love with you? Please help Krissie, Oskar."

When he could stop crying, he said, "I'll try I guess." She laughed and hugged him again, very tight. "So you can get married with Hank Berntsson and live happy ever after?"

"You could be a Quiz Kid," she said, and wiped his eyes and nose and mouth with a Kleenex. "And mum's the word about *gangsters*, okay? Half the trick in life is knowing when to clam up, trust me," his Aunt Kristina said.

"Mum's the word," he said. She hugged and kissed him, then had to wipe off the lipstick on his cheek.

The Professor snored long low snores, stirring the fringe of his snowy mustache with each breath. A blue vein pulsed in the glossed, papery skin at his temple, fluttering movement visible beneath his eyelids. Oskar watched him to avoid looking at his wife in the chair across the room. He had to look at her when she began to speak to him.

"Bad boy," Mrs. Berntsson said. Her voice was very high and clear, like a little girl's. "Dirty boy," she said, "Dirty pig!" There was something like a smile on her tiny face. He could see the perfectly even edges of sparkling white dentures. Her small recessed eyes flashed, her head and torso quivered as she spoke, louder. "You are a dirty, nasty boy!"

"I'm not doing anything," Oskar said. His own voice sounded weak to him, as if he were trying to keep from crying. He knew he could not let himself start to cry. "I'm just sitting here," he said. Professor Berntsson's snoring was very loud when they did not speak.

"Go away. Get out of here right now. Go, dirty thing!" She began to rock in the cocoon of her afghan, as if she meant to get out of the chair, come across the room at him. *"Go!"* she screeched.

"I can't! I have to stay here. I have to visit my aunt to see if my mom and dad have to have a divorce."

"Nasty," she said.

"My Aunt Kristina said I have to stay here all day while she goes to work with Elsa." He tried to talk loud enough to wake the Professor, but his voice was too weak.

"Dirty, dirty," Mrs. Berntsson said with the edges of her false teeth showing.

He stopped answering her. He tried to make himself think of other people, his mother and father and brother Lars, his Aunt Kristina and his Aunt Anna, of Elsa and Gene and Hank Berntsson, the Professor sleeping beside him, of the dead man killed by gangsters who was not really a gangster his aunt almost married a million years ago, of his Uncle Knute who was killed in the war he mixed up with the one that just was. He tried to think their names and faces, things they had said to him, where each one was this minute, but still he heard Mrs. Berntsson speaking to him.

"Nasty, dirty," she said. He made himself look away. He looked at the propped mirror reflecting himself, hands clutched in his lap, the sleeping Professor, the easel and the Professor's unfinished self-portrait in oils.

* * *

In the darkened room, Oskar could see only the darker shape of his aunt bending over him. He heard the tinkle of ice in her highball glass, saw the sudden glow of her cigarette when she drew on it, heard the whooshing sound as she exhaled smoke. "Don't let the bugs bite," she said.

"You have to hear my prayers," he said.

"Lordy. I just bet your mama doesn't miss a night, does she." The end of her cigarette glowed again, and he heard her drink, the ice rattle in the bottom of the glass, her sighing exhale of smoke. She knelt beside the folding cot. Very close, he smelled her perfume, the stale odor of her cigarettes, the tinge of alcohol on her breath from the highball nightcap she had just finished.

"You can say it with me if you remember it," Oskar said.

"I never trust to memory," she said, and he said the Lord's Prayer in Swedish. She said amen with him, but in the dark he could not see if she had folded her hands as he prayed. She laughed. "Who but your mama would teach you that," she said, laughed again.

"What's funny?"

"Nothing. The fact I recall Annie trying to teach me that hoo-ha when I was no more than your age, but either I wasn't having any or I was too dense or a combination. I'm not laughing at you, Os, it just cracks me up not hearing that for umpteen years and then you come out with it every night like you're just off the boat."

"That's us," Oskar said. "Swedes. From the old country, like the Professor," he said.

His aunt said, "I won't tell if you won't," and laughed again.

"I have to bless people now."

"I promise not one peep out of me. I think it's sweet." He could feel her fold her hands now, close to his on the cover, thought he could see her bow her head in the darkness this time before he closed his eyes and asked God to bless his mother and father and brother Lars and Aunt Kristina and Aunt Anna, and to help him be good and love all people. She said, "Amen?"

"I have to ask for special helps."

"Scuze me please?"

"Please," Oskar said, "help my mom and dad not to have a divorce so I can go home and Lars can go home from visiting Aunt Anna and everything works out fine."

"Ossie, I think that's so nice."

"And please make Mrs. Berntsson stop calling me names when the Professor takes a nap after we eat."

"Dearie," his aunt said, "she can't help it. She's senile. She's probably terrified they'll stick her in a home or she'll die or both."

"Really?"

"It happens when you get real old, knock on wood," she said.

"I'm not done. Please God help the Professor finish his picture of himself."

"Oskar, that is so sweet of you."

"And please help Hank Berntsson not be so nervous from the war so he can get a job and get married with my Aunt Kristina." He heard something, but did not realize for a moment she had begun to cry.

"And please let Elsa Berntsson and Gene Berntsson like it so they won't try to stop them getting married to live happy ever after." Then he knew she was crying. He tried to think of things to say to help her stop. "How's come Gene Berntsson's so funny? Funny strange I mean." She stopped crying at once, laughed, hiccuped, put her wet cheek next to his. "Isn't he funny strange?"

She laughed, said, "Do you know what a pansy is? Your old man's the one to tell you about that." He said nothing more, lay there with his aunt's head beside his on the pillow, her arms holding him lightly. He closed his eyes again, felt her damp cheek, the movement and sound of her breathing. They lay together like that for a time, and then she got up and went away to her bedroom, and Oskar fell asleep.

Oskar whispered, "Can I ask you a question?"

"Of course. What's the matter?" The Professor's voice was loud in the room, restored by his nap.

"I don't want her to hear me." The Professor looked at his wife.

"She's asleep," he said. "She's tired. We're all tired. Pretty soon, the folks get home, we'll maybe have a little party, huh? What's the question?"

"Does she have to talk mean to me when you take a nap?" Oskar said, afraid to raise his voice. Mrs. Berntsson slept with her eyes partially open, glassy slits catching the last dull light of late afternoon. The Professor cleared his throat loudly before he spoke.

"She can't help that. Kris told you? It's a sickness, you have to ignore things like that."

"It's hard."

"Sure it's hard." Professor Berntsson looked at his sleeping wife, then away from her. "Everything's hard. Life is hard. You better get used to that. Keep your mind on your business, otherwise all you do is worry how hard everything is." He looked at his unfinished painting on the easel, colors indistinct now in the fading light. He laughed a very small laugh.

They sat together in silence on the sofa, waiting for Oskar's aunt and the Professor's children to come home. It felt to Oskar like they sat for a very long time without speaking. Then he said, "If my mom and dad don't have a divorce, I can probably go home tomorrow if they call up on the telephone and tell my Aunt Kristina."

"That's what Kris tells me." It was almost dark in the room now, but they did not turn on the lights.

"But if they have a divorce I don't know what happens then." When the Professor did not speak, he said, "Do you think my mom and dad will have a divorce or stay married?"

"You have to learn to be patient. Patience is a virtue. Things you don't understand, later, if you're lucky you understand things, it all can make sense."

"Do you think Hank and my Aunt Kristina will get married with each other?"

"That's another question. You said one. Anyway, it's complicated," the Professor said.

"How come?"

"People," the Professor said, "have opinions. Opinions, you understand? Some people don't think it's such a good idea."

"Elsa and Gene don't want them to," Oskar said.

He said, "I don't try to understand why people have opinions. It's hard enough to paint pictures." He looked at his pocket watch. "Time Hjalmar and everyone should be home. Who knows," he said, and laughed loudly, "maybe my son got a good job today, he can afford to marry and move to China, whatever he damn wants." Oskar was going to ask if Hank Berntsson might really take his aunt to China if they married, but Mrs. Berntsson woke up.

"Isn't he a pretty boy?" she said. The Professor got up, went to her.

"Hello, Karin," he said, "did you have a good sleep? Karin, let's go to the bathroom, pretty soon folks get home, we'll forget your worries, have a party, will you like that?"

Oskar waited. He got up and turned on the lights, sat again, looked at the painting, the easel, the pictures hung on the walls, his reflection in the large mirror, waiting for the party they might have when everyone got home.

They thought he was still asleep, but Oskar woke when Hank Berntsson laid him on the cot in his aunt's apartment. He felt the constant tremor that ran through Hank Berntsson's arms as he lowered him to the cot, waking to that unceasing shiver, opening his eyes just enough to see they had not turned the lights on to avoid waking him.

He pretended sleep while his Aunt Kristina slowly undressed him where he lay, covered him with a single, light blanket. "Poor guy, he's dead to the world," she said. He felt her pat the blanket once. They moved away from his cot, and when he heard the sound of their shoes on the tiles in the vestibule, he turned his head toward them, opened his eyes enough to see them, listened.

The corridor's light fell through the open door, silhouetted his aunt and Hank Berntsson, his aunt moving to Hank, the sound of her spike heels on the hard tile, putting her arms around his neck, their heads touching, the wet smack sound of their kiss. "Stay a while," his aunt said. "I'll build us a drinkie. We can talk in the kitchen. He won't wake for the last trumpet. Please?" She kissed Hank Berntsson again, a long, quiet kiss, the silhouette of her head rolling slowly with his.

Hank Berntsson moved away from his aunt. Oskar saw the shuddering of his head as he spoke. "I better not, Kris. I don't need another drink," and, "I need to get an early start in the morning."

"Take a day off tomorrow," she said. "Come keep Krissie company for a little bit. Pretty please?" She rose to her toes, put her arms around his neck again. Hank Berntsson moved his head away from hers.

"No," he said. "You know Papa expects me to get out every day. If I'm not out wearing out my shoe leather he'll get so upset he won't even be able to paint, I'll hear about it from Elsa and Gene until I'm blue in the face." The catch in his voice became a stammer as he talked.

"Pretty please," Oskar's aunt said, and, "Stay. I'll skip work tomorrow, we can spend the day out, nobody will ever know. Stay," she said. "You can stay here all night with me if we want, Hank."

"No," he said, and removed her hands from around his neck. "Elsa's waiting up for me to get back." He stepped back, the corridor light falling between them, two silhouettes. When his aunt spoke, Oskar caught his breath, held it, pinched his eyelids shut.

"The hell with goddamn Elsa waiting up!"

"You'll wake him."

"The hell with all this crap! I give a good goddamn!"

"Kris—" Hank Berntsson tried to say. Oskar opened his eyes, saw his Aunt Kristina, hands raised, clenched into fists, Hank Berntsson in the doorway to the corridor, head, body, shaking.

"What the hell is this?" she said. "Are we going to get married or is this a goddamn game I'm playing? What the hell should I care what your goddamn old maid sister does or doesn't!" She started to cry.

"I suppose it's my fault I'm sick," he said, stuttered, choked between the words. "Papa's so old," he said. "Elsa wants Mama in a nursing home. Who pays for it all if I don't get well and work? Elsa and Gene carry everything. I can't just say I'm getting married at my age and walk away from everything." He choked so hard he had to stop speaking.

"So go," his aunt said through her crying. "Get your ass to goddamn hell back to your old man and your crazy old lady, Elsa, and your faggy brother!" She closed the door after Hank Berntsson without slamming it, walked quickly through the dark past Oskar's cot to her bedroom, weeping softly.

Oskar held himself as still as if he were dead. He said his prayers to himself without folding his hands, said amen, then asked God to bless his aunt and Hank Berntsson and everyone he knew and everyone else in the world, and then prayed and prayed again the Lord's Prayer in Swedish to himself, until the words became nonsense, dizzying him, until he fell asleep.

They played pinochle. Hank Berntsson moved the Professor's easel to make room for the card table and chairs in the middle of the room. Gene Berntsson brought a tea cart with bottles of whiskey and glasses with little knitted coasters fitted to the bottoms, mixed highballs for everyone. "Papa, will you partake of a snort?" he said, and to Oskar, "I have cola and some uncarbonated orange that must surely be prewar if it's a day," and Oskar chose the orange. Elsa Berntsson and Oskar's aunt fixed bowls of snacks, peanuts and chips and some tiny chocolate-covered mints Gene Berntsson said were exquisite if you dissolved them on your tongue with a highball.

"Have you been doing me proud today?" his Aunt Kristina asked him.

"Are you learning to draw from Papa?" Elsa Berntsson said, and, "None of us inherited a lick of all his talent." Oskar asked Hank Berntsson if he had found a job today, and Hank said no such luck.

"Confess," Gene Berntsson said, "did you *look* for work or did you just look for work, Hankie?"

Hank said, "That's a cold world out there," with a little pause between each word.

"You're telling *me* it's a cruel world?" Elsa Berntsson said.

"We can't do more than give it the old college try, can we, darling," Oskar's Aunt Kristina said, and patted the back of Hank's hand.

"Is this pinochle I'm kibitzing or just a gang of Swedes want to gossip all night?" the Professor said. Hank Berntsson and his aunt were partners against Elsa and Gene. The Professor sat on his painting stool, high enough above them all to see their hands and kibitz the tricks they won and lost. Oskar sat on the sofa, drinking uncarbonated orange soda. He watched them all at their game, could see them all, could see himself in the Professor's mirror, the easel and the canvas, covered with a cloth now. He could see Mrs. Berntsson, wrapped in her afghan, watching him and everyone playing pinochle.

They slapped their tricks down on the table. They laughed a lot with each trick taken, kept the score on a pad. Between hands, Gene Berntsson got up and mixed more drinks at the tea cart. They played and drank highballs and ate snacks. The Professor kibitzed on his stool. Hank Berntsson's fanned cards quivered in his hands. Oskar's aunt moved her chair close to his, patted his arm or hand or shoulder often, leaned over to give him little kisses on the cheek when they took a trick or a hand. Mrs. Berntsson never answered anyone who spoke to her.

"You wouldn't believe these cards she's giving me, Mama," Elsa said.

"Did you have a pleasant day today, Mama?" Gene said, and his father said yes, Karin had a nice day today.

"How are you holding out, doll-boy?" his aunt said to Oskar, and, "Just put your feet up and snooze if you want." He drank the last of his soda, went to the bathroom, then fell asleep on the sofa while they laughed and drank and talked and played pinochle.

Everyone was shouting when he woke. His aunt was crying, and Elsa Berntsson had tears in her eyes, shouting at his aunt. He was suddenly wide awake. They stood up and shouted, then sat back down again. The highball glasses were empty and all the snacks were gone. Mrs. Berntsson was not there, taken to bed while he slept. Oskar pretended he was still sleeping. The Professor sat on his painting stool. When he tried to talk somebody was always up, shouting, so nobody listened to him.

Elsa said, "Gene has his responsibilities and I have mine, and Hank has to take care of his like the rest of us!"

"Who the hell appointed you to tell people's responsibilities!" his aunt shouted back at her. When she stood up and spoke, Elsa Berntsson sat down. His aunt sat down and took hold of Hank Berntsson's arm with both hands. Hank moved his lips, but no words came out.

Gene Berntsson said, "Kris, what Elsa means is we have a situation with Mama and Papa, we have to do what has to be done."

The Professor started to say something, but Oskar's aunt let go her hold of Hank, stood up, and shouted, "We're two adults, we can damn well get married or shack up or run off to Timbuktu if we damn well feel like it!"

When she sat down, Elsa said, "That's lovely language."

"I'll use any damn language I please!" his aunt yelled without getting up, then began to cry harder.

Gene said, "We're only saying you don't understand our situation. We can't just keep Mama here until she rots, can we? And Papa," he said, and the Professor tried to say something, but they did not hear, "Papa," Gene said, "he's old, he'll need the same care. Who's going to provide it if we don't? We need Hank's help, Kristina."

"I can't even help myself," Hank Berntsson said, choking, shaking.

"So where the hell does good old Kris come in?" Oskar's aunt stood up to say. "Old Kris holds her breath until everybody conveniently croaks, is that it?"

"You've lived your life without a husband this long," Elsa said. "What's the mad rush? Maybe my brother's just convenient right now. Is that it?" His aunt was crying too hard to answer her.

Gene said, "It does strike me a little silly. The both of you can hardly be said to be spring chickens. I frankly don't fathom all this passion."

"See, Kris, I told you," Hank Berntsson managed to say, "we're too damn old for this."

Then they were done shouting. His Aunt Kristina cried harder and harder, until Gene Berntsson gave her his handkerchief, and the Professor got off his stool and went to her, put his arm around her, and then Oskar could hear what he said because everyone else was quiet now. "Come on, Kris," Professor Berntsson said, "I'll help you, come wash your face, you'll feel better. We have no business talking about all this after drinking. We should be ashamed. We're all so tired. Just look how your nephew sleeps."

When she came back from the bathroom he pretended to wake. "I fell asleep a long time ago," Oskar said. His aunt, trying to smile at him with her weepy eyes, said it was time to get up and go.

"I don't even remember when I fell asleep," he said. The Professor stood beside his aunt, smiling at Oskar. Elsa Berntsson was very busy, cleaning up the card table. Gene Berntsson mixed himself another highball and said he knew every time he would regret the last one in the cold light of morning. Hank Berntsson sat at the card table while his sister wiped away the crumbs and ashes and drink spills. He sat with his arms folded in front of him, body quivering, muscles in his forearms flexing, a tic flickering along his jaw. Oskar blinked and rubbed his eyes as though he was still too sleepy to see well.

"Goodnight, Professor," he said. "I'll see you in the morning unless I get to go home tomorrow."

"The hell with tomorrow and the whole damn shooting match," his aunt said, taking his hand, pulling him after her to the door. The Professor said goodnight. Elsa Berntsson continued to move about the room, picking up ashtrays to empty. Gene toasted Oskar with his highball, winked. Hank moved his lips, but could not speak.

His aunt said, "Say your prayers if you have to, but say them to yourself." Oskar undressed. His aunt went to the kitchen to make herself a nightcap highball. He listened to her talking to herself. She said, "Shit!" and, "The goddamn hell!" and he heard her light a cigarette, the sound of ice in her glass as she drank. He had his pajamas on when the telephone rang. She came in from the kitchen carrying her drink and cigarette and said, "Beg, damn you, you beg for a change. How's that for the old switcheroo?" before she picked up the receiver and said hello very loudly.

Then she said, "Would you mind saving the guff for somebody wants to hear it?" and, "If you don't like the hours I keep you can tell his mother to farm him out to someplace else when she gets in a fight," and, "Look, Annie, do you have something to say to me or do you want to talk to the kid or what?" and, "None of your damn business," and then she began to cry again. She took the receiver from her ear, held it out to Oskar. He put it to his ear, waited for his Aunt Anna to speak.

He watched his aunt find an ashtray for her cigarette, a coaster for her glass, sit on the small chair beside the telephone table. She continued to cry, so he looked away. There was no voice on the phone, just the unbroken whispering sound of the long-distance circuit and his aunt's crying. Then she stopped crying so hard, wiped at her eyes with the back of her hand, took a drink.

"Hello?" Oskar said.

"Oskar? Is that you?" his Aunt Anna said.

"Hi, Aunt Anna," he said. "I'm fine; how are you?"

"Where were you this evening, Oskar?"

"We had a party real late." He looked at his aunt, who laughed and blew her nose into a hankie. She lit a new cigarette, crossed one leg over the other, began to bounce it. She took a long drink from her drink, smoked, tipped her head back to blow the smoke up at the ceiling.

"I can well imagine," his Aunt Anna said, and, "When it rains it pours." Looking at his Aunt Kristina in the chair so near him, listening to his Aunt Anna's voice, he tried but could not imagine how she looked, if she sat or stood as she talked, her face or hair or hands, what room or house she was in as she spoke. Her voice sounded different, as if he heard her on a radio program. "Here's your mother, Oskar," she said.

"Oskar?"

"Hi, I'm fine. I'm being real good," he said. "We had a party and now I'm going to bed." He could not imagine exactly what his mother looked like. He wondered if she had been close by all the time or just now came to the telephone. His Aunt Kristina laughed again, shook her head, like it was the only way she could stop laughing and crying.

"Listen to me," his mother said. "You're to come home tomorrow. I don't know what's going on there, but you tell Kristina you're to be put on the train just as soon as possible tomorrow. Do you hear me?"

"Okay," he said. "I'll show you how I learned to do real good drawing from the Professor. He's real neat. He's Swedes, just like us. He was even born there," and, "Can I say hi to Dad too?" There was a short silence on the telephone. His Aunt Kristina held her drink in one hand, a new cigarette in the other. She was not laughing or crying.

"Would you like to say hello to your brother?" his mother said. He said sure, and almost at once Lars was on the telephone. Oskar tried to imagine them all there, close to the telephone, even his father.

"You sure must of been out late someplace," his brother said.

"Hi," Oskar said. "A party. Are you home already from Aunt Anna's?"

"Where else would I be talking to you from? Don't be dumb," Lars said.

"I'm coming home tomorrow, I guess," he said, but it was his Aunt Anna who answered him. He tried a last time to see them all there by their telephone.

"Let me speak to Kristina at once."

"Can I say hello to Dad first?"

"We'll talk about that when you're back where you belong," she said. He said good-bye and held the receiver out to his Aunt Kristina.

She stood up and laughed and said, "Jump in bed and cover up your head, Os, the air's going to burn around here shortly." He pulled the covers over his head, but still heard what she said. She was still talking, not so loud, when he fell asleep that way, forgetting to pray because he concentrated on listening and trying to think what was said to her to make her say what she did, trying to see all the other people, how they looked, wondering still if there was a chance his father was there with them by their telephone.

Professor Berntsson sat on his stool at the easel, but did not work. The unfinished canvas was still covered with the cloth. He had not opened his tubes of paint, mixed nothing on the palette. Oskar watched the Professor and the image of the Professor and the covered easel and himself on the sofa reflected in the large mirror. Mrs. Berntsson sat in her afghan across the room, smiling, not speaking. "How's come you don't paint any?" he said.

"What's the good?"

"You're almost done."

"Sure," the Professor said, and moved his hands up to cover his face.

"I'm going home today," Oskar said. "When my Aunt Kristina comes home from work we have to go right to the train station. My mom and Aunt Anna said. My brother Lars is already home. Him and my Aunt Anna went home already."

The Professor said nothing, sitting on the stool with his face hidden in his hands. Then he said, "You told me. Kris told me." His voice, muffled by his hands, sounded like he was talking to Oskar long-distance over the telephone.

Oskar looked at Mrs. Berntsson. She smiled harder at him. He looked quickly back at the Professor and said, "I think my mom and dad are having a divorce. I think my dad's already gone away. It didn't all work out in the end," he said, and, "I don't know if it makes sense," and, "My Aunt Kristina says it serves him right." When Professor Berntsson did not speak, he said, "My Aunt Kristina's mad at my mom and my Aunt Anna. I think she's even mad at me, and I didn't even do anything. I behaved . . ." he began to say, then saw the Professor had begun to cry almost silently into his hands. His shoulders moved up and down with his weeping, hunched on the stool.

"Don't," Oskar said. He had never seen a very old person cry. He had cried a lot, and his brother cried a lot before he was thirteen, and his mother and both his aunts. His mother cried when she showed him a picture of his dead Uncle Knute and told him his Uncle Knute was her brother and had been dead a long time and Oskar would never know him. He believed his father must have cried when he was a little boy once. "Don't," Oskar said.

"Oh!" Professor Berntsson said, and then stopped, took his hands away from his face, took off his glasses to dry his eyes, tried to laugh, said *Oh* again.

"Is it funny funny or funny strange?" Oskar said.

"Sure," he said. "Damn funny. Live all your life, and then Karin they put away to die, my daughter tells me what I must do like I'm a child, my sons . . ." he said, but could not finish what he meant to say.

"Hank's not getting married with my Aunt Kristina," Oskar said.

"Sure," he said, and "Hjalmar, Eugene," and then he started to cry again, covered his face. Oskar got up, stood next to him, patted his shaking shoulder. *Oh Oh Oh* the Professor moaned. Oskar looked at Mrs. Berntsson, who was still smiling at them.

"Maybe you could stop and you could paint on your painting and I can do some more drawings," Oskar said. "I think it's real neat doing drawings and paintings all the time. Thanks a lot for teaching me how to do drawing," he said. "When I get home I'll show my mom and Lars and my dad if he's still there how I learned how to do neat drawing."

Mrs. Berntsson began to speak, saying wasn't he a lovely boy, wasn't he a sweet boy, but Oskar did not listen to her. He kept his hand on the Professor's shoulder and thought of all the drawings he would do when he got home.

He made himself try to imagine all the people, their faces, he could draw. He did not listen to her or the Professor. He made himself see all the pictures he would make, all the people he knew. He imagined them all, and then he made himself think how he would ask God to bless each one by name, every night, after he said the Lord's Prayer in Swedish. He would make himself remember all the names until he made pictures of everyone he knew. He would draw pictures of everything, and then he would never forget anything. He could always hold a picture up to the light and remember anything he wanted, and then he would understand it all.

The Good Man of Stillwater, Oklahoma

An end, the end is come upon the four
corners of the land.

—Ezekiel 7:2

I SLEEP BADLY, wakened again and again by vague, troubling dreams. I sleep, dream, wake, realize I have been sleeping, dreaming, that I am now awake. I sleep again, wake, and in this state, not sleeping, not fully awake, hear the distant growl of summer thunder. I sleep again, wake to the storm, the metallic crack of lightning that flashes like strobes at the bedroom windows, the guttural thunder, howling wind, slashing torrents of rain. I am instantly, fully awake, shocked, frightened by the noise and sporadic light.

"Norvetta," I say, turn to my wife who continues to sleep soundly beside me, touch her bare shoulder, shake her gently. "Norvetta," I say, and, "Norvetta, hear that? It's coming down in buckets. Who says it doesn't rain in Oklahoma. Norvetta, wake up, it's raining like hell."

She stirs, groggy, rises to one elbow, looks at the lightning's fierce blare at the windows, hears its crack and crackle, the thunder, wind, rain. "Raining," she mutters, socks her pillow plump, lies back down. I lean over her, hear the purr of her snoring beneath the storm's raging.

"This'll wake the kids," I say, and, "This is a real gully washer," and, "This is the kind of rain you get with a tornado, except we'd be hearing the sirens right now if it was. Norvetta?" She sleeps, deeply, peacefully.

I sleep no more. I snuggle closer to my wife's warmth, huddle under the blanket, close my eyes tightly, but the storm is too loud, seems to me to be directly overhead, hovering over my house where I lie next to my sleeping wife, our children asleep in their bedrooms upstairs. I squeeze my eyes shut, clench my hands into fists beneath the blanket, imagine this awful storm directly over Stillwater, Oklahoma, over my home, my family.

I imagine a great black, boiling cloud in the black night sky, expanding, south toward Perkins and Shawnee and Oklahoma City, north to Ponca City, Wichita, creeping eastward to Mannford and Tulsa, west to Hennessey, to Guymon in the Panhandle. The great storm heaves like a violent yeast, shoots out bolts of jagged lightning, spews rain.

81

I hold myself rigid to keep from trembling. What if the noise of the storm wakes my sleeping children, scares them? Should I rise, go upstairs, check their bedrooms? Should I rise, walk barefoot through my dark house, see that no windows are open, no rain blowing in? Should I get up, see that all windows are latched, front and back doors locked against intruders? I imagine a maniac, an escapee from the state prison at McAlester, murderous, sex-crazed, roaming the streets of Stillwater under cover of this storm; he breaks into my home, kills me and my son, ravages my wife and daughters, our mutilated bodies not found until days later, after the rain ceases.

"Norvetta, Norvetta, hold me!" I whisper, my voice a faint, dry croak; she sleeps soundly. I lie awake all through the night, listening to the whipping rain, afraid. The thunder and lightning are so loud, even now the tornado alert sirens might be screaming, a black funnel bearing down on my home in Stillwater, Oklahoma, coming to kill us all, and we cannot hear the warning through the crashing, banging, moaning of this horrible storm!

Norvetta and I watch the weatherman on the cable channel from Oklahoma City. He has maps, a pointer, a crayon with which he writes the number of inches of rainfall recorded at various locations in north-central Oklahoma. The weatherman explains the static condition of colliding frontal systems, unseasonably cold winds sweeping southeast off the Colorado Rockies, very warm, very moist Gulf air flowing north out of Texas.

"More of the same again," Norvetta says.

"Where are the kids?" I ask.

"I don't know. Why? Upstairs probably. Jesse may have gone out for a while."

"They should be home in weather like this," I say, do not take my eyes off the television when I speak to her.

"Really," she says, and, "He's seventeen years old. You forget. Kim will have her nose in a book, and Cissy always finds a game." I listen closely to the anchorwoman's wrap-up. There will be flash flooding in low-lying areas, delay and potential damage to expected wheat harvests if the rain does not end soon; numerous isolated storm cells are revealed on radar, but no tornado watch is announced.

"You keep Cissy inside," I say, and, "You keep those children in this house. They're susceptible to colds," I say when she asks why. There is no thunder or lightning, but the rain falls thick as a beaded, translucent curtain, fogs the windows, the sound of it a loud hissing I hear everywhere in my house.

I find my son in his room. Jesse does not see me, hear me enter. I open the door, find him seated Indian-fashion in the soft depths of his bean-bag chair beside his stereo, earphones clamped on his head, a record-album jacket in his hands. The stereo's turntable spins silently; Jesse, eyes closed, sways like a snake charmer, rocks forward and back, as if he prayed to the rhythm of the music only he hears. I hear the sibilant, steady rain, slanting down out of the dingy sky. I think: Jesse, Jesse, my son! Jesse, bearer of my name into posterity!

The rain slants to the earth, splashes against the panes of my son's bedroom windows. I hear an occasional mumble of muffled thunder, the slanting rain's shrill whisper, look upon my son Jesse.

His long hair is snarled, still smudged and spiked from sleep. He wears soiled jeans, a frayed jersey. His fingernails are dirty as a mechanic's, bare feet a sickly white. I sniff the muggy air of my son's bedroom. Has he been smoking cigarettes again? Is that tinge of sweetness the lingering aroma of marijuana? Oh Jesse, my son!

What if my son is a confirmed doper? What if he should come to manhood without knowledge or skills or interests or character? What if he should run away, work for a traveling carnival, have himself hideously tattooed? What will I do if my son becomes a shame to me?

My son Jesse is a dull, lazy, juvenile thug, unprepared, unable and unwilling to assume the approaching responsibility of adulthood, to be a credit to his family, community, nation. What if my son were to suffer brain damage from drug abuse? What if, today, tomorrow, the next day, he were to suffer a permanently disabling injury while stupefied by narcotics, be a vegetable the rest of his life, fed through his veins, evacuating through tubes into plastic bottles? What if he never recovered consciousness, never again knew he was Jesse, my only son!

I back slowly out of his room, careful not to disturb him. I close his bedroom door silently, stand in the hall outside, hear only the muted patter of the rain.

Restricted by me to the house because of the rain, my daughters do their best to avoid boredom. Kim sits in my recliner chair in the den, feet up and crossed, face hidden behind the tattered Judy Blume paperback she has read again and again through these days of rain in Stillwater. Cissy, my baby, sprawls on the carpet, doing a dot-to-dot book. The Flintstones are playing on the cable channel from Dallas that runs only cartoons and black-and-white movies. I step across Cissy's body to change the channel to the all-news-and-weather service.

"Hey!" Cissy cries.

Kim speaks from behind her Judy Blume paperback. "She was watching that, Dad. You come in and just change it like a dictator, that's gross and rude."

"I just want to check the forecast is all," I say, but they do not respond as I turn back to the Flintstones. I move away from them, stop in the doorway to the kitchen.

Kim turns a page in her book, bobs her foot. Beside her, on my smoking stand, are a crumpled bag that held Doritos, the red residue of a soft drink in the bottom of a glass. Kim makes a sucking noise with her lips against her braces as she reads. Cissy works her dot-to-dot, surrounded by her clutter, shoes and socks where she removed them, paper dolls, crayons and Magic Markers, the brown crumbs of something she has eaten flecking the carpet's nap.

I think: Daughters! What will happen to my innocent daughters? Grow up dopers under their brother's influence? Worse, become promiscuous, secretly taking birth control pills? Worse yet, become pregnant by redneck boys from Perkins or Coyle or Cushing, go to Oklahoma City for abortions! Worse, marry rednecks from Perkins, Coyle, Cushing, wife-beaters, child-abusers, be divorced, forced on welfare, work for tips as Sambo's waitresses! Cissy! Kim!

Today's rain is intermittent, sometimes only a mist in the sodden air, sometimes a light sprinkle, then a drizzle, fading to a sprinkle, a mist. My daughters do not know I have left the den.

It is Norvetta's ironing day. The rain is loudest in the utility room, drumming on the low roof, smacking on the patio flagstones just outside where water pours out of the gutters. The utility room is very noisy with the rain, the vibration of a load of wash in the spin-cycle, the steady clicking of another load in the gas dryer. Heaps of sorted clothes wait on the linoleum floor. Norvetta makes a dry slapping sound with the steam iron as she irons a hankie, another, another.

"I can't stand this weather anymore, Norvetta."

She speaks without breaking the efficient rhythm of her work. "You've been an absolute bear all this time. If you're going to be such a grouch I don't want to hear about it."

"I'm sorry, Norvetta," I say. She continues to wield her steam iron, fold hankies, stack them. I look at my wife. I look upon Norvetta, my love, my helpmate, mother of my children, my darling! Her eyes show crow's-feet at the corners; ropy muscles flex in her throat, her forearms; bluish veins stand in relief in the back of her hand that grips the steam iron; the Lady Clairol hair coloring she uses is all wrong for her complexion. Leaning over the ironing board, there is a permanent hunch in her narrow shoulders. She is too thin. Norvetta!

"I am sorry, Norvetta," I say, and, "Maybe this is just some atmospheric effect getting me. Biorhythms. The phase of the moon. But don't you ever sometimes get thinking, Norvetta," I say, "about your life, our lives, life? Do you ever get philosophical about what's the point of it all? I guess maybe it's just this rain. I get to brooding, moody. I keep thinking I should be asking and answering some important questions, but the trouble is in the end I can't even come up with questions. It's like I can't see over a blank wall I run into." She sets the steam iron on the board, covers her face to cry into her hands. I see her shoulders shake, but cannot hear my wife crying through the noise of the washer and dryer, the pounding rain. I say, "I truly am so sorry." Now I hear her weeping through the rain's noise.

"Dammit!" my wife shouts, faces me, her eyes wet, streaming. "You should just be grateful for what you have! Who cares if it happens to rain more than it ever has? We're not the ones get evacuated to go sleep in the armory when Duck Creek floods, are we? No flooding can get us, can it? Think of something really terrible if you like to feel so depressed! What if one of your lovely beautiful children who adore you were truly sick or was kidnapped! How would you feel then? What if you suddenly lost your job? What if I took the car out shopping and was mangled in an accident? What if a tornado came and suddenly blew us all to smithereens? Think what *could* happen!"

"I know," I say.

My name is Pease, and I am a good man. I am a good husband and father. I am good at my job. I pay my taxes, and I pay my bills on time. I do not like to think I have anything to be ashamed of, no reason to be afraid.

I watch the rain through the big glass patio doors in the breakfast nook, falling relentlessly. "The story in the Bible," I say, "as I remember it, it rained forty days and forty nights. How many days is it in a row it's rained now in Stillwater?" I ask.

Perhaps I did not speak, only thought these words, spoke to myself?

Norvetta is busy cooking and serving our family breakfast, sets a plate of eggs and sausages before me, another plate, hotcakes, pours me a mug of coffee, glass of tomato juice. Jesse is already eating, head down; I wish he would wash his hair more often, cut it, comb it before coming to breakfast. Kim has her Judy Blume paperback propped against the salt and pepper shakers; I should remind her to close her mouth when she chews. Cissy, my baby, does not like eggs or sausage, eats hotcakes with her fingers, leaves sticky prints on her milk glass, a milk mustache on her upper lip; Norvetta should blow her nose for her. My breakfast grows cold on the plate before me.

The greensward of my backyard is awash, puddles gathered in every dip and hollow, overflowing, running to join together in shallow running streams. My backyard is like a shallow pond, its surface pocked with tiny bubbles, the rain that keeps falling, lightly, unbroken, from the ashy sky. The glass patio doors are streaked with rain.

I think I am as good as most men. I am a registered voter. I attend the First Methodist Church of Stillwater. If you could find people who knew me well enough to ask them about me, I think they would say: *Pease? Pease is a pretty good man.*

Cissy spills her milk. It runs off the table, onto Jesse's lap. He jumps up from the table, utters an obscene word. Kim says he dare not say that word. Cissy begins to bawl. Norvetta tells Jesse he should be ashamed of himself, asks Kim to please mind her own business, tells Cissy it is not serious, wipes up the milk with a paper towel.

"Don't you feel it?" I ask. "Can't anyone but me feel it? Am I the only one feels this way?"

"These are my only jeans I wear," Jesse says.

"If *I* say a bad word everyone in the whole world tells me to shut up," Kim says.

"I hate eggs and I hate sausage meat and I hate all this stuff except pancakes!" Cissy, my baby, says.

"I know a certain family got up on the grumpy side of bed this morning," Norvetta says.

Perhaps I did not speak?

Thank God or whatever, the rain has stopped. I expect to feel better now that the rains have ended in Stillwater. My family seems to feel so much better now that the rain has stopped. "I really think it's over," I say to Norvetta.

"It looks like it at last, dear," she says, and, "You'll be miles late for work if you don't hurry, dear. That's no way to start off the first day of the new month," and, "Oh, I tell you, I'm just going to throw open all the windows and get some fresh air in this musty house and just clean this house from top to bottom today!" I am certain it has stopped; the sky outside is very clear, a very pale blue.

"Can I go to a friend's house today after I eat if I want to?" Kim asks.

"Surely you can, love," Norvetta says, "but I want you to take your umbrella if you go far. We never know if it might change its mind and decide to rain some more."

"No," I say, "I'm positive it's done. Don't ask me how I know, I just know."

"If I play outside can I still wear my new rain hat even if it isn't raining?" Cissy asks.

"You may," Norvetta says, "and I for sure want you to wear your galoshes. The sun's lovely, but the ground's going to be spongy for days even if it stays nice like this." The sun is very bright in the sky, the light very hard; when I try to look at the sun it hurts my eyes, makes me blink, squint.

"I have to go see some guys today," Jesse says. When Norvetta asks when he'll be back, Jesse says he does not know, they are just going to mess around some. She says he is to come straight home if it clouds up to rain again. Jesse says it will not rain; Norvetta says he cannot know that.

"He's right," I say, and, "Call it psychic ability if you want a name for it, but I know for certain there won't be any more rain."

"You scoot unless you *want* to be late to work!" Norvetta says to me, and, "Oh, the wheat farmers are going to be thrilled with this weather! I could bottle it and sell it!" My wife is very happy. My daughters make plans for this first, lovely day of July, happy, my son happy to be free to leave the house for the day. I look out through the patio doors.

The sky over Stillwater is palest blue, the sun blazing, a hard, hot light everywhere. My neighbors' roofs glisten in the searing light. The soaked land steams in the heat of this sun. The rains have ended. I know.

I should feel good about this.

It is not over. The rains that fell all through June have ended, but it is not over. Something is happening.

The rains are over, and the sun is out, bright and hot, every day. The days are hot, steamy, the nights humid and very warm; the air does not seem to cool after the sun goes down. I have trouble sleeping because of the close, warm nights, and because I think something is wrong. Something is happening in Stillwater. First we had the rain, now this.

Nobody else seems to suspect. My wife, my children, people I see at work, at church, they talk of how they love all this sunshine, of how everything is so lush, so green, in Stillwater, Oklahoma, grass and weeds shooting up to this rich sunshine, trees and shrubs a dark green, greening, flowers blooming as if the city were a florist's hothouse, backyard vegetable gardens thriving like tropical jungle growth. But I can feel it.

I say to myself: *Pease, I think you're a darn good man. You work hard, selling insurance is hard work, and you're honest in your work, your dealings with people.*

I can feel it. Nobody else seems to notice. If I were to try and tell them, I do not know how I might say it. But I think I know something they do not.

Everyone seems happy, but if they knew, if they felt what I feel, they would not be so happy.

There is a toad on the front steps. "Norvetta!" I call back over my shoulder, step back into the front hall, let the screen door close. "Norvetta!" I call out. It is the largest toad I have ever seen. It is sitting on the top step, facing me, the front door of my house. The morning sunlight falls directly on the huge toad; its warty skin is bleached gray-white by the sunlight. "Look!" I say to my wife when she comes to the front hall, asks what I want, what is the matter with me.

"Oh," she says, and, "It's a big frog."

"It's not a frog," I tell her. "It's a toad. Frogs are green. Frogs don't have warts all over them like that. That's a toad. I'm not leaving this house until it's gone from there."

"Silly," Norvetta says, "step over him or go around. Frogs don't bite you."

"I don't want it to touch me. It might jump up against me if I go out there," I tell her. My wife says I am like a silly child. The enormous toad on my front steps does not move. It makes no sound, no grunt or croak. Its large, deep eyes do not move, blink. I look into its eyes, look away. "Who put it there?" I say, and, "A toad doesn't just come up on my doorstep by chance. There has to be some reason for it. There's some cause for it being there when I come out of my house."

Norvetta says, "You are so preposterous." Our children join us from the breakfast nook.

"Yuck!" says Kim when she sees the toad.

"It's the biggest toad I ever saw," I say, and, "Something brought it here, it's not just coincidence."

"Neat," my baby, Cissy, cries, and, "Can I keep him for my pet? You always say no when I want a pet for my very own."

"Go to work," Norvetta says to me. "Go finish eating, children."

"I won't risk touching it," I say, and, "I will *not* leave here while it's sitting there." The toad breathes, warty, sun-bleached skin pulsing.

"Squish it," Jesse says. "You want me to squish it for you?"

"I'm not budging until it's gone away," I tell them.

"Double-yuck," Kim says as we watch her brother prod the toad with the toe of his shoe, nudge it off into the flowers that bloom so extravagantly beside the steps.

"Now I can't have it for a pet!" Cissy says, begins to bawl.

"You'll be late for work," Norvetta says, and says that for the life of her, she cannot understand a grown man afraid of a little bitty froggy: do I believe that superstition about warts, she wants to know, and do I want to be late for work with people depending on me for their insurance?

"What's so big-deal about a toad?" Jesse says, and, "I'd of squished it except I don't want it all over my shoe sole." Kim comforts Cissy, tells her frogs do not make good pets.

"It was a toad. An enormous toad," I tell them as I leave for work. "They don't just appear on your doorstep by chance."

The toad has disappeared into the flowers beside the steps to my house.

I have questions. I have questions about everything.

I want to know why it rained all through the month of June in Stillwater, Oklahoma, when it never has before. I know what the weathermen from Oklahoma City and Tulsa said, but that is not what I mean when I say I want to know why there were the rains. I want to know why it stopped raining when it did. I want to know why a huge toad was on my doorstep, these things that are happening now that the rains have ended.

So many questions go through my mind, I cannot concentrate on my work. It would be terrible if I could not do my work, if I lost my job because I was always thinking of these questions instead of doing my work. I sit at my desk in the Allstate cubicle at the Sears Catalogue Store; I try to think about Allstate insurance, but cannot.

What if I lost my job? What if the rains had not ended, all of Stillwater swept away in a flood? What if my house burns down to the ground? What if something terrible happens to my wife and children? What if a tornado destroys Stillwater? What if these things happening are not just things happening?

I cannot work. I sit at my desk in the Allstate cubicle, look out through the glass half-walls, watch the Sears catalogue clerks behind their counter, the customer traffic crowding the service counter, wandering the showroom, pricing the refrigerators, washers and dryers, television sets on display. There is a red light on my telephone that flashes instead of rings when I get a call. When the red light flashes, I punch another button, put the caller on hold. I put a caller on hold, then watch the white light flash until the caller hangs up; the light goes off. I have too many questions to care about my work.

I watch the Sears clerks, three of them, women. One is divorced, must work because her ex-husband has fled to Clayton, New Mexico, contributes no child-support. One still has a husband, but he is underemployed, works only part-time at a Quick-Trip store, paid the minimum wage. The third is a student at the old agricultural and mechanical college, working part-time to afford to live in a sorority house.

When they are busy, they are very busy. They call out the numbers of waiting customers, run back and forth to the stockroom to get catalogue orders, check merchandise order numbers in the many catalogues chained to the service counter. They are all trained to smile when they handle a customer, say they appreciate the customer's coming to Sears, that they hope the customer will come in again soon. When the customers are not looking, the clerks make funny faces at each other, stick out their tongues, pretend they smell something that stinks.

When the traffic slows, the store empties, they do nothing. They are supposed to straighten the catalogues chained to the counter, file receipts and back orders, take returned merchandise back to the stockroom, but they do nothing. They take turns making trips to the rest room, and then they lean against the service counter, watch the television sets on display if the soap operas are playing; they do not like game shows. The divorcee smokes cigarettes. The college girl combs her hair. The woman who still has her husband does nothing at all. I watched them from my desk in the Allstate cubicle; they do not know I can also overhear them.

"My kid," says the divorcee, "has these awful damn nits. In his hair. The middle boy. He was itching his head so I looked this morning. I parted his hair and there's these millions of tiny nits crawling through his hair."

"It must be going around," says the woman who still has her husband. "My sister's kids all have that. You should smell the stuff she got a prescription for, she has to wash their heads three times a day or something, wash all their sheets and clothes, shampoo her rugs and all."

"Cut it out you guys," says the student from the old A & M college. "You make me puke just hearing about it. I heard there's a whole entire dorm at OSU infected with lice or fleas I don't know which." She scratches her head lightly with her little finger.

When customers come in they have to stop talking, be busy. I listen and watch, try to imagine them when they are not working here at the Sears Catalogue Store. I cannot imagine them. One has a son with millions of nits crawling over his scalp; I try to imagine her washing her son's head with ordinary soap, but that is all I can imagine. The woman who still has her husband also has a sister; her sister has children who have nits, a house infested with nits, the smell of prescription medicine. But that is all. The girl who is a student at the old agricultural and mechanical college they call OSU now has heard a rumor of a dormitory overrun with fleas or lice, some vermin. I cannot imagine anything more.

I watch the customer traffic, but I cannot imagine them before they come in the door, after they leave with their catalogue purchases. I should be working, answering my calls, calling people, processing the claims and applications stacked in my in-box, but I cannot imagine it means anything beyond the papers neatly clipped in manila folders, the flashing red and white lights on my desk telephone.

When customers see me watching them, some nod, smile. I pretend I have not been watching them, look away, try to look like I am busy. There is a large Allstate sign on my cubicle, so they know I cannot help them with Sears business. Once in a while somebody says hello, passing my cubicle. I pretend not to have heard; it almost always works.

"Some weather now after all that rain," a man says. "Hot. You can stand on the corner and watch the crease go out of your pants it's so humid out there." There is something wrong with his face; it could be severe acne, but I think it is something else, a fiery rash, eczema.

"I'm with Allstate," I say, point with my thumb toward the Sears service counter.

"I know that. I can read your sign," he says, and, "I'm needing to talk about a little insurance here is why I'm out sweating my buns off on a day like this." He has very frizzy hair; the hair on his head is like pubic hair. I put one foot up on the chair beside my desk to keep him from sitting in it to talk to me. "So this must be the place," he says to me. When he talks I can see his cheesy teeth.

"It is," I say, "but I'm not the regular man."

"So when's the regular man here?"

"Check tomorrow or the next day," I say, and, "Call first, or you might come in and be wasting your time out in this weather. This weather doesn't look like it's going to break now the rain's over. It's not determined when he'll be back." The man frowns, looks around the Sears store, back at me. There are dark tufts of hair visible in his large nostrils. "He came down with something," I say, and "Nits."

"Nits?"

"Body lice. What some people call crabs. He had to see a specialist in Tulsa. He may be hospitalized for observation for all I know if they can't clear it up right away."

"Crabs?"

"Vermin," I say, and, "There's a lot of it going around in Stillwater all of a sudden since the rain stopped. All those three ladies you see working at the counter have them. Don't say I told you. See how they're scratching themselves secretly while they wait on customers?" He looks. The backs of his hands are nicked, reddened. The college girl is digging at her hair with the eraser end of a pencil. The divorced woman is rubbing her forearm against the edge of the counter while checking in one of the catalogues with a customer. The woman who still has her husband digs at her belly with her free hand while writing out a returned-merchandise form.

"Really?"

"Really," I tell him. "Check back in a couple weeks, or, better, go downtown. There must be a half-dozen agencies have downtown offices, they'll fix you up. You can't tell what you might pick up hanging around here." There are faded spots on the fly of the man's trousers.

"You're no salesman, I'll say that for you," the man says, walking backwards away from my desk, toward the door.

"Honest though," I say. "I could have let you get body parasites and not said a thing. Be grateful. If somebody mentions Pease to you, you tell them he's a good man, honest, kept you from getting infected." When he is out the door, I cannot imagine him at all.

Sometimes I just watch the cars and trucks passing outside on Boomer Road, the Sambo's across Boomer, the Baskin Robbins that is always announcing new management. I cannot imagine the point of working. Everybody is busy, but I cannot imagine why. Things are happening in Stillwater, Oklahoma, and I wonder that nobody else seems at all aware of it.

I do not get much sleep. I stay up late, pretend to work at the same insurance claims and applications I carry back and forth to work in my briefcase each day, pretend to watch television with Norvetta and my daughters, pretend to worry along with my wife when Jesse stays out at night to all hours, eat, pretend to be hungry, to enjoy the dinners Norvetta cooks.

When the girls are in bed, Jesse home, gone to his bedroom to sleep or smoke cigarettes or marijuana, listen to his trashy music on his stereo, I go to bed with my wife, pretend to sleep until she sleeps. I cannot sleep because it is happening, and I begin to think I understand why. This should make me very afraid, but I tell myself I am a good man, no harm will come to me.

I lie awake in bed beside Norvetta, listen, hear it. I hear everything, Norvetta's light snoring, the occasional thump, tick, or creak of my house as the beams contract in the cooling night air, the muffled chug of the plumbing, soft hum of the refrigerator's ice-cube maker. I hear all this, the tired sigh of my own breathing, muted pock of my heartbeat, the coursing of my blood in my ears. I hear all of it, but listen to the insect noise outside.

It is happening. The huge toad at my front door, the epidemic of lice raging among children, college students, the insects I hear through the screened windows of my bedroom; it is happening, here in Stillwater, Oklahoma. The rains, now this.

I do not speak of it to anyone, do not know if I will. They would say it is normal, after such rains, to have such a great hatch of insect life. Mosquitos breed in the evaporating pools of rainwater; Cissy's legs and arms are swollen, scabby with bites she scratches until she bleeds. I hear the high whine, like a faraway tornado siren, of clouds of mosquitos hovering outside my bedroom window screens. There is a residue of the scent of the chemical fogging city trucks spray in ditches each evening.

They say it is normal, the season's great hatch of cicadas after such rains, their churning chorus filling the night outside my house. The *Stillwater News-Press* has printed an interview with an entomology professor from OSU; he says this hatch of insects in Stillwater is only unusual, not abnormal. Mosquitos, cicadas, roly-polys, beetles, wasps, fire ants, ticks. The entomology professor warned of Rocky Mountain Spotted Fever, said mothers should examine their children frequently for ticks embedded in their skin, how to disengage the ticks safely, the symptoms of the fever that can be fatal.

I do not sleep until I am exhausted. I listen, hear everything, the noise of all the insects outside, until it begins to sound like a roaring to me, like a storm, a cyclone. I hear them, think I can hear them flying, crawling, hear the sound of their movement in the grass of my lawn, the shrubs planted along my house's foundation, in the leaves and needles of the trees in my yard. It is happening.

I try to at least ask the questions I ask myself.

I take a call on the desk phone in my Allstate cubicle at the Sears Catalogue Store; the red light flashes, I push the hold button, watch the white light flash. It flashes for a very long time. When it will not stop flashing, I push the red button, answer the phone. It is Hackett, my regional supervisor, calling from Wichita.

"Pease?"

"Hello, Hackett. How are things in Wichita? Is it happening up in Wichita the way it is here?" I say.

"Pease? Man, what are you doing down there? I'm getting incredible scary feedbacks on you there, Pease. Did you have a client there with you, you keep me on hold so long? Would you like to guess how many times I've tried to call you this month? Pease? Are you opening your mail or am I sending letters out to you like messages in a bottle I might as well drop in the river to get to you?"

I can tell Hackett is trying to keep his temper in Wichita; he would not be a regional supervisor for Allstate if he lost his temper easily. He has a four-state region to supervise. I supervise a sub-district here in Payne County. I used to like to think, talk with my wife about it, before it began to happen, that I might someday get a full district, even a region to supervise. Like Hackett, if I was a good enough man for the job. "Pease? You still there? Can you hear me on this line?"

I say, "It must not be happening in Wichita. It is here, Hackett. You could see it right away if you'd read July's issues of the *News-Press.*"

"Pease? What the hell are you talking about? Why in hell's half-acre would I be reading your dinky newspaper up here in Wichita? Pease?"

"I'm serious, Hackett," I say, and, quickly, before he can speak, "You could see if you'd ask yourself a few easy questions. For instance, just one, why does a humongous big toad wait for you on your doorstep in the morning? Why is there suddenly an epidemic of nits—"

"What?" Hackett says.

"—nits," I repeat, and, "body lice, vermin, crabs we called them when I was in the army, mechanized dandruff. Haven't you heard about the Rocky Mountain Fever here? That stuff travels, Hackett, it'll get to Wichita in time. You probably don't know bugs are overrunning Stillwater, do you. It's in the paper here, it'll be on TV in Tulsa and Oklahoma City soon enough I'd bet. Maybe you'll see it on network if it doesn't let up. And I have this very strong conviction, don't ask me how, it won't let up, Hackett. Do you get Oklahoma TV on your cable up there?"

Hackett says only, "Pease? Pease? Is this a joke you're doing to me on the phone, is that it? Pease, stop talking so I can talk to you, will you? Pease?"

I push the hold button, watch it flash white. It only flashes a little while. I am trying to tell someone, even if I can only ask the questions I ask myself. I watch to see if Hackett puts through another call to me from Wichita, but no lights flash on my desk phone.

The women behind the Sears service counter are screaming; I am thinking, concentrating so hard on the questions I want answers for, that I do not realize they are screaming. It is as if their screaming were only a kind of music that accompanies my thoughts, my questions. Then I realize that the women are screaming, scrambling out from behind the service counter, scattering files as they flee, knocking catalogues off the counter.

They scream, "Snake! Snake! A snake!" There are only two customers on the other side of the counter, a woman, also screaming, "Snake!" and a man who retreats from the counter, dances a frightened jig, like a man with St. Vitus, among the refrigerators, washers and dryers, television sets playing soap operas and game shows. His mouth is open, hands fluttering, as if stricken with palsy, but he is not screaming.

I get up, run out of my Allstate cubicle, run to the counter. At first I see nothing, only the empty lane behind the counter, floor littered with spilled files, order and reorder forms, returned-merchandise acceptance forms, the catalogues swinging on the ends of their chains. The women stand with the man in the middle of the display area, surrounding him, as if he hid behind, among them; they are pointing at me, the counter, screaming, "Snake! Snake!"

I am frightened for only a moment, because I do not see it. There is an instant when I am very afraid; my stomach churns, as if I had eaten too much, or eaten nothing, a metallic taste in my mouth, a tingling current in my arms and legs. I imagine a snake close to me, hidden in the shadows under the counter, about to strike; I feel a prickling in my feet and ankles, hot spasms in the backs of my knees. They scream, "Snake, a snake!"

I see the snake, and fear leaves me; there is nothing for a good man to fear. It lies a dozen feet from me, looped upon itself like a thick brown rope. It is not moving, and then it moves, slithering, looping back upon itself, out of the shadows now, where I can see it is a snake, mottled, a rattlesnake, and it coils tightly, too far away to reach me if it strikes, rattling its rattles now. I can hear the dry rattling even though the women continue to scream.

"Of course!" I yell at the women, the male customer who crouches behind them. "Are you surprised?" I yell, watching the rattlesnake coil tightly upon itself; the sound of its rattles is a dry buzz as I try to watch it, shout at the women and the man on the other side of the counter, screaming, grope like a blind man for something to use as a weapon. The rattlesnake's head moves slowly forward and back, wavers slightly, as if trying to locate me exactly. "It's a damn rattlesnake!" I shout, and, "He probably crawled in through some hole to nest. The town's alive with snakes and rats and roaches and toads, don't you read the *News-Press!*"

My hand finds a tall carton leaning against the wall. I step back a step, pick it up, set it on the counter; it is a set of Sears Best golfing irons. The rattlesnake moves, unfolds its coil, slithers deeper into the farthest corner, recoils, begins to shake its rattle again.

"You're a fool if you're surprised!" I yell at the screamers. The rattlesnake's rattles buzz, the women scream, a telephone is ringing in the stockroom; I have to yell very loud to make myself heard. I tear open the carton, pull one of the irons free. "You don't even have to see it yourself, you can read the paper!" I yell, and, "First rains, then toads and salamanders and lizards and horned toads, cockroaches and silverfish and termites in everybody's house in Payne County, all those kids getting lice in their hair! Mine have been lucky, some of us are lucky, but believe me it's happening!" I am screaming.

I am screaming, but I move very carefully, slowly, toward the coiled rattlesnake. "Record insect hatches, snakes turning up in people's yards and garages, why are you surprised!" I miss the first swing at the snake; it moves too quickly backward, uncoiling, coiling, trapped in the corner when I swing again, feel the soft feeling of the golfing iron hit the snake. It strikes the club before I can lift it for another swing; I feel the vibration of the strike in the club's shaft.

I lift the iron, swing again, feel the softness of the hit; the rattlesnake is uncoiled, writhing, trying to find something to strike. I swing again, again; it is hard to hit the snake's whipping head. "We had abnormal rain!" I scream. "Now snakes and toads and lice! What do you think it means! What do you think we've done in Stillwater to get this!" I hit the rattlesnake again and again; there is blood on the floor behind the counter, flecks of blood on my shoes and trousers, on the head of the golfing iron. The rattlesnake is still moving, trying to roll away from me, no place to escape.

"Ask yourself!" I am screaming as I swing the golf club again and again, pulp the rattlesnake's head. "Ask yourself why these things are happening!" I scream. "If we'd all ask those questions we might get some answers we need!"

The snake is dead, no movement left in it, and I stop hitting it with the golf club. The women have stopped screaming; they are silent or sobbing, weeping quietly, cowering about the sole male customer among all the Sears appliances on display. I am the only one screaming. I stop hitting the dead rattlesnake, but I am still screaming at them.

All they have to do is read the *News-Press*. "Look," I say to Norvetta, "here's another one. There's so many they don't even make the first section anymore, they stick it back with sports and stocks." I hold the paper up for Norvetta to see. It is a picture of an old man named Campbell who lives out near Perkins; he looks like Pappy Yokum. He is posed, holding a five-and-a-half-foot rattler he killed with a hoe in his melon patch. The caption says he found the snake asleep, sunning. In the picture, the old man named Campbell from Perkins is grinning, some teeth missing, holding the limp snake out at arm's length.

"I'm out of Raid. Remind me to pick up Raid when I shop this weekend," is all Norvetta says, and, "If I don't keep after under the sink we'll have ants everywhere."

"There's another article on ticks, too," I say. "They've had another case of Rocky Mountain Fever at Stillwater Memorial. Are you checking yourselves for ticks like I told you?" I ask my daughters.

"Gross," Kim says.

"Ticks is bugs. I'm not afraid of bugs," Cissy says.

"You think your snake you killed's so hot," says my son, "you should see the skin they got hanging up in the front window at First National Bank, that sucker's six feet long!"

There is an announcement in the *News-Press*, buried in among the daily reports of divorces, marriages, civil suits, the Stillwater police blotter, of a seminar to be held at the university; open to the public, faculty from the biological sciences will explain the recent dramatic increase in insects, rodents, and reptiles reported in Stillwater and surrounding Payne County. A professor is quoted as saying it is very logical, due to the June rains, the hot weather this month, normal cycles invigorated by circumstances. "They can't explain it away like that," I say aloud.

"What? Dear?" Norvetta says.

"Ticks is only just bugs is all," Cissy says.

"If I found a tick on my skin I'd die," Kim says.

"I'm not kidding, six damn foot from the end of his nose to the last rattle on his tail. You could make a damn belt from it. Cool," says Jesse, and, "Did you hear about the black kid swimming out at Boomer Lake swam into a whole damn nest of moccasins, got bit to hell, damn near drowned?"

"Did you say something, dear?" Norvetta asks me.

"Nobody listens to anybody!" I say, and, "Nobody listens to what I'm trying to say. Somehow in this world I'm going to find a way to make people listen to me or die trying!" I throw down the newspaper.

"Mom," says Kim, "it's no fair if Jesse can say damn and I can't."

The sound of the locusts is like humming, like the humming of the children's choir at First Methodist Church of Stillwater, a light humming, the way the humming of the children's choir in the loft will stay in the air under the church's vaulted ceiling at the end of a hymn, after they have sung *amen*.

"You should hear it, it sounds like a choir humming, like at the end of the hymn. When it's over but you can still hear it," I say to Hackett, calling long-distance from Wichita. "Can you hear it at all?" I take the receiver away from my ear, hold it out towards the Sears store's big window, the traffic on Boomer Road, the locusts. *What? Pease? Pease!* I hear him saying on the telephone before I hang it up, go back to watching the locusts out the window, listening to their hum.

The sound of the locusts is a harsher whirring now, the flutter of their wings like the approach of a helicopter flying in to Stillwater to pick up an emergency case for transfer to Oklahoma City. It is a whirring, a clicking noise at the center of it, like the metal blades of a helicopter chopping the air over Stillwater. "It sounds like a helicopter, doesn't it," I say to the women behind the Sears service counter.

"Gives me the creeps," says the divorced woman.

"I think it sounds about like my blender if you ask me," says the woman who still has her husband.

"Or maybe like my Lady Norelco shaver," says the student from the old A & M college they call OSU now.

"And what do you think it means?" I ask them, and, "I mean, put it together with the lice your kids got, the snakes, the toad on my front steps, the rains in June. Have you asked yourselves what it all means for us?" They do not say anything to that.

The noise is a buzzing, like swarming bees, like a rattlesnake, and there is a continual popping as they fly against the glass of the Sears store's big window, a popping sound, like a Christmas tree ornament breaking, and the Sears store is darker because the sun is obscured by the thickening moil of locusts in the air outside. If the door were opened there would be thousands of locusts in the Sears store, but there are no customers, nobody on the streets of Stillwater because of the locusts.

So we close the Sears store, run to our cars to drive home, and the locusts fly against our faces and hands like driven rain. I swat at them, brush them off my clothes, out of my hair, feel them, hard and brittle, against my fingers, squash them on my clothes as I slap at them, the sound of them a roaring in my ears, like a rainstorm. I hear the women yelping as they run to their cars, because the locusts are tangling in their hair, flying against their eyes and mouths.

Driving home, my wipers sweep them off the windshield like rain, smear the windshield yellow, gray, dark brown; I am lucky to make it home, the sky dark as dusk with locusts, the locusts in my headlight beams like heavy, blowing rain.

"You're all so shocked," I say to my wife and children, and, "What shocks me is you're so shocked by it!" Some locusts come in the front door with me, flit about the living room, light on the carpet, the walls, lamp shades, the TV screen, where a man is talking about the locusts in Stillwater. "Couldn't you see it coming?" I ask Norvetta, my children. "Think back," I say, "the rains, the toad that morning, mosquitos, the rattlesnake I killed at work, nits in everybody's hair. Now this. Don't you see it?"

Norvetta takes a broom after the locusts flying in our living room. Cissy is screeching, standing on a chair, hugging herself in horror. Kim stomps a locust to mash on the hall tiles. My son holds a wiggling locust in his fingers, up close to his face, examines it; the locust struggles, shudders, is still as Jesse pinches it to death between his fingers, drops it, looks at the mess on his fingers.

"I suspect a purpose in this," I tell my family. "I won't say I can explain it very well, but these things came here for a purpose, maybe to tell us something. It's not just coincidence. Are you listening to me?"

"Dad, crap, it happens every so many years," Jesse says, "a generation or something, I forget."

"The TV said they eat everything they can and then they all just die," Kim says. Cissy has stopped screeching, come down to the floor to poke and prod at a crippled locust trying to crawl on the carpet.

"Do you seriously think this is the end of it?" I ask them. "Do you truly in your heart of hearts believe they'll eat up every green plant in sight and then die off or go away and that's the end of it?"

"Is that the tornado alert siren I'm hearing?" Norvetta asks. We are all quiet to listen.

"No," I say, "it's just the locusts." They sound like a heavy rain on our roof, like a wind, like hail against our doors and sealed windows. There is a sound in it like the tornado alert sirens, but it is only the locusts. "It's not over. I'm telling you it's not," I say, but they will not listen to me.

"Are you going to just sit there?" Norvetta asks. "Are you just going to sit around the house like a zombie for the rest of your life?"

"A drought," I tell her, "is like a siege. Do you know what a siege is? You sit it out. There's nothing you can do but wait for it to end. You wait it out, and when it's over you either won or you lost." She does not say if she knows what a siege is.

"What's going to become of us?" my wife says, and, "Are you going to sit there without a job until we starve to death? I don't understand you!" she says, and now she is angry, weeping; it is hard to listen to her because she is crying as she talks, and I do not like to see my wife cry—no good man wants that—but there is nothing I can do about it. "Have you just decided to quit living, is that it? You won't talk to me!" she says before she can no longer speak through her hurt, angry crying.

"It's no use," I tell Norvetta, and, "I don't talk to you because *you* don't listen to *me!* You, the children, you can't seem to see it, no matter what I say, so I don't try. Hackett, up in Wichita, he can't see it, he won't listen, so he gives me my walking papers. People at work, customers, the counter girls, nobody wants to hear it. So either I wait and keep it to myself or I can go out and try to tell somebody else. That's why I said it's like a siege. We have to wait this drought out. Then maybe we'll all know what I know."

My wife is crying too hard to listen to me; I stop talking. I wait while she cries the tears she needs to cry. I know she would like me to get up, go to her, hold her, help her stop crying. But I know if I wait she will stop, or leave the room to cry alone. What I have to do is wait; if I wait, she will stop or go away where I cannot see or hear her. If I just wait, this drought will end. Or I could try to tell somebody.

The snakes are gone. The nits and beetles and wasps and cockroaches are gone. The toad is gone. The locusts are gone. The drought has killed them. Insects and reptiles and rodents cannot live in this drought. I think we can survive this drought if we will only wait.

I am not sure where my wife and children are. I think they are somewhere in the house; nobody goes outside in this heat unless they have to. Nobody wants to be outside in this drought. Whenever I am in my house, not out in the drought, I think Norvetta takes our children somewhere else in the house—upstairs, into one of the bedrooms—where they will not see me. I would like to see Norvetta, Jesse, my daughters, but I do not mind, because I would not say anything to them if they were with me. I have my severance pay from Allstate, so they will not starve while we wait for this to end.

Waiting, there is not much to do. When I cannot think of anything else to do, I watch television. I try not to miss the weather reports on cable news from Tulsa and Oklahoma City. They talk about the drought. They do not know. They say it is stationary centers of high pressure, blocked, static masses of dry air, show charts of average monthly rainfall patterns, interview wheat farmers and cattle raisers who say they think they will be ruined by this drought if it lasts much longer.

"That," I say aloud, to the TV, myself, the empty room, "is what *you* think." My voice sounds strange to me in the empty room. Like the voice of the weatherman on the TV, as if it came from far away, not real, not a human voice; I think to myself: That does not sound like the good old Pease I know!

I think this is because I have stopped trying to tell people. Maybe I need to tell somebody while we all wait for it to happen. "Will anyone listen to me?" I say aloud in the empty room with the TV on, and I recognize my voice. It is Pease's voice. It is a real, human voice I hear.

The sun is like iron, the heat of this sun like a great weight I feel pressing down on me when I am outside. The sun is too hot, too bright to look at, like iron heated until it is red, orange, white, molten, pouring down upon me. Sweat beads my face, runs out of me, soaks my clothes, plasters my thinning hair to my head. Walking, my feet feel like they are on fire. Sweat runs out of me; I feel myself drying under this burning sun, like the land, drying, in this drought that has come to Stillwater, Oklahoma.

The last amen sung by the youth choir of the First Methodist Church of Stillwater hangs in the air above our heads like an incense, like the sound of flying locusts, like the dust motes that float constantly in the hard sunlight outside since this drought came. Like an echo of my thoughts. I wait for Reverend Bob Yantz to give his benediction to the congregation.

I sit in the last seat in the pew, on the central aisle, where I will be easily seen when I stand. In the center of the church, where I can be heard. Norvetta wanted to sit somewhere else, off to one side, under the stained-glass memorial windows, but I insisted. She holds her worn confirmation Bible in her free hand, grips my hand with the other. I do not think she will really try to stop me.

Beside her, Kim holds her white imitation-leather confirmation Bible with both hands; I see her expression stiffen, suppressing a yawn, as Reverend Bob Yantz speaks his benediction. Cissy is off with her Sunday School class; they color in biblical coloring books, downstairs, in a soundproof crying room. My son will not attend church with us. I do not know where he goes these days, in this drought.

"Lord," says Reverend Bob Yantz from his pulpit, "we also ask You to visit Your mercy upon us, to send us moisture as a sign of Your mercy, to end this drought that has caused our ranchers and farmers and all of us so much suffering and concern."

Reverend Bob Yantz is very popular in Stillwater, because he is young, and because he gets on so well with our youth. He is the city council's unofficial chaplain, opening and closing their weekly public meetings with prayer, and each Easter, Thanksgiving, and Christmas is featured in the *News-Press* for his ministry to prisoners in the city jail.

"Also, Lord, before I forget," he is saying, eyes closed, hands clasped under his dimpled chin, "we ask Your special mercy on behalf of our elderly people in the hospital and in nursing homes here in our city. They suffer especially in this terrible heat, our invalids and our shut-ins in Stillwater, some of them don't have air-conditioning," he is saying.

Reverend Bob Yantz is a handsome young man, except that I do not like his hair since he began to have it styled in an Afro. I think it makes him look like a pretty young woman, but Norvetta says lots of men do it these days, famous men who appear on television with Johnny Carson. Bob Yantz has a cold sore on his lip that never seems to go away.

"Amen," he says, bowing his head. I feel Norvetta tighten her grip on my hand, but she releases me when I stand. I speak before the organist can begin the recessional music.

"What if it was the Lord sent drought to us for a purpose?" I say. I recognize my voice; it is me, Pease, speaking, very loud. They hear me. The organist does not play. Reverend Bob Yantz lifts his head, eyes open wide. I look above his head as I speak, to the large cross suspended in mid-air on invisible wires above the altar; I can hear the congregation—three hundred souls? four hundred?—shifting in the pews, turning to look at me as I speak. Norvetta takes hold of my right arm, tugs, but she cannot, will not stop me.

"Have you forgotten the rain in June?" I say, and, "How many of you had to call Orkin or A & M Termite Control to exterminate the bugs in your house last month? Raise your hands." I look, now, at the congregation, pivot slowly where I stand in the central aisle. They are all watching me, but no hands are raised. Reverend Yantz is watching me from the pulpit, mouth hanging open.

"How big was the biggest toad you ever in your life ever remember seeing?" I say. I hear my voice louder now; it is me, Pease. "Who says the locusts just naturally happened? Who can prove it beyond a doubt? Raise your hand if you think you can. Nobody?" Norvetta stands, takes my right arm with both hands, pulls me off-balance, but I do not stop. I can hear Kim begin to cry with embarrassment. Norvetta makes a throaty noise through her clenched teeth.

"This heat and drought we have now is part and parcel of it all!" I shout. Reverend Yantz leaves the pulpit. People begin to talk, get up from their pews. The organist starts to play. "Wait, if you won't listen!" I am screaming at them. "Wait! This drought will end, but then what? Are you ready? What if it was your Lord you're praying to to end it sent it in the first place, then what? What's next?" I scream.

Norvetta tugs and jerks on my arm, people brush past me in the aisle, the organ is very loud. So I stop. Because no one can hear now, nobody listening.

I believe the purpose of this declares itself. The rain, insects, reptiles, rodents, drought. If only I could read it. I walk out into the heat, the drought, to read its meaning. I am one of the few in all of Stillwater, Oklahoma, who walks the streets in this drought.

I see groups of children, walking to Couch Park to swim, a few who still gather to play softball on the dusty diamonds under the sweltering sun, an occasional child pedaling a bicycle; they pass me, and I watch them recede into the shimmering heat waves dancing in any direction in the distance. I screw my eyes up against the sun's awful glare, blot the sweat from my face with my sleeve, try to read the purpose I know declares itself in all this.

There is no sound beyond the thick plopping noise of my shoes on the blistering concrete, the whoosh and spit of sprinklers as the citizens of Stillwater try to save their parched lawns. Sound is diminished, lost in the relentless heat of the sun that envelopes me, everything, drying everything. I am one of the few, out and about in Stillwater, Oklahoma, trying, in the hot clutch of this August drought, to read its purpose. If I could know its purpose, exactly, be sure, then I could tell them what is happening to us here. The chugging, dripping air-conditioning units sound like the voice of this drought to me.

The Stillwater City Council meets in public session in the Municipal Building each Monday evening. Their public sessions are broadcast on the local channel, a cable subscriber's service; I have told Norvetta to watch if she wants to see me tonight.

The council members are always reelected; the *News-Press* always refers to them as our City Fathers. They boast of their public sessions, that any citizen can be heard, that the public's business is open to the public, broadcast into every home in Stillwater receiving the cable service. Tonight they hear anyone interested in the proposed emergency water rationing statutes. I will be the last to speak. I wonder if Norvetta and our children are watching the local channel at home.

The chairman, our mayor, recognizes the president of the Stillwater Garden Clubs Association; she protests that the severity of the proposed rationing will destroy floral gardens that have required countless hours of loving care, and which, she reminds him, have done so much to establish the reputation of Stillwater, statewide, as a city of residential beauty and gracious living. Our mayor tells her, speaking on behalf of not only the entire elected body of the council but for all the citizens of Stillwater, that she and her colleagues are to be commended for their achievement and dedication, but, he reminds her, when a community's welfare is so seriously threatened, he ventures to say that some things, even appearances, must be sacrificed to essential priorities.

She yields the floor, telling the council she intends to file her protest in writing. The owner-operator of three automatic carwash facilities in Stillwater rises to address the council. He wishes to point out to council that the rationing they propose will put him out of business; this will mean the end of many jobs, a loss to the city, county, state, and nation of tax revenues and consumer purchasing power generated by his business. Our mayor thanks him for his opinion, assures him the economic impact of the rationing statutes is still under study by council and staff; he reminds the businessman, and all present, and those viewing over the cable channel at home, that this hearing is designed to elicit information from the public, not to act rashly with a snap decision.

There is only one television camera. I wait, after standing, until I can see its lens point at me; I want Norvetta, my family, to see me when I speak. If they are watching. Our mayor recognizes me, tells me I have the floor and council's attention.

I say: "Can you not, can we not all think in terms that transcend taxes and jobs and how things look if they're not washed?"

"I ask the gentleman please identify himself before presenting his view," our mayor says.

"My name is Pease," I say, and, "I like to think I am a good man." I speak up loud and clear. "I live in Stillwater. I work—I worked—until recently in Stillwater. I'm still paying taxes here. I'll be living here and paying my taxes at least until my severance pay runs out. After that I don't know where I'll be, but I have something to say to all of you." Our mayor says I have the floor and council's undivided attention. I look into the television camera as I speak.

I say: "There's a purpose declared in this we can maybe read if we'd just give it a shot. June was rains. July we had roaches and rats and snakes and the locusts they tried to tell us was only natural. Now drought."

"Council doesn't exactly follow. Can you elaborate a little?" our mayor asks. I continue to speak as if I had not heard him, directly into the camera's lens.

"This will not end," I say, and, "Oh, sure, this drought will come to an end sooner or later, but you don't really believe that's all, do you? It has some purpose. We can understand it if we try. Something with a purpose can be understood if we'll stop talking about jobs and watering the grass and asking college professors for all the answers for a minute. I'm trying to tell you we don't ask the right questions." I do not stop trying to tell them. Our mayor covers his microphone with both hands, confers with his fellow council members; I see Reverend Bob Yantz, who gave the opening prayer, huddling with the council members. They are not listening, but I try to tell them.

"Either," I say, "we try to know what's happening now, before it happens, or we learn when it's too late. It's up to you, to us, take your choice. Are you listening to me? Are you deaf? Are you blind? Don't you *want* to know!" Our mayor is waving his hands at the television cameraman.

I do not stop speaking. I do not stop for the policeman, even when he takes hold of me, twists my arm behind my back; I only stop when I see the television camera swing away from me. Then I stop, let the policeman march me out of the council chambers.

"You're hurting my arm," I say to the policeman, and, "You can let go, I'm going. I'm not going to say anything more to anybody. Please let me go, you're hurting my arm," I say, but he does not release me until we are outside, on the steps of the Municipal Building, in the heat of this drought that does not ease, does not relent even with the sun gone down to end another day.

He releases me, says, "If I was you I'd get myself home where I belonged, Mr. Pease is it?" He leaves me there. I look up into the black night sky, feel the radiating heat, stored in the dry earth through the day, rising up into the sweltering night sky. If only I could read the meaning of what I see, the white-hot points of stars in the black night sky. I believe it declares itself, like a book in a strange language.

It is happening. The dust storm is a sign. I believe it is happening. Soon.

The dust storm began this morning. When I woke I thought it was earlier than it was, the sky outside the bedroom windows a dull gray. "What time is it, Norvetta?" I asked my wife, and, "Is the alarm clock right?"

"The same time it always is when we get up," she said, and, "I don't want to talk to you. Please don't say anything to me."

"Look, Norvetta, the sky outside!" I said. "That's dust blowing in the air! It's so dry now the wind's blowing the topsoil away!" She left the bedroom without speaking. I looked out the window at the dirty gray sky, lighter where the sun rose behind all that blowing dust. "Keep the children indoors today!" I shouted after my wife. "This is no weather to risk letting them outside in!" She did not answer, but kept our children in; only I went out into the dust storm.

I did not stay out long. There is no one else walking the streets of Stillwater, no one to tell. They will all know, soon I think. The dust storm is red with the fully risen sun glowing behind it now. Everything a redness, whirling in the air, a reddish coat of dust over the withered grass and shrubs and leaves, a caking of dust on my clothes, a paste of red dust stuck to my sweating face and arms and hands; I cover my mouth to breathe, choke and cough as I walk the streets of Stillwater, looking for someone to tell. The dust blinds me. I do not stay out for long in this dust storm. There is no one to tell. They will all know soon.

Jesse says, "I vote we get in the car and cut out for the university like a scalded-ass dog. There's plenty buildings with basements there."

Norvetta says, "We could do that or we could go to the church basement. They have it marked for a shelter."

Kim says, "Before next time we should dig a hidey-hole in our yard. I know this girl her parents made their own private hidey-hole in their backyard."

Cissy, my baby, says, "I can taste dirt when I breathe in my mouth," begins to cry.

I tell them: "It doesn't make any difference where we go if it wants to hit us." They do not seem to care what I say. The TV is turned to the local channel where Stillwater Civil Defense monitors the tornado watch. Cissy cries, my son argues with his mother, Kim watches them. I watch the TV; the tornado watch area covers all of Payne County, touch-downs reported to our west and south, no injuries or property damage confirmed yet.

"We have got to *do* something!" Norvetta shouts at Jesse.

"That's what I've been telling you since June," I say, and, "Now we'll all find out, won't we."

We are shouting at each other when the rain comes. The sky goes from dark red to black, like a total night falling in the middle of this late afternoon. The rain is driven by high winds.

"Oh help us help us help us!" Norvetta cries. My daughters are screaming, my son standing helplessly beside the TV set, fidgeting, hopping from one foot to the other, hands in his jeans pockets, babbling.

"Help?" I yell, and, "There's no help! Wait! Now we'll all know, all of you! Shut up!" I yell, and, "Hear it?" We are all quiet, and there is the battering rain, the shrill winds, and then they hear it too, the tornado alert sirens going off all over Stillwater. It is like hysterical screaming; it is like a terrible wailing, as if all of Stillwater, Oklahoma, cried out in terror at the approaching tornado.

"Now!" I say to my wife and children, have to shout to be heard. "Now!" I yell against the rising keen of the tornado. And they come to me, Norvetta, Jesse, Kim, Cissy, and I take them, huddling, close to me. I feel their hands on me, their faces pressed to me, feel their shaking bodies as the tornado becomes a roaring. I lift my head, look toward the windows to see the tornado come upon us, but it is only a blacker roaring in the black, lashing rain that sweeps about its roaring center.

"Now!" I cry out, feel the pressure of the air against my ears, hear the windows burst, the grinding of our house beginning to crumble. "Now," I am able to say, hold my family close to me, lift my face to look into the whirlwind for a sign, a purpose I think I can read, listening for a voice I know I will hear.

Whiskey, Whiskey, Gin, Gin, Gin

> . . . use a little wine for thy stomach's
> sake and thine often infirmities.
>
> —1 Timothy 5:23

A CONSTRUCTIVE WAY *to begin would be for you to make the simple admission, statement, if you like, that you're an alcoholic. Are you able to say that about yourself?*

Not on your life! Not on my life. What we're really talking about is my life here. No way. Never. Far from it.

When he had something to celebrate, my father celebrated; he was a moody man, but he knew how to celebrate.

World War II for example. The war was very good to my father, at least for a time. He sold machine tools, a part of a machine necessary to make a machine that made something in some way vital to the war effort. Riding the crest of cost-plus contracts and military delivery priorities, he did extremely well until the war began to wind down toward victory over the Axis.

I like to think of him, remember him, celebrating.

I can see him, as clearly as though it were yesterday; my memory of things is like that, exact, alive, more real as memory than the fading facts ever were.

We are in a bar. I do not know which bar, what time of day or night it is. I am six. Seven? It is 1944? Memory can be like a dream, cause and effect nonexistent, the reality all the more vivid for its isolation in a void of particular time and place.

It is World War II, we are in a barroom, my father and I. My mother is not there. She was not a woman who enjoyed barrooms. My brothers are away at the war, Milton in Belgium, Leonard en route to the Philippines.

My father stands at the bar, celebrating. A winning contract bid? A commission paid? His return from another flying trip to Washington, where he confers with Dollar-A-Year men? He stands at the bar.

His suit coat is open, thrown back, one hand cocked on his hip; one foot is up on the rail. His chest is thrust forward. Satisfaction? Pride? Bravado?

Chin up, he talks, brags, throws back his head to laugh often, loud. The bar-room, people, seem arranged for him, a stage setting. Everything, everyone is arrayed about him; he is the center, focus of attention.

With his free hand, elbow on the bar, he manipulates his Pall Malls, a Ronson lighter, a shot glass. Again and again. Memory is like that, incredible, yet more real than the possible.

Again and again, he lifts the glass to his lips, tosses off his drink. Some-thing colorless. Gin? Schnapps? He tosses off his drink, raps the bar top with the empty shot glass, casually nudges money toward the bartender, flips a Pall Mall out of the pack lying in the tangle of bills and change, places it in the corner of his mouth, thumbs his Ronson, blows smoke, still talking, a cloud of smoke that shades into the layers that drift below the indistinct ceiling, obscures the faces of men and women who surround him, wait on his words.

Again and again. This is how I remember him. He tosses off his drink, calls for another round, lights a Pall Mall, blows redolent, luscious smoke. My father celebrates: the war, his success, himself.

Where am I in all this? Somewhere. There. I cannot remember when or how. I am there, observe. This is what I remember, how I remember it.

But my father was not a drinking man, what could be called a *drinking man*. Later, years later, I recall asking my mother if he drank a lot. Did he *drink?*

"No," she said, and "Your father didn't have the courage for that."

"What?" I said. "What does that mean?"

"He was too afraid of hangovers to drink much. Your father wasn't the sort of man to face the morning after the night before."

"I can't believe that," I said, "I remember being with him in a bar once, way back when, he was tossing off shots like he had a hollow leg."

"You're imagining things," my mother said, and, "Your father was a coward about physical pain. He'd never take the risk."

I was old enough to understand she meant more than she said. Another time, I might have asked another question, invited her to go on, speak about how she really felt about him. But all I was interested in at the moment was his drinking. I remember thinking that was funny, a man not drinking for fear of a hangover.

My father could be moody. I have another memory of him.

There was still the war, but it must have been almost over; it must have been the summer of 1945. The cost-plus contracts were evaporating, military delivery priorities revoked. The world war that was so good to him, for him, was ending, no longer a good war for my father.

We are at home, my father and I; my mother is there, but not in the room. It is the time when they are seeing lawyers, haggling over dwindling assets. Our home is dominated by long, tangible silences between them, broken only after I am put to bed for the night. I lie awake in the dark of my bedroom, listen to their strident voices, his hoarse shouting, her weeping. I lie awake, listen, try to assemble, make sense of references to a woman named Irene who lives somewhere he travels frequently on business. I have never understood the whole story, no longer care.

My father and I are there, my mother somewhere else in the house, my brothers still gone to the war that is ending. Milton will return from Europe soon. Leonard is missing in the Philippines, will never be found. We do not know this yet.

My father and I listen to the radio. Mr. Anthony. People come to Mr. Anthony, tell him their problems. He asks them questions, deliberates, gives them, judgelike, solutions to the difficulties of their lives. My father listens. I listen, watch my father. He slumps in his easy chair, an expression of deepest, blackest depression set in his face like stone. It is night; the only light in the room comes from the large dial of the Philco console. A Pall Mall smolders in the ashtray at his elbow; in his hand, he holds a highball, ice melting in the thick summer air.

Mr. Anthony, says a man with a problem, *my brother-in-law has lived with me and my wife for six months. Not once has he so much as lifted a finger to pay his share for groceries and the rent money.*

"Holy Jesus," my father says. He rattles the melting ice in his highball glass, lifts it to his mouth, no more than wets his lips.

Mr. Anthony, says the man's wife, *my brother has tried hard to find a suitable employment. He was 4-F for his bad back and also he got injured in a car crash shortly after.*

"Jesus H. Wept!" says my father. He twirls the chips of melting ice in his highball with his finger.

Mr. Anthony says, *I think we have a situation here where two people who should have, failed to talk freely about what concerns them.*

"Sweet jumping Jesus," says my father, looks into his drink, does not drink it. I do not understand; Mr. Anthony seems to be solving their problem. "Promise me one thing in your life," my father says to me.

"What? Sure," I say.

"Never do anything in your life the way I did. Okay? Promise me."

"I don't catch on," I say, and "What?" again. Do I begin to cry? Do I try to listen for the sound of my mother in the house, hope, pray she will enter the room, turn on the light, tell me it is past my bedtime? I cannot remember.

"Promise!" my father says, drowning out Mr. Anthony.

"I promise," I say, and we sit there in silence together, listen to people's life problems being solved by Mr. Anthony's mellow voice. In the dark with the Philco's glowing dial, while the world war is ending outside, my father's fortunes crumbling, a woman named Irene waits for him, my mother waits for my bedtime, waits to begin her screaming accusations. My brother Milton waits for his rotation home from France. My brother Leonard is missing on the island of Luzon, though we do not yet know this.

My father was a moody man. Too depressed even to drink. Or afraid of a hangover. This is another of my memories. And I probably garble literal events, trying to tell it now.

I'm confused. What's the key here? You associate drinking with his exuberance, is that it? Drink is celebration? And this conflicts with your resentment of his philandering and his business failure? I'm thoroughly confused. The key's your image of your father?

Not at all. Of course, you're confused. You can't see it with my eyes. You don't have my memories. My way of seeing it.

In 1947 there was a record blizzard; they always mention 1947 when we have a hard winter. I remember the two days and two nights of snow, the way the streets looked drifted over, the bite of the wind on my cheeks when I played in the tunnels and forts I burrowed in the huge snowbanks, the crunching sound my boots made on the frozen crust, walking down the narrow lane plowed in the middle of a main street, my breath like smoke.

This is vague, a kind of collage, but the year was 1947, a matter of record.

I woke suddenly in the night. I was not dreaming, or if I was, I did not remember the dream when I woke. I was not frightened. I was sleeping, deeply asleep, and then, in an instant, I was wide awake, and all I knew was that I was awake in the darkness of my bedroom, only a pale moonlight at the window. I did not know what time it was, just that it was very late at night. My bedroom was cold; I wrapped myself in the quilt, went to the window, looked out at the cold stillness of the night, moonlight glittering on the snowdrifts, the high, plowed banks, the crusted streets. Then I heard them singing.

I do not remember what they sang. Songs from the war, dirty limericks, nonsense. Then I saw them, dancing, staggering in the street, and I recognized my brother Milton and his friend, Edmund Henry Clark. Milton wore his army fatigue jacket with the imprint of his chevrons still on the sleeves. Edmund Henry Clark wore his navy peacoat, black watch cap. They danced in circles on the snow-crusted street, slipped, fell into the frozen snowbanks, sparred with each other, sang, shouted, cupped their gloved hands to their mouths, called out obscenities to the sleeping neighborhood.

They stumbled out of sight. Then I heard them on our front steps, their booted feet stomping on the porch, the front door pushed open. I climbed back in my bed, sat up, huddling in the quilt, listening. I heard them creep through the house, heard Edmund Henry Clark curse when he bumped into something, Milton's loud whisper shushing him.

My brother opened my bedroom door, snapped on the light, and they stood there for an instant in the glare of the sudden bright light, grinning at me. Then my brother said, "Fancy finding you all up and alert at this wee hour," and Edmund Henry Clark laughed and Milton said, "Knock off the static, you want to wake up the *mater?*" He pulled Edmund Henry Clark into the room and shut the door, and the two of them tiptoed in slow motion to my bed, sat down beside me, still grinning.

I said, "I heard you guys yelling and it woke me up."

Milton said, "That was my compeer here," and, "Swabies can't hold their grog like GI's can." Edmund Henry Clark laughed so hard he fell over on his side of my bed. Milton said, "Brother of mine, brother-boo, I have a little proposition for you, now you're awake anyhow." Edmund Henry Clark fell asleep, a gentle snoring sound in his breathing.

My bedroom felt warmer with them there, as if they brought a source of heat through the subzero night into my room. They seemed to glow in the harsh light. Snowflakes dotted my brother's hair, melted to dewdrops. Powdery snow dusted his fatigue jacket, Edmund Henry Clark's peacoat and wool watch cap. Milton leaned close to me to speak; I smelled the tart, yeasty odor of beer.

He said, "Unbeknownst to you because of your tender age, the bars in this burg remain open for a good solid hour yet, but me buddy-boo and me finds ourselves temporarily tapped for funds. Now I happen to know you must have ample in yon Mr. Pig there"—he turned to look at the large, pink plaster piggy bank on my dresser—"which with your permissible permission I and this dumb swabie here would like to borrow like a fin or maybe even a tenner at most, after which we'll tuck you in, say good *nacht* to all and to all good *nacht,* and be on our way in a trice if not a thrice or even quicker than that. What do you say?"

My memory is that he sat close to me on my bed, grinning, smelling of beer, warming my room, and we were silent for a long moment. My brother Milton grinned at me, wavering a little as he sat. Edmund Henry

Clark snored lightly on the foot of my bed, and my memory tells me that I believed, in that very long moment of silence, that my brother and his friend were very happy.

They had come home from a world war, and the government paid them twenty dollars a week for fifty-two weeks to buy cigarettes and beer while they pondered college educations on the GI Bill or pretended to look for jobs that would lead to satisfying and productive careers.

I believed, as I remember this moment, that the freezing black night outside, the city choked with snow this record winter of 1947, held joy and promise for them. They had come from a war, and they had no money, and our family had been broken by divorce and death, the future was so opaque as to be nonexistent, but my brother Milton, nodding, drowsy with beer now that he was out of the terrible cold, was ecstatic as he waited for me to speak, say he could raid my piggy bank for beer money. And I believed Edmund Henry Clark, passed out on beer in his navy coat and hat, dreamed pleasant dreams at the foot of my bed.

"Can you help us out, bro?" my brother said. Before I could answer, my mother opened the bedroom door, tying her bathrobe closed, blinking against the light, furious.

"Do I have to have this!" she shouted. "Everything else, do I have to have this thrust on me on top of everything in this damnable life!" She jerked at her bathrobe tie, stood for an instant with her hands on her hips, hair mussed from sleep, blinking at the light, then came to us, stood over my brother and me to shout at him. "Is it enough his father's deserted him for a slut, must you add to our misery!" she shouted at Milton.

Edmund Henry Clark woke up at once, sat up straight at the foot of my bed, stood up as straight as if he were on parade, walked, mumbling what may have been apologies, out of my bedroom, out of the house, into the night's bitter weather.

My brother did not answer her. "Leonard dead and gone in some God-forsaken end of the earth, rotting in the jungle for all we know, your father's a louse, is this the fine example you mean to be for your baby brother!" she shouted. Milton lowered his head, gloved hands in his lap, seemed to deflate, shrink under her words, the room chilly again.

I do not remember how it ended, how long before Milton and our mother left my room, turned off my light, the house dark and quiet again. I think I remember lying awake a while after it was over, snuggled under the quilt. And I suppose I thought of my father, my brother missing and presumed dead, my mother trembling with rage, weeping tears of hurt and anger, Milton with beer on his breath, melted snow in his hair, Edmund Henry Clark somewhere outside in the record cold and snow of the winter of 1947.

And then I suppose I must have gone back to sleep.

Traumatic. Or at least it would be, in context. Point?
The point is I am nothing like them. My father or Milton. My point is
it's a mistake to leap to easy conclusions. The point is that such memories
are what you make of them.

Beer. Another winter. 1953? 1954? Somewhere along in there. No special
winter, no record cold or snow. Just a winter night. I am sixteen or seventeen,
and my two best friends and I are drinking quarts of Gettleman beer. We
are parked in my rickety old Nash, lights out, motor running to keep the
heater going, on a country road, having set out to drink as much beer as
we can stand.

"It's warm enough you could take a bath in it," Nick says from the
backseat as he takes the bottle from his lips, burps.

"Stand outside and drink it if you like it so much cold," I tell him.

"Next time," Larry says, popping the cap off a fresh bottle, "you be the
one goes in to buy it, ask for refrigerated, show your spiffy fake I.D., they'll
laugh you off the premises."

"Shut up," I say, "and drink your share before I get it," and, "Anybody
gets sick cleans up after themselves."

"Anybody gets sick blames it on warm beer's a dork," Larry says.

"Big deal," Nick says, and, "Like it's real talented to be so overgrown
you can pass for twenty-one."

"More than you can do, short Greek dork," Larry says, tips up his quart
of Gettleman with both hands.

"Are we drinking beer or what?" I say.

"That's real neat," Nick says, and, "Maybe when you're twenty-one
actually you can pass yourself off for thirty or so, huh?" He begins to
laugh, says, "Imagine old Lar here the rest of his life, he can look real older
than his age!" He laughs, gags when he tries to drink his beer.

"I never talk to short Greek dorks, it's a new rule I just made up," Larry
says.

I tell them, "While you're yacking I'm drinking."

And then we do not speak for a long time, sitting in the dark of winter on
a country road, drinking Gettleman quarts, my old Nash's motor running,
the faulty heater clacking, the beer tepid. The only light is the dull winter
moon, the points of stars in the black sky, the Nash's orange dash lights
that make silhouettes of us as we lift our bottles to drink, wipe our mouths
on our coat sleeves and the backs of our hands, the smack and gurgle of
our drinking.

I do not know what made me think to speak as I did. I do not remember.

I said, "Each one say what he wants to be. Seriously. I mean in life, when you're an adult."

"When Nick grows up if he ever does he'll be this real short, real Greek old dork," Larry says.

"Seriously," I say.

"And you'll be this old man can pass for a hundred when you're say fifty," Nick says, laughs.

"I mean really," I say, and, "Just say, right this very minute we're sitting here, getting sloshed, unless one of you two pukes first, each one say your best guess on what you want to be in your life. Seriously," I say.

And then we are quiet again in the winter dark, drinking our beer, and it would not have surprised me if nothing more had been said, or we began to tell jokes or talk about girls or school or the atomic bombs they were exploding in Nevada, half-drunk-on-warm-beer-talk among three boys age sixteen or seventeen.

But Larry said, "I'm getting serious as hell about b-ball. I'm knocking off smoking and drinking except for like parties, and working out on a schedule so I'm honed down in shape to get me a scholarship." I expected Nick to laugh, mock him, but he did not. Larry said, "I've got the size and the talent for college ball, and you make a lot of good contacts for your career in varsity sports. I'm joining the Masons for that too when I'm old enough."

When no one spoke, I said, "Nick?"

Nick said, "I want to grow up to be a short old Greek dork."

I said, "Seriously," and Larry said he was only joking, Nick should know that.

Nick said, "I'm going to college and majoring in business. I'm having my own business someday. Marketing or finances or something."

Larry said, "Sounds extremely boring," and, "Only joking, Nickie."

Nick said, "My old man's a goddamn waiter in a restaurant, man." When we were silent again, Nick said to me, "So what about you, Mr. District Attorney?"

I said, "You know, until I just now asked you guys, I never even once thought about it. I honestly have not got the foggiest." Nick laughed, and Larry said it was boring, and I was boring, and we opened more quarts of warm Gettleman beer to drink in my car, motor running, lights out, on a country road one winter night.

We spoke no more of it. I would guess we went on to tell jokes or talk about girls and high school, or the atomic bomb tests in Nevada, to get drunk and sick on beer. But I know I sat and thought about what they, what we had said about our lives, our futures. I imagined Larry playing college basketball, developing contacts that led to a career, joining the Masons. I imagined Nick, whose father spoke just enough English to wait tables in a hotel restaurant, majoring in business administration, founding a successful company, something in marketing or finance. And I thought of my future. And though there was nothing specific I could imagine, I believed in it; for all its vagueness, it was as real as the winter night or my Nash or Gettleman beer, and the whole of the future, for all of us, seemed natural, definite, tangible, a sure and certain path leading to the way things would and should be.

I'm lost.

So was I. Larry never finished high school. He joined the air force, but they gave him a mental discharge. The last thing I heard he was still in and out of veterans' hospitals for mental illness. Nick, the last I knew of him, was an accountant for some corporation. I'm sure his father must have been very proud of him. And I don't drink beer, haven't since I was in the army. I hate the taste and smell of it to this day.

I said, "Why do I love these quiet moments in life? Can you tell me that, Fat?"

Vos said, "Cut him off, Fat, he's starting to get all philosophical already."

Stu Pinzer shook the dice cup, rolled a full house hand of poker dice out on the bar top, said, "Read and weep, Fatty, you lose."

Fat poured all around, said, "If I win, I win. If I lose, I still win."

"How do you figure?" I said.

"Don't I get a drink too?" Fat said, and put away his rye.

"Really," I said, "I can't get over how good I always feel this time of day."

"It's called stinko," Vos said.

"That's just the buzz you're supposed to feel," Stu Pinzer said.

Fat said, "I don't feel a thing," and, "But don't mind me, maybe I'm numb on my way to bombed."

It was the quiet time in Fat's Bar, the slow hours between the time the graveyard shift came off at the steel fabricating plant across the street to wash away the heat and metal dust at the bar, before the second shift came in for eye openers in the early afternoon.

Fat opened his doors at six in the morning for his regular winos on pensions and Social Security, stayed busy until nine-thirty or ten. The second shift started drifting in as early as one-thirty or two, and after that the bar was crowded, noisy until Fat locked up at two in the morning.

We did our drinking during the quiet, slow time, late morning to early afternoon, the summer after my discharge from the army. It was a hot summer, the sun beating the city into stillness and immobility. Everything seemed idle to me, waiting. I had my mustering out pay and some Soldiers Deposits savings, nothing I needed or wanted to do while I waited through the summer to start college in September.

I said, "These are the perfect hours," Fat lost another hand of poker dice, set up another round.

He said, "This is the perfect life, but then you kids are too young to appreciate my wisdom." Fat believed he had it made in life; he owned his bar, had plans to buy another in the same neighborhood.

He was only a few years older than we were, but he was married, to a fat woman we called Mrs. Fat, who spelled him as bartender, had two fat children as ruddy and red-haired as he was, was making some money, and liked to remind us, as we got drunk at his bar each day during the slow, quiet hours, that he drank more in a day than the three of us combined, yet never showed the effects. I think it was his size; he was six feet seven inches tall, weighed at least three hundred and fifty pounds. His face grew rosier and puffy as he drank, but I never saw him lurch or fall, never heard him slur a word.

Vos rolled the dice, said, "Be good to The Vos, he's flat busted!" It did not matter if he had to pay for a round. Fat carried his bar tab, and Vos paid up every two weeks when his unemployment compensation came in. He lived and took his meals with his mother, who had a good job with county civil service. When I once asked him if he ever felt guilty for sponging off his mother, he said, "Why should I find work at twenty a day when I can steal ten a day from my old lady?" He said she only nagged him if he laid around the house too much. "What the hell you think I hide out here every day for?" he said.

"If I thought like you I'd cut my throat," Stu Pinzer said. He attended extension night school, sold insurance, studied on his own for the Certified Life Underwriter's examination. He drove a company car, carried business cards, and always wore a necktie. He drank the least of us because he had to get out each afternoon and evening to run down prospects; he only killed the quiet time with us at Fat's because there was no sales percentage in chasing prospects in the middle of the day; nobody he tried talking to seemed to want to think about dying when the sun was high overhead. He said, "When I'm rich living off policy renewals, remind me to have my chauffeur cruise me by here and buy the house a round for old time's sake."

Fat said, "Pinzer, I can buy you and sell you now, and I can buy and sell you the best day of your life."

Vos said, "Yeah, Fat, but he gets to wear a hat when he works," and, "Pour, Fat, put it on my tab."

I said, "You know, there's no place I can think of I'd rather be than right here and now. My brother writes me a letter, says come on out to California with him, go to school there, it's a paradise, my mother loves it already, but I can't see it."

"Fruits and nuts," Stu Pinzer said.

"That's because you're already half in the bag and we just got started," Fat said.

"Pour," Vos said, and, "Your dice, philosopher," sliding the cup on the bar to me.

But what I remember, what was most important, was the quiet. There might be a couple of winos at a table or nodding in a booth, and we could hear the hydraulic punch presses from the plant across the street, feel their vibration in the floor, and Fat's inefficient air conditioner chugged in the window, but we did not talk much, and I remember the quiet of those days, that long hot summer I killed time waiting to start my college education.

It was as if there were no time, no place except Fat's Bar. We heard cars pass on the street, and the blazing sunlight flared at the edges of Fat's dusty Venetian blinds. Fat had a Sylvania television on a corner shelf high above the bar, and a big Seeburg jukebox with colored lights, but we watched no soap operas or game shows, and nobody played the jukebox.

Sometimes I talked about what I might study in college come September, that I was considering pre-law. Stu Pinzer talked about a sale he had made or hoped to make, and Vos always tried to borrow a few dollars before we broke up for the day, and Fat laughed at us and told us how he had life made. We played liar's dice or poker dice or horse, and we drank away the quiet time of each day that summer. Whenever Vos or Stu Pinzer or I told army stories, Fat made fun of us because he had been in combat in Korea when we were still in high school.

But it was how slow and quiet and complete it was there, then, that I like to remember. And I remember how bad it felt to leave each day, walk outside, sun-blind for a minute, heat bouncing up from the concrete walks, softening the macadam street, the wet spot on the sidewalk just under the window where Fat's air conditioner dripped, how we stumbled to Stu Pinzer's company car, the suffocating, superheated air inside that rushed out when we opened the doors to get in.

There was each day, the mornings before we gathered at Fat's, and there was the bad, drunken, nauseated feeling when we stumbled out into the heat of the day, Stu Pinzer's company car, before the rush of second-shift steelworkers crowded in for eye-openers, the stink and noise of the factory.

But I remember most the time between, different, special, because there seemed no time, no before or after. I remember saying to Vos and Pinzer once, as we lurched out of Fat's, "You know, these are probably the good old days we'll talk about when we're all a bunch of old men." I do not remember them saying anything.

And you mean to tell me you can't discern pattern here? Or is it won't?
Can't, won't, don't care to. It's just something I remember clearly.
And what became of these people?
How should I know? That was years, ages ago.

Mornings, starting each day, were horrible; I often think that if I had learned how to handle mornings I might still be married, have my family. The problem was I had the idea a man should tough out his hangovers, since I had earned it the night before—if I had been willing to stash a bottle someplace, a closet, under the bathroom sink, I think it would have been fine. I might still be a man with a wife and children, but I never stashed a bottle at home, so I suffered hangovers, and lost my family, that phase of my life.

Mornings. Hangovers. Naturally I was hungover. Cheryl was already up and doing by the time I sat on the edge of our king-size bed in the master bedroom of our new split-level; we designed that house as our dream house, had it built. I sat there, looking at the bedside clock, trying to wake up through a monster hangover, listened to my wife move about our dream house, in the bathroom, waking our boys, washing and dressing them, in the kitchen, turning on the portable Sony on the breakfast bar to get the network wake-up shows.

It was morning, starting another day, and I listened to the sounds of my wife and sons in our dream house, and I looked at the bedside clock as if I thought it might speak the hour to me, encourage me, and suffered my well-deserved monster hangover. My arms and legs trembled, and my hands shook; my stomach knotted and unknotted, my head throbbed, my eyes and lips were gummed shut from sleep, my mouth and throat so parched I could not swallow.

I sat there and suffered this, and listened to my wife and children talk, scrape chairs, the clack of spoons and knives and forks on their plates, the portable Sony television on the breakfast bar. I watched the second hand sweep around the lighted face of the clock, heard its faint electric hum, until I could force myself to stand, walk to the bathroom, shower and shave, dress, go to the kitchen to join Cheryl and my sons, Max and his little brother, Leonard, named for my brother who died in World War II.

"Do you feel like something substantial, or just toast or a roll?" Cheryl might say. Sunlight blared at me from the big picture window, reflected in watering eyes off all the chrome and glossy formica in the kitchen of our dream house; when I could make myself look out the big window, I saw our patio slab, the natural stone barbecue, my lawn that was so even and green it looked artificial, the rear of my neighbors' dream houses, their patios and green carpet lawns.

"Just coffee," I would tell her.

I wish I could remember my sons from this time. I have photographs, and I know what they looked like, blond like Cheryl, very fair complexions. I can say how tall they were, details, but when I try to think back to then it is as if I never saw them there in the kitchen at breakfast, as if I had only seen their pictures, been told details about them. I had to try to keep my stomach down and my hands still as I sipped my coffee; it is as if I never looked at them.

They were normal, noisy boys. They spilled their milk, giggled, fussed at each other, chattered at their mother. I cannot remember speaking to them, them speaking to me. All I seem to remember well is the terrible sunlight in the kitchen, the ache of my hangover, that it was morning, starting another day, the Sony's drone.

"You need to eat something for breakfast," Cheryl might say as I left for my office.

"What I *need* is the Hair of the Dog!" I remember telling her once. I remember how she looked at me, and I looked at her, squinting because my eyes burned, and then, after a moment, she tried to smile, and then I left for my office.

The Hair of the Dog, then, when I was married, had sons, was the New Mecca Cafe, across the street from the county courthouse and the Commercial Building, where I had my law office. I saw a lot of the men I worked with—lawyers, police detectives, civil service people, a judge or two—in the New Mecca Cafe to get their Hair of the Dog. Some sat at the little round tables for coffee, doing business already, cutting deals, but most of us stood at the long bar, quiet, bleary-eyed, trying not to let our hands shake when we lit cigarettes, lifted glasses. We were silent, stared at ourselves in the back bar mirror as though we saw our faces for the first time, could not recognize ourselves.

My Hair of the Dog was two double whiskeys, a house brand called Our Very Own, always at a special price, with half a glass of water to ease the rasp. The first one put my head and stomach and my tremor to rest; that was how I really woke up, ready to begin a new day. I stood a little straighter, looked at the men around me I worked so closely with each day, smiled, said hello, breathed deep. I looked at these men, and almost liked them, admired their affluence and success, the cut of their suits, the styling of their hair, the delicious smell of their talc and tonic and lotions.

After the first double Our Very Own whiskey I was sure who I was, there with these men in the New Mecca Cafe, about to go to work across the street, a lawyer with an office in the Commercial Building, next door to the courthouse, and center of the city, a family man, married to Cheryl, and I had two young boys, Max and Leonard.

The second double Our Very Own put me into motion. I was a *good* lawyer, doing better every day, married to a lovely woman, had two fine sons! Then I could step to the cash register stand, pay my tab, buy a packet of Sen-Sen for my breath, leave the New Mecca Cafe, start to work for another day, get on with my life.

I do not remember when I began taking a late-morning nip to set me up for lunch. If I spent the morning in court, maybe I began to take a nip when I checked back in at my office for phone messages, felt I needed a jolt to clean out what went on in the courthouse, set me up for the long lunches at the New Mecca, where lunch was always business at one of the small round tables, trying to cut a deal with a client or another lawyer, once in a while with one of the judges.

I drank the New Mecca's famous martinis at lunch; they kept their glasses in the freezer, served coated with a thick frost. I must have eaten something for lunch, but I do not remember anything I ever ordered, though their delicatessen sandwiches were also famous. "I guess," I would tell the waitress when she came to our small round table, "I'll open with one of your famous martinis. Make it a double. Rocks. It's been that kind of a morning. No olive, no onion, no twist, okay? And just whisper *vermouth* at the gin on the way out of the bottle. Dry. Just the unadulterated juice of the juniper." I suppose I often sat at lunch with people, clients, who did not drink their lunches, but do not remember any of them.

The New Mecca was very crowded from noon until two o'clock, when court recesses ended, the air cloudy with cigarette and cigar smoke, noisy with the babble of conversations, deals being cut, waitresses carrying heavy trays, squeezing between tables. I ordered another famous martini, suppose I ordered something to eat. And I talked and listened, made notes sometimes in my pocket calendar, cut my deals. With the second famous double martini I could talk and listen, make a note, did not see the crowded bar and jammed tables, did not hear the clamoring voices. I could do what I had to do to be the good lawyer I was. I drank a third famous martini while I watched the clock over the bar, always careful to get back to court at the end of a recess.

I paid my bill at the cash register stand and bought more Sen-Sen for the afternoon.

The nip I took in my office before I drove home was to handle a lot of things. It washed away the day's work, the courthouse, my clients, the deals I cut or failed to cut, all the men I had to work so closely with but did not like or admire or respect.

This nip was a kind of little bridge between my office and my home, and it set me up for the rush hour traffic. And it stopped any edge of daylight hangover that might start to creep in behind my eyes along about five o'clock. By *nip* I mean I kept a pint of bourbon in the deep-well drawer of my desk; I always closed my door so the secretaries could not see, then just took the bottle out of the drawer, unscrewed the cap, turned it up for a swig.

Then I could leave my office, say, "Goodnight ladies, and a goodnight to you," and go home to Cheryl, and to Max and Leonard.

I loved Happy Hour; when I think back on this time of my life, remembering the good times, I always remember Happy Hour as one of the best times of all.

We were all together in the den, with the big console Zenith on, the local news, and then the network news, but we really did not watch it closely. I mixed up a pitcher of manhattans, and Cheryl fixed snacks and soft drinks for the boys. I sprawled in my easy chair, sipped my manhattans, looked at the news a bit, watched my sons eat snacks and drink soda pop, glanced at the newspaper, listened to Cheryl talk about her day. I cannot remember anything specific she ever said—she talked about the boys, cute things they had said or done, about shopping, money she saved at a sale, a letter she got from her mother, an old girlfriend from college who called. Max and Leonard made a mess of their snacks, played at my feet.

What I loved was how it all made a kind of sense, the day, my life. I had finished another day. I had worked hard, done well, made some money, would make a lot more, faster, soon. And now I was home, and my wife told me about her day, and my children played at my feet, and the local, national, and world news ran in marvelous lifelike color on the big remote-control Zenith in the den of my dream house. I kept up with Vietnam, Watergate, whatever, but did not have to pay close attention, did not have to read my newspaper.

Cheryl told me things, and I responded, asked me questions I answered, and I spoke to Max and Leonard, touched them when they came close to my easy chair, and I kept up with what was happening in the world, but did not have to care about it. I sipped my manhattans, the tall pitcher on the coffee table close at hand. My family was close to me, and I was in our dream house, listening but not having to listen to all the voices, and it made a perfect, logical sense to me. I remember that feeling very clearly.

We ate a formal, family dinner. Cheryl was a wonderful cook; I remember how she planned our dinners so carefully, gourmet recipes, and we ate together. The boys were not fussy eaters, so it was very pleasant. There was always wine, and I opened the wine at the table, poured. I had some interest in good wine, and Cheryl tried to share that with me, but she had to supervise the boys' eating. I always enjoyed our family dinners, but I suppose I could not really taste the wonderful food my wife prepared, did not do it, or her, justice.

I spent my evenings back in the den. I read briefs and depositions, did some light paperwork for the next day's court appearances. Cheryl was busy clearing the dinner dishes, getting the boys ready for bed. She brought them in to kiss me goodnight, and I hugged and kissed my sons. I remember how fresh and clean they were, how their blond hair smelled, their perfect skin. While she put them to bed, I got out the brandy, and after that I drank brandy until I went to bed.

Cheryl might join me once Max and Leonard were tucked in, and we often watched a night-owl movie on the television, but I did not pay attention to the movie. We sat in the den with the lights off, just the glow of the TV screen, did not talk. I drank the warm, warming brandy, and sometimes I dozed off there in my easy chair; Cheryl woke me when the movie ended, television signing off with a sermonette.

"Time to go to bed," she might say.

"What? Oh. Right," I would say, waking. I woke in my chair, head fuzzy with brandy, all the lights off, our dream house quiet. "Right," I would say, and, "Morning's going to come too soon to suit me," or, "I'm not sure I've got the will to get undressed when all you have to do is get up and dressed all over again in a few hours."

Cheryl might say, "You'll regret this in the morning," as she picked up my empty snifter, put the bottle away.

"How," I remember telling her once, "can you be so sure? You don't know how I feel."

And so you drank yourself out of a marriage. Lost your family.

Put simply, yes. Things are never so simple. And it worked out well enough.

Are you joking about this?

No. Cheryl remarried, very happily from all I understand, and my sons are fine young men. Max is in college now, and Leonard graduates from high school in another year. He attends a military academy, high-class boarding school, really. They're both really excellent young men.

What you'd call a happy ending, is that what you're telling me?
There's more truth than not in that.
Now I know you're not serious.
But I am. Everything largely depends on how you look at it. How you
see it, and where you're at at the time. That's what you can't understand.
Nobody understands that.

My only drink now is vodka. Straight. Beer, whiskey, gin, cocktails, fancy mixed drinks—I never touch them. Vodka is pure. Cold. I drink it iced, with ice. *Purity,* I think is the quality of it that appeals to me. Cold, clear, like pure water.

Why do I drink? What do I mean when I say: I *drink?*

Not to celebrate, not to indulge my moods in any way. I am nothing like my father was. And my father is dead, and my mother, and of course my brother Leonard—somewhere in the Philippine Islands, almost forty years ago. My brother Milton is alive, but lives out in southern California, a grandfather several times over; it has been so long since I saw him, was in contact, he might as well be dead. This has something to do with my drinking.

Anyone, everyone, is born into a family. I have a father, mother, brothers, and my life with them remains with me, a part of me, forever. My family is broken by divorce, a world war, death, distance, time. It could make a man nostalgic. Sad.

I think of them, remember, and might be sad, but I drink. Not to forget. I drink. I fill my glass with ice, vodka that looks like purest water, drink. And I remember: father, mother, brothers, myself as I was then. And I am not sad. A man is born into a family, and they die, separate; that is the way it is. There is no reason for sadness, no point in nostalgia.

I fill my glass, drink. It is clear, cold, pure. It chills my mouth, warms my throat, my belly. I feel it soften me, relax my arms, legs, feet, hands. There is no aroma, no aftertaste. Things are the way they are.

A young man is ambitious and foolish. His ambitions are foolish. He has fools for friends. A young man believes whatever he wishes will come to be, is certain he will succeed. A man's friends, like his family, die. Surely Fat must be dead now. Or a friend can go mad, like Larry. Perhaps they succeed; Stu Pinzer is surely a success. Or they might as well be dead or mad, wherever they are. Where is Nick? Vos? I was young and ambitious, and I believed. And I succeeded.

So of course my success was foolish because I was too young to know what to want for my life. I dreamed the wrong dreams; what I realized of them is not what I should have wished for. But I do not regret my youth, that I was a fool. How could it have been otherwise?

I drink vodka, and it seems right to me that young men are fools. Such regret as I might feel for my life dissolves, dissipates. What else should a young man be but a fool? There is no regret, no nostalgia in this. I drink my vodka, and this is clearly the way things are, and should be.

And I fell in love, and married my love, fathered two beautiful sons all the while I was creating the fool's success I had imagined for myself when I was a young fool. And then my wife fell out of love with me, and took away my sons. I lost my love and my children, and this could hurt a man terribly for the rest of his life. But I am not hurt.

I do not hurt for this loss because I drink vodka, and can understand that this happens to many men, is what can happen for so many reasons. The woman I loved has a new love, and my sons are fine, excellent young men. I am sure they have ambitions, dream, and I suppose there is a chance they are not wholly foolish. But they were not hurt, I think, by me, and their mother is not hurt that I know. Why should I hurt? My vodka is clear and cold and pure; when I drink I see that things are the way they are, no reason for them to be any other way. I do not hurt.

When I drink vodka, I remember, whatever I remember, and understand, accept, feel no pathos, no self-pity, no anger. I remember whatever I remember, see myself, as I was, as I am, and there is only a great sense of the necessity of things, given time enough. I never wished to be tragic or pathetic, and I am not. I think I drink vodka only when I am confused. I am not confused when I drink.

Sometimes I am afraid of what will happen next, what may happen eventually. But then I drink, and I do not wonder about what is yet to come. I am not afraid when I drink.

I think anything, a man's life, my life, can only be known to me. No one else can know. When I am drinking, I am sure I know. No one knows a man except the man himself; I think drinking is how I know things, myself. I do not *drink*. It is simply a way that I am, who I am, have been. The way the world changes could confuse a man; when I drink vodka I am sure about what I know.

Is that all you have to say? You haven't anything else to say for yourself?
Nothing. Now, I think I'd like to leave. Talking about this is confusing.
I am beginning to feel confused.

The Parts of Speech

> I tell myself that a healthy imagination is like a healthy appetite and must be fed. If you do not feed it the lives of your friends, I maintain, then you are apt to feed it your own life, to live in your imagination rather than upon it.
>
> —Peter Taylor, *Daphne's Lover*

I AM A WRITER, a man who makes fictions. I take things, real things—people, events, language—and I make them into fictions. I take the real people I know or have known, and what happens to them, and what they say to me, or what I have heard them say to others, and to one another, and I think about all this, and sometimes, when I am working well, I am able to make real people's lives into fictions that are more real than what I began with. Sometimes I am not able to achieve this, and there is no fiction, and the real people and their lives remain just that—real. When they do not become fictions, I forget them as soon as I can, and I go on to the next people, their lives, their words, the next fiction.

Making fictions is a craft, and a writer is a craftsman. He needs skills to practice his craft successfully; the skills can be learned if he works hard. And he also needs something besides skills. Some people call this *talent*, what the writer needs in addition to the skills he can learn by working hard and using his imagination. I do not know what *talent* is. I do not call it *talent*. I do not know what to call it, this other thing the writer needs. But it exists; it is there. I use it all the time when I make fictions out of all the real people and lives and words I have experienced in my life.

I do not worry that I have no name for this quality that enables people to be writers, make fictions. Though I do think a lot about it. And sometimes I am not entirely certain it is a wholly good thing. Which is not to say I have any doubts about the value of fiction. I am a writer, and I love writing, and I love fictions and fictionmaking. There are times I wish I could love it unreservedly, without any doubt about what it is a writer uses besides his skills and his imagination to make real people into fictions.

125

This is a story, in three parts, about myself, and about my being a writer, and about the way I make my fictions. The first two parts of this story are true, as accurate as my memory will permit; the last part is not. The whole of it is a story, a fiction.

In 1954, when I was sixteen, my family moved from the east side of the city of Milwaukee to its far west side, to the suburb of Wauwatosa. So I transferred from Riverside High School to Wauwatosa Senior High School to begin my junior year.

Like many adolescents, my response to my daily agony of self-consciousness was to present a studied, intense facade of jaded indifference to everyone—my parents, my teachers, the other students, who seemed to me to occupy received positions of security and self-confidence so firm that nothing could ever shake the suburban foundations of their juvenile social orders. I was struck dumb, near panic, by their seemingly effortless competence in classes, their ease in the organized busywork of clubs and sports, the subtle, rich flux of their sexual pairings, innocent, but spiced with unknown hints of permissiveness, casual sophistication, the occasional serious romance.

In short, a stranger, a trite and stereotypical outsider, awkward and boorish, a touch homely, ambitious and timid, cunning and ignorant, paralyzed by the tension between my natural dreams of popularity and the fact of my obvious inconsequentiality, between the necessary vision of my special individuality and the dull certainty of how ordinary I was, I withdrew inward.

To the world—parents, teachers, peers—I offered a stony and stoic indifference bordering on perfunctory hostility. Inwardly, I seethed, so deliberately sensitive I registered nuances like a psychological seismograph. To the world, I showed myself a rock of placidity, emotionally dormant, on occasion skeptically, cynically observant, rarely puzzled, almost never interested. Inside myself, where I could live, was chaos; my thoughts raged with contradictions, my eyes dazzled by the strobe-flash opacity of life around me, ears numbed by its din, flesh and feeling a riot of puberty's multiplying cells, my inner voice an unbroken shriek, the whole of me perpetually churned by my frenetic glands.

My ethos, if I could be said to have had one at age sixteen, in 1954, was: I see, but am not seen; I hear, but do not speak; I know, but am unknown.

My routine was to arrive at school late enough each day to miss the clusters of students gathered near the main doors to tease and gossip until the final tardy warning bell rang; while they jostled and flirted, their voices carrying to me like the taunt of sirens on the clear early morning air, I lurked angrily behind someone's maroon Ford hot rod in the student parking lot, smoking a last bitter cigarette, poised to spring when the bell clanged its inevitable gloomy summons.

In the crowded, noisy halls, I threaded my way to my locker like some preoccupied commuter; as I opened the combination lock, threw my gray, anonymous jacket on the hook, found the textbooks I would need for the day, I shot furtive glances at the girls who took time for a last primp in the mirrors hung on the insides of their locker doors, the excessively jocular boys who shouted across heads to one another, traded mock-punches, slammed their locker doors shut, snapped locks in place.

I might as well have been invisible, watching sidelong and silent from the shadowy nook where chance—for once in my favor—had assigned my locker.

I slipped into my homeroom with great skill, never among the first to enter and take my chosen seat—in the last row, of course, back to the wall— never the last, always shielded within the median and mode, that stumbling group, the majority, who funneled in together, spread out to their seats as though by osmosis. In my seat, I assumed my obligatory slouch behind the stained and nicked desk, elbows braced on its surface, head propped against my hands, as if shading my eyes from the window's dusty sunlight—as if I nursed a migraine or hangover headache, as if I meant to doze through the first half-hour of the morning, as if I had drawn an opaque, impenetrable bubble about myself.

Inscrutable, thus impervious, I took in the sensations that played about me in homeroom class, absorbed them the way a sponge might take on water splashed randomly against it.

I listened to the rustle of my classmates' clothing as they fidgeted at their desks—the crackle of crisp shirts and blouses, shuffle of shoes on the scuffed wooden floor, the whispered slide of legs crossing, uncrossing. I listened: click-click of ballpoint pens, rip and rustle of notebook paper, dry slap of books opened and closed, the rattle and ring of bracelets, the tedious rhythm of long sighs, muffled giggles, sotto voce exchanges, a snort, coughing. From the front of the room, Miss Myrna Klemp, Latin teacher, our homeroom monitor, cleared her throat daintily as prelude to calling the roll.

The morning sunlight from the windows fell on me like a warm bath, and I smelled the odors generated in the room by its accumulating heat: the flat, dry smell of the wooden floors mixed with the oily tinge of the janitor's sweeping compound, spiced with the worn varnish on desktops; the powdered scent of chalk, blackboards, chalk trays; the day's first perspiration blunted by a melange of flowery perfumes and colognes; the residue of cigarettes on my fingers.

Peering out from the tunnel of my cupped hands, my eyes moved from the scruffy, pimpled back of the neck of the boy seated directly in front of me to the embryonic sideburns being cultured by the boy to his left, the wispy tendril of a loosening spitcurl floating beneath the pearly ear of the girl to his right, the impossibly broad shoulders of an athlete, straining his lettersweater, the exact bas-relief of a fat girl's brassiere.

I considered—and dismissed—my classmates as Miss Myrna Klemp chirped their names in alphabetical order: Ardith Anne Allen (fat girl with enormous breasts, rigid brassiere, too much jewelry, her lilac scent a purple miasma hovering about her, left behind in her wake) . . . Sidney Brodson (only Jew in the junior class) . . . William Fifer (candy eater, cheeks always swollen with suck-hards, flecks of licorice between his dingy teeth, in the corners of his sticky lips) . . . Sue Gralman (most popular, unfailingly cheerful, greets even me with a toothy slash of a smile, waves at everyone in her field of vision, both *nice* and *cute,* thus hateful) . . . Leonard Leff, Jr. (president of the Foto Club, Leica suspended on a strap from his neck, gadget bag on his hip, totes a tripod, distracted, smug in his technical competence) . . . Oscar Southard (considered dirty, shunned by all girls and many of the boys because he swears, carries a condom pressed in his shabby wallet, delights in sharing his obscene picture books) . . . Melinda Tate (so spectacularly beautiful no boy dares approach her, reputed to date college men, uses a sunlamp to maintain a perpetual Florida tan the exact shade of breakfast waffles, a superior creature beyond even my scorn) . . . Geoffrey Walker (class brain, a shoo-in for valedictorian, vain and pompous, utterly devoid of physical grace, winner of regional science fair competitions, almost as friendless as I) . . . Eduardo Walkiewicz (brutish, a hulking football player and wrestler, child of a Mexican mother, Polish father, his swarthy face possesses a cunningly Oriental cast that contradicts his unmitigated stupidity) . . . Jeanmarie Young (notorious slut, an untouchable) . . . Mary Helen Zimmerman (very short haircut, darkly haired forearms and calves, incipient mustache, suspected of liking girls more than boys) . . .

Some say *present,* some say *here;* when Miss Myrna Klemp calls my name I respond with a contemptuous grunt, like the grumpy protest of a hibernating animal disturbed out of season in its cave.

And so it was, school day after school day—the weekends and holidays my only reprieves—that I coped with, survived both the upsetting move to Wauwatosa Senior High School in my junior year and the excruciating burlesque of adolescent self-consciousness I inflicted upon myself when I was sixteen, in 1954.

Moved from homeroom to first-hour class, from first-hour to second, class to class throughout the day by clamoring school bells, I wove my way through the jammed halls, up and down the thundering wooden stairs, never bumping, brushing, never touching, never touched.

In American History, I retired behind my massive textbook, let Mr. Rollins's flow of comment on current events (Joe McCarthy was still a celebrity), relieved by personal anecdotes from his experience in World War II, slide around and over me while I read and reread a paragraph, or simply stared at the page until the words blurred, Mr. Rollins's voice became a husky buzz. In Solid Geometry, Mrs. Cook scarce knew I existed; her back to us, intent on the constructs she chalked on the smeared chalkboard, she struggled with truncated cones and parallelograms, pyramids and rhomboids, while I doodled on my graph paper. In German class—an alternative to Miss Myrna Klemp's Latin—I sat up straight for Frau Rognebakke, loaned my reluctant voice to the class chorus as we bent our throats to repeat her umlaut sounds, chanted the conjugations of irregular verbs. I enjoyed Geography, received my best grades from Mr. Warren, who loved maps, and so appreciated the clean lines I drew in colored inks to limn the borders of states and nations, the meanderings of great world rivers. There was no threat in Art Appreciation; in good weather, Mrs. Pixton took us outdoors to sketch. It was appropriate for me to take shelter behind a tree to scratch out the shape of the school's towers against the sky with a soft pencil—I varied the cloud pattern, always added a bird or two in flight, suggested the off-the-page sun with planes of shading. And in Physical Education, Harold "Wristlock" Mathias, rumored to have been an NCAA wrestling champion at Oklahoma A & M in the impossibly distant 1930s, was content as long as each boy generated at least a visible film of perspiration; he considered team sports and games unmasculine, so allowed us to work out, as he called it, individually. Often, I did lazy sit-ups. When no mats or weights or punching bags were free, I escaped by jogging slowly around the gym floor perimeter, picking up my pace whenever I felt Wristlock Mathias watching me, hands on hips, torso still muscled under his tight white T-shirt, shaking his head in resigned disgust at the flabby, indifferent generation I exemplified. In Chemistry, since Mr. Davis did not trust us to use chemicals, I could perch on a table at the rear of the laboratory to watch him create chlorine gas under a bell jar or gingerly transfer a lump of sodium from a can of kerosene to a tub of water to demonstrate its volatility. I passed his course by memorizing the Periodic Table of Atomic Elements.

So I coped, survived. My stance and my strategies worked, and no one— my parents, teachers, fellow students—challenged me. Except in my English class, taught by Miss Agnes Keintzle, who began each class with a drill designed to compel us to demonstrate a thorough knowledge of the parts of speech.

It was a large class, at least thirty students. The most remote seat I could find was the second-last in the row next to the windows, where I could bask, dormant, in the mote-filled late afternoon sunlight that fell into the stuffy room, ignore the teacher, think my own twisting thoughts, observe, as anonymous as I was in German or Chemistry or Solid Geometry.

Miss Agnes Keintzle was notoriously undemanding, never assigned essays to be written outside class, her homework assignments calling only for short readings in the anthology of excerpts from English and American literary classics that was our text, expected no one to venture any opinion about poetry or fiction or drama, never asked anyone to speculate as to the relationship of literature to life or other potentially embarrassing subjects. She loved her students, knew them all well, called them by their first names, had taught most of them as freshmen and sophomores, was universally popular because she seldom gave a grade lower than B. The only matter on which she took an unshakable stand was the parts of speech.

She began her classes with a drill on the parts of speech. Thereafter, she chattered about the day's reading assignment, the form of the ballad stanza, the characteristics of tragic heroes, the symbolic ambiguity of Hester's scarlet letter. On occasion, she read passages aloud with no more than a minimally silly injection of feeling interpretation; rarely, she asked open questions to test our reading, counting on her reliables, a claque of sycophantic girls and Geoffrey Walker, the class brain, to answer promptly, fully, and accurately.

I was, I thought, safe. I could, I thought, warm myself in the sunlight, muse, watch, read at random in the textbook, doodle in the margins. Survive. But there was no refuge from her parts of speech drill. It was a convenient substitute for calling the roll, and it was her sole pedagogic passion, the one body of finite information she had taken to her heart, determined to impart to the generations of students who passed through her charge, semester after semester. And she succeeded in this, if only by the inexorable pressure of routine, embedding this knowledge in her students, as if her drills on the parts of speech were a perpetually renewed drop of water that imperceptibly wore away the rock of our ignorance.

Agnes Keintzle was a merry, bouncy woman, always smiling—the shine of her too-white, too-even dentures struck me as predatory; her too-red lipstick matched the glossy polish on her talon-length nails; she wore expensive clothes, too-young fashions color-coordinated with the purse that sat on her desk, her high-heel pumps that cracked on the wooden floors as she moved about in front of the class, conducting her drill on the parts of speech; her hair was always set in an elaborate coiffure, glinting, a hopelessly artificial, metallic platinum, no strand out of place; her watery eyes were magnified by thick lenses set in flamboyant bows, secured by a garish ribbon around her neck; the peach shade of pancake on her cheeks and forehead contrasted with the raised, dark veins in the backs of her hands, the ropy muscles dancing in her forearms, the trembling crepe of her throat.

I feared her, knew I was not safe in her classroom, that junior English would expose me—to her, the other students, myself. As she brought out her flash cards, slipped the wide rubber band off the pack, I tightened myself against disaster, hunched deeper in my seat.

Her voice veered back and forth between a girl's lilt and a crone's croak. I tried to will myself dead. "Everybody ready?" she asked. "Everybody alert today? Here we go, class!"

She drilled us on the parts. She had been drilling my classmates as freshmen, sophomores, so they were ready. They knew her, knew the drill, had responded for two years to the same worn pack of flash cards, memorized the correct answers, could call out accurate responses as readily as I might spit in the gutter to express feigned disgust. They lifted their heads, squared their shoulders, sat up; they were ready, and I was not.

"Why do we do this, class?" she asked. "Because it teaches us what we have to know if we want to know our language, doesn't it? And we all know our language is the most marvelous tool for living we have, don't we. Because it's very, very precise, and it's also flexible, so we can take that precision and adopt it for anything we need, can't we. Because we know it's not an instinct like an animal barking. It's not a mystery, is it. And if you can say what you want to you can achieve anything you set out after, can't you."

The class looked at her; some returned her stiff smile, some nodded. And when she had finished telling them—as she had told them when they were freshmen, sophomores—of the flexible precision of language that would enable them to be and do whatever they chose in life, and how the parts of speech were solid little foundation building blocks—they could think of punctuation marks as little fasteners that held the parts of speech together in sentences—that all this, if mastered, would lead them to successful careers and satisfying lives, she began her drill. Easy in their familiarity with her false, bubbling enthusiasm, easy in their collective sense of themselves, the certitude of who and where and when they were, they began. They stood her drill on the parts of speech with a communal tone of security so alien to me it might have been a formal dialogue in a foreign tongue, a rite performed in an ancient religion, a game played on Mars.

"Now," Miss Agnes Keintzle said, and took the first card from the pack, held it above her head, waved it like a semaphore flag. Starting with the first seat in the first row, nearest the door, she proceeded. Down that row in order, front to back, to the first seat, second row, down that row, to the first seat, third row. Agnes Keintzle flashed her cards, snapped her glistening dentures in approval as each student in turn gave the correct answer.

And I sat hunched at my desk, watching the inevitable approach of her attention to the last row, second-last seat, the irresistible march of the parts of speech toward me.

I was not ready, knew I could not do it. At Riverside High School, we had not studied the parts of speech. As a freshman, I was required to read *Julius Caesar* and *Silas Marner,* to write synoptic book reports that I do not recall were ever evaluated, no grade assigned until the perfunctory end-of-semester C. In my sophomore year we read some poetry and *The Merchant of Venice,* and I earned a B by matching quoted lines and passages of dialogue with the names of poets and Shakespeare's characters.

I was ignorant of the parts of speech. I was ignorant of grammar, of punctuation, could no more diagram a sentence than I could have delivered a discourse on formal rhetoric.

I was not ready; I was ignorant, laughably so, and when Agnes Keintzle reached me with her flash cards, she would know it, all my classmates would know it, and the stance and strategies of withdrawal that were my way of living as a transfer student in the junior class at Wauwatosa Senior High School in 1954, when I was sixteen, would be destroyed. I would have no way of living, no way to survive, to be who and where and when I was.

Of course I had known about her drills before I entered her class. I knew a great deal, eavesdropping, about teachers, classes, other students at Wauwatosa Senior High School. So I knew it would happen before it happened, but did not really believe it would happen—like most teenagers, the only true reality for me was the immediate, excruciating present, the moment I occupied in time and space. Yesterday was a figment of memory, tomorrow a shifting, unreliable rumor.

Agnes Keintzle gave the first week of class over to organization and orientation, the second to lectures on the vital significance and seductively interesting nature of language arts studies, though she did mention what she intended, and why, for the parts of speech. It was only in the third week, a Tuesday, that it came to pass. Memory and rumor merged to create the present, and I sat, hunched, waiting for it to happen to me as it happened.

Down and down and down the rows of desks she went. Everyone was confident, competent.

"Ardith?" said Miss Keintzle, waggling the flash card at her: *school.* And fat Ardith Anne Allen smirked, drew her enormous breasts up in a deep breath, said, "Noun. Also it can be a verb if you say like for example, *He was schooled in Latin.*"

"Excellent," said Agnes Keintzle. "And that's a common noun when it's a noun, isn't it, Ardith." She tucked the card in at the back of the deck, flashed the next off the top: *Milwaukee.*

"Proper noun," said the girl seated behind Ardith Anne.

"Excellent. Which functions to?"

"Name a particular person, place, or thing."

"Fine. Next?" *Drove.*

"Verb."

"What kind?"

"Transitive."

"Used in a sentence?"

"He drove his car to the game. Or, he drove the golf ball far," said Leonard Leff, Jr.

"Perfect. Billy?" *Is.* William Fifer swallowed the juice of whatever confection he was eating, pushed it to one side of his mouth with his tongue, wiped his wet lips on his sleeve, answered that it was a linking verb, used it correctly in a sentence.

Down and down the rows went Agnes Keintzle. Verbs; the properties of verbs (tense, mood, voice, transitive-intransitive, linking, verbals, participles, gerunds, infinitives); adjectives (positive, comparative, superlative); adverbs (those changing form to indicate comparison, those which cannot); prepositions; conjunctions. Row by row, seat by seat.

Sue Gralman simpered over a conjunctive adverb; Oscar Southard leered wickedly, stumbled on a relative pronoun, recovered almost immediately; Melinda Tate's serenity was unaffected by the challenge of creating a set of grammatical equivalents on either side of *but.* Even Eduardo Walkiewicz, eyes blank as a statue's, was able to haltingly join a subordinate adverbial clause to the main clause of a sentence with *because.* Class brain Geoffrey Walker was ludicrously untested by an interjection.

And then Agnes Keintzle reached me with her flash cards.

I do not remember which card Miss Keintzle held up for me. It did not, does not matter. My ignorance of the parts of speech was such that she might as well have asked me to translate a calligraph or a rune; I only remember sitting, frozen, time in that moment frozen, seeing Agnes Keintzle, the smile of her feral dentures, red smear of her lipstick, matching nails clutching the card aloft, the platinum helmet of her hairdo, her gelatinous eyes bright behind her magnifying spectacles.

I was frozen, paralyzed—there was no movement of time, no sound I heard, as if some translucent screen separated me from Agnes Keintzle, the cryptic card she held up for me to see, the rows and ranks of students who seemed caught in suspended animation, waiting until something happened to bring us all, everything, back to motion, sound, life. I do not know how long this moment of horrible stasis might have lasted.

What happened, what saved me, was the correct response, the answer whispered from behind me, from the last seat in my row, whispered in my ear by Cynthia von Eschen, the girl who sat behind me in Miss Agnes Keintzle's junior English class at Wauwatosa Senior High School, in 1954.

I do not remember the answer she whispered—only the perfect, clear, soft quality of her voice, so faint, yet as distinct as if it were my own articulate thought. And I knew, was absolutely certain in the instant I heard her whisper, that no one else in the classroom could hear her. It was totally unexpected, unhoped for, a miracle—I sat, frozen on the edge of disaster; Cynthia von Eschen whispered the correct answer to me; I repeated it, loud, emphatic; Agnes Keintzle said *excellent* or *fine* or *very good,* or she tightened her fierce smile a notch, put away her flash cards, took up a poem or a novel excerpt from our text. And it was over, and I was safe again, safe forever, could live as I had to live, then and there and thereafter.

I did not, do not understand what happened, why. I had never paid the slightest attention, taken the slightest notice of Cynthia von Eschen, would not have known her name, perhaps not even recognized her in the halls before that day she saved me.

From my withdrawn stance I had considered—and rejected—the students in my homeroom: Ardith Anne Allen, surrounded by the wall of her lilac scent, bovine breasts straining her blouse, was a pathetic fat girl who vainly sought femininity; Sidney Brodson was a Jew, doomed to the isolation of inarticulate prejudice; William Fifer's candy addiction rendered him childlike, hopelessly immature; Sue Gralman's programmed affability was patently bogus, a naked social politics; Leonard Leff, Jr.'s Leica and gadget bag defined his own inscrutable, eccentric space; Oscar Southard's nasty fascination with filth enabled anyone to feel a tangible moral superiority; Melinda Tate's beauty was quite simply otherworldly, no more real than a painting or a photograph; Geoffrey Walker's straight-A grades were beneath contempt; Eduardo Walkiewicz's crude bulk and blatantly slow mind made it almost possible to pity him, his athletic prowess only minimally mitigating; the reputed sexual extremity and perversity of Jeanmarie Young and Mary Helen Zimmerman cast them both outside the pale of conventional decency.

There was no one I noticed from within the fastness of my self-imposed alienation, no one with whom I was thrown together in homeroom or classes, from whom I could not distance myself. But I had never noticed Cynthia von Eschen, and it took an effort to do so after she had saved me in the parts of speech drill.

I did not speak to her that day in class, did not thank her for what she had done for me when we were at last dismissed by the raucous bell. But I did, from my sullen remove, now observe, take notice of her—in the halls, taking my seat in English class before she reached hers behind me, remaining there when the bell dismissed us, watching her leave the room.

Cynthia von Eschen was surely the plainest, least remarkable girl in the junior class. She moved about so unobtrusively, spoke so seldom, greeting only when greeted, she might have been only the shadow of her plain substance; she appeared to embody, as naturally as light or air or motion itself, the impenetrable anonymity I made for myself through unblinking alertness and unstinting effort.

Cynthia von Eschen wore her pale brown hair in a short ponytail, just a little out of fashion—junior and senior girls had begun to blaze peroxide streaks back from their hairlines, to frame their faces in white-frosted tips, to clip their manes, shave the backs of their necks in gamin cuts. She wore glasses, of course, but not the thick, distorting lenses of a Miss Keintzle or the harlequin frames, so recently popular, that her peers sucked on coyly as much as they wore them; her lenses were small and round—they seemed to constrict her face, pinch her small eyes even closer together. She wore no makeup that I could see, her brows unplucked, her thin lips bloodless, no earrings, no rings on her fingers, her skin white enough to show light blue veins at her temples, her wrists. Her nails were a washed dull white with large, whiter half moons, trimmed blunt. She was thin, her flat chest absurd in contrast with the cone-breasts most girls flaunted. Her dresses were buttoned to the last button, dowdy when seen against the cashmere sweaters and teasing cleavages popular then, the hobble skirts that stressed the fullness of thighs and calves. Her legs were sticks, and she did not affect the conventional posture, one crossed over the other, foot bouncing seductively as Agnes Keintzle droned on about language and literature. Cynthia von Eschen skittered in and out of English class, her steps mincing, as if her slightly too-large feet had been bound from infancy. She stood and walked slump-shouldered, clutching her books and ring binder to her bony chest, as if they were a shield, armored her against any accidental encounter. Her eyes, tiny behind her pinching spectacles, were always down, as if measuring her tiny steps or counting the tiles, memorizing the pattern of the floorboards.

Cynthia von Eschen was the plainest, most unattractive, most inconsequential girl in the junior class at Wauwatosa Senior High School in 1954 and I had not a grain of curiosity or interest in her, but she knew the parts of speech as well as even Geoffrey Walker, and she whispered my answers to me, day after day, all through that semester, spared me—for a reason or reasons I cannot know—the shame that would, without her rescue, have destroyed me, as I was, the year I was sixteen years old.

She saved me, day after day, week after week, through the semester. Miss Agnes Keintzle grinned her terrible grin, flashed her cards, seat by seat, row by row. Noun and pronoun, verbs transitive and intransitive, verbs expressing the qualities of tense, mood, and voice, linking verbs and verbals, participles, gerund and infinitive, adjectives and adverbs, positive, comparative, and superlative, prepositions, coordinating and correlative conjunctions, conjunctive adverbs, subordinating conjunctions, relative pronouns, interjections—which, Agnes Keintzle never failed to remind us, were generally to be avoided in formal writing.

We drilled the parts of speech, and, always, Cynthia von Eschen's clear whisper sounded in my ear alone, the correct answer; I almost began to think I was actually learning, coming to master the parts of speech, that Cynthia von Eschen's delicate whisper was only a confirmation of my growing expertise.

And the semester ended, and I received a final grade of C+ from Miss Keintzle, and I passed to another teacher, another class for the second semester of junior English, and I was never again in a class with Cynthia von Eschen, but it did not matter because no other English teacher at Wauwatosa Senior High School seemed to care about the parts of speech, those finite foundation building blocks of our marvelous, precise, and flexible language.

I never thanked Cynthia von Eschen for what she had done for me. I never turned in my seat just before or after class began to say thank you to her. I never caught her outside the door, before or after class, to say thank you. I never stopped her on the rare occasions when we happened to pass in the crowded halls, never thanked her. We never shared another class, but I saw her two or three times a week for the next year and a half. I stood close to her in the line of graduates, dressed in our gray gowns and mortarboards, as we marched through the auditorium to the stage, paced by the organ rendition of "Pomp and Circumstance," in June of 1955—the last time I saw Cynthia von Eschen. And I did not speak to her, never thanked her.

Why did she do it? I cannot know that. Like the parts of speech, it was a mystery I did not care to solve. Pity? Kindness? Did she, perhaps, from within her mousy inconsequentiality, express some boy-girl interest in me? I can never know the answer to this.

I simply did not care, then. I sat back in my impregnable stance, watching and listening—contemplating the big breasts of Ardith Anne Allen, the infuriating, self-serving camaraderie of Sue Gralman, the unattainable beauty of Melinda Tate, the sluttish allure of Jeanmarie Young. I never learned why Cynthia von Eschen came to my rescue, and I did not care, then. It is now that I think about this, often. But I can never know the answer or answers.

Who I was then, who she was—the *then* of then, this is always a mystery, and memory only invokes it, never answers or resolves.

This is the first part of my story. Here is the second part, the shortest of the three I promised; it is also true.

In 1965 I lived in New York and received an invitation, forwarded from my parents' address, to attend the first reunion of Wauwatosa Senior High School's class of 1955. It was impossible for me to travel a thousand miles; I was very busy becoming a writer of fictions. So I wrote Susan Hackett (née Gralman), class secretary—the payoff for her unremitting effort to ingratiate herself with everyone. I wrote to her and said I was becoming a writer of fictions now, unable to attend. I sent a check for three dollars, so that I would receive the information-packed souvenir directory that would be published, that would tell me all about my former classmates, where they had gone, what, who they had become in the ten years since graduation.

I thought no more about it. Weeks passed, the reunion was held, but I had forgotten about it. When, several months later, the souvenir booklet arrived, bent, the envelope tattered, I read it. It gave the names, addresses, occupations of all my former classmates, and I was surprised at how few of the names I recognized, how little I cared about where they had gone in life, what they had become. It was interesting only because some of them ran so true to form, while others seemed to have defied all the laws of probability.

Ardith Anne Allen had become Ardith Anne Zucker, was one of four graduates with four children; a prize was given at the reunion to a girl named Gail Speer (née Gooch), who, with five, had the most children. I did not remember Gail Gooch, but could imagine Ardith Anne Allen nursing her infants with ease. Sidney Brodson was married, two children, very successful in banking and insurance, prominent in the Anti-Defamation League. Melinda Tate had, of course, married well, the heir to Milwaukee's Gettleman Brewery. Geoffrey Walker had earned a doctorate in physics at the University of Wisconsin, was already an associate professor at Penn State, listed publications concerning research on laser beam applications. The order of these destinies, governing logic, was clear.

But William Fifer, who also failed to attend, was listed as a television weatherman for one of the major Chicago stations. Oscar Southard had graduated from Purdue, then founded his own engineering consulting firm in California. Leonard Leff, Jr., owned and operated a Phillips 66 station on Milwaukee's south side. Sue Gralman Hackett was twice-divorced.

Jeanmarie Young had attended college, married, had a child, was a successful part-time Avon lady; she described herself as a contented homemaker. Eduardo Walkiewicz listed himself as employed by the Wauwatosa Municipal Sanitation Department, made no mention of having gone on to college football or wrestling. I found no logic—only wonder, the suggestion of mystery—in these new identities.

And there was a description of the dinner dance held at the Pfister Hotel's ballroom, the professional master of ceremonies who awarded the prizes: for the woman (née Gooch) with the most children, the man with the least hair, the fattest man, the graduate who traveled the greatest distance to attend (a career Air Force officer on furlough from his post in Alaska), the most famous (William Fifer, television weatherman). There was mention of the teachers who came, but neither Myrna Klemp nor Agnes Keintzle was among them—I thought of the parts of speech.

And there was a short necrology, on the inside back cover of the booklet, like an afterthought—that, in addition to all these life-changes, higher education, occupations, careers, marriages, children, travel, there was, lest we forget, one more, greater, final change.

There were six people listed, six of the more than four hundred graduates of Wauwatosa Senior High School, class of 1955, who had died during the preceding ten years. Of the six, I recognized only the name of Cynthia von Eschen.

I read her name on the list of the dead, and I thought of her, remembered her, Miss Keintzle's class, the parts of speech. I remembered all that very clearly, and I am sure it was sad to think she was dead, but I could not really imagine it.

A little over a year later, I went back to Wisconsin to visit my parents. I borrowed my father's car and drove about the city of Milwaukee, the suburb of Wauwatosa, past the high school, and it was purely by chance that I met Eduardo Walkiewicz.

I stopped behind a municipal sanitation truck, and there he was, emptying a trash can into the dumpster; I did not recognize him at first, he had gained so much weight, his overalls and gloves so dirty, his black hair shot with premature gray. Then I recognized him, and after only an instant's satisfaction at seeing him—what, who he was now—I leaned my head out of the car window, called to him, and he came over, leaned on the car, spoke with me for a minute before he had to go, follow his truck to the next house on its route.

I am not sure why I called out to him.

I smelled the sour stench of garbage on his clothes as we spoke. I mentioned the reunion, and he told me who he remembered seeing there.

He had been most surprised at what had happened to Sue Gralman; with three children, twice-divorced, she subsisted on Aid to Dependent Children, welfare, food stamps; he remembered her as such a nice girl in high school, friendly. I mentioned seeing Cynthia von Eschen's name among the dead, and said I wondered how she had died. He had talked with someone at the reunion who knew the story of her death. And he told it to me, a brief sketch, before his driver honked, shifted the truck's gears, and Eduardo Walkiewicz followed on foot after the truck to the next house on the garbage collection route.

What follows, the last part of my story, is not true; it is a fiction I have made out of two sources, what Eduardo Walkiewicz, the garbage collector, told me that day, and from my fiction writer's imagination. What he told me was already a kind of unself-conscious fiction, a fabric of the truth so remote from the experience it related as to be wholly unreliable, passed through at least two unreliable, incompetent sensibilities—Eduardo Walkiewicz and whoever told him what he told me. And my imagination is only remotely tied to whatever facts came to me; I have my own reasons for making the kind of fiction that follows, and even the best intention has to be manifest in words. I take everything I know, everything I am, have been, and I have to use words, and the words are the fiction, what follows.

Henry Peña was born and raised in the Santa Fe barrio. The youngest of seven children, he was small and sickly as a child, skinny and weak as an adolescent, and the most notorious liar in the barrio.

When he was seven, he told his best friend, Luis Roybal, that his true father was not the man who lived with his mother; his true father, he told Luis, was a rich man from Old Mexico, a *patron,* who had come across the border just long enough to father him, then gone back to his rancho where he raised racehorses and fighting bulls, and someday soon he would come back to Santa Fe to find Henry, take him back to Old Mexico to live with him.

"You lie, Henry. You always lie. I heard your mother say to my mother your father was this guy from Clovis lived with her until then you were born. Why you always lie, Henry?"

"It could as easy be my mother telling lies, Luis," Henry said.

"Except it ain't," his friend said. "Henry, you the worst big liar I ever know. Hey, if you got to tell lies, make something people already don't know the truth about, maybe then somebody believe you, hey?"

When he was fourteen, Henry stole change from his mother's purse, bought a bottle of blue-black ink, borrowed one of her sewing needles, and tattooed *Pachuko* crosses between the thumb and forefinger of both his hands. He kept his hands in his pockets until the swelling went down and the tattoos scabbed off. Then he showed them to Luis Roybal. He told him, "Man, you see this bad crosses? Means I am *Pachuko,* see? I join up with these bad dudes, you don't know them, Luis, they not from the barrio, see? Really bad they are, man. Now I belong, anybody messes with me, I give them the word, man, *Pachuko* all come, even from as far as Los Angeles if I say, kill anybody messes with Henry Peña, see? Same for me, I gang up on anybody bothers my *Pachuko* brothers, see?"

Luis Roybal said, "Henry, you done that yourself with a needle. Man, everybody know, your sister saying she seen you poking ink in your skin with a needle, man. You a damn liar ever since I know you, man!"

"No, honest, I'm telling you, I join up with the *Pachuko,* man! It's true. We the toughest people in Santa Fe, Luis!"

"The only place you tough is in your mouth always lying," Luis said. "And so where's your knife? *Pachuko* is always got a big knife, no? You don't even got no knifes! Liar Henry is your name, man!"

Of course he lied about having women too, but everybody did that, even Luis Roybal.

When he was seventeen, he joined the army with his friend Luis Roybal. He said to his mother, "We will be paratroopers. You get to wear shiny boots all the time, and the pay is extra because it's so dangerous to jump out of airplanes with only a parachute, see? Paratroopers is the most dangerous and toughest soldiers in the whole damn army, Mama!"

That was not supposed to be a lie, because he and Luis did enlist for airborne training. Luis was accepted, and went off to Fort Campbell, Kentucky, to join the Special Forces, but Henry Peña was rejected, found physically fit only for conventional duty. He took basic training at Fort Leonard Wood, Missouri, failed the advanced infantry training test, and was sent to Fort Riley, Kansas, assigned to Headquarters Quartermaster Company of the First Division.

His duty consisted of spending every Monday taking in all of division headquarters' dirty sheets; on Tuesdays he shook out all the dirty sheets and folded them for the post laundry. Wednesdays he loaded the folded sheets on a two-and-a-half-ton truck, rode to the laundry and unloaded them. Thursdays he rode the empty truck to the laundry, loaded up clean sheets, rode back to his company supply room, and passed out clean sheets. For the Saturday half-day's duty, he was supernumerary. That meant he tried to look busy around the supply room; if he failed, they sent him over to the dayroom to help the orderly clean up to get ready for the weekend. Off-duty at noon each Saturday—unless he came up on the rosters for KP or guard mount—he spent his weekends wandering on the post.

He sat in the Service Club, because it was air-conditioned, and because he could hide behind a magazine and watch the Special Service girls—blondes, redheads, tall women who wore high heels and stockings with seams up the backs of their long legs; he could smell their perfume when they passed close to him. He pretended to read, watched them conducting bingo games and Ping-Pong tournaments. He drank coffee and Cokes in the big snack bar over at Camp Funston. He tried reading books in the post library, but his English was not good enough to read much. He drank 3.2 beer at the outdoor tables at the central PX, but he got sick easily on too much cold beer, and his head ached in the hot Kansas sun with all that beer inside him. Sometimes he walked all the way over to Camp Forsythe to watch the guard mount at the post stockade, found a spot of shade and watched the prisoners file in and out on fatigue details, armbands with a big black letter P, the guards with their shotguns and lacquered helmet liners that reflected the bright sunlight.

He wished he was a stockade guard so he could carry a shotgun, get one of those special helmet liners. He had heard guards got an automatic transfer if they shot an escaping prisoner. If he was a stockade guard, Henry Peña thought, he would get a transfer, get to be someplace else, be something else instead of the one who had to shake out the dirty sheets for all of division headquarters at Fort Riley, Kansas. Sometimes he even wished he was a prisoner, wore an armband, marched in and out of Forsythe's old limestone cavalry barns that were the stockade barracks now.

He tried lying. Monday mornings, when the other men in Quartermaster Company complained about their hangovers and talked about the women they had in Manhattan and Junction City and Lawrence and Topeka and Kansas City, he tried with them. He said, "You guys got to go all the way off to Kansas City to get you some. Me, I got me womens right in Junction City and Manhattan, see? I go in and stay all weekend, this one I got even pays for my beer I drink."

"Sure thing, Peña," one man said to him.

"You hear this?" another said. "Peña gets all he wants right here close to home. Must be you tapping all them sorority girls at K-State, right, Peña?"

"If he is he wasn't this weekend," said another, "since I happen to have personally saw him walking around like a lost dog over at Funston when I was coming back from Junction City in a cab. You got a woman lives on the post, Peña?"

"Peña," another said to him, "you could make a fortune selling that crap for fertilizer, man."

"Hey, Peña," a man said, "tell the truth for once in your life. You ever really ever slept with a woman in your whole damn life?"

So there was not even anyone he could lie to.

Evenings, he sat alone at the EM Club, sipped a glass of 3.2 beer, listened in on all the drunken stories told by men who had been in Korea, stories about fighting the Chinese and the gook Koreans, stories about whores, Japanese women. Listening, he finally got his idea about how to make a lie that would work.

He was listening to two men talking one night, late in July. One was an older man; he looked as old as the man who lived with Henry Peña's mother but was not his real father. The older man was a corporal. The other man was much younger, only a few years older than Henry; on his sleeve were the fresh impressions of corporal's stripes only recently removed; the younger man had been busted down for something. They were both so drunk they could barely keep their heads off the table while they argued.

They argued about the use of the 60 mm. mortar. The younger man said, "I been on crew-serve weapons all my life, and now you're going to tell me from mortars?" The older man smiled, reached into his pocket and pulled out a Combat Infantryman's Badge, held it up to show to the younger man; it had the star between the tips of the wreath, which Henry Peña knew meant the man had been in two wars. The younger man snorted, said, "Seventy-five cents in the damn PX." Both men laughed. They talked about a whorehouse in a place near Pusan they had both visited, and Henry Peña had his idea about how to make a lie work.

Henry Peña figured he needed two things to make a lie work: proofs, something that would look like proofs, and the right person to tell the lie to. After that, it was the telling it, telling the lie right so it would be believed, as real as anything real.

Getting proofs was the easiest part. He had to wait two weeks to do it, because he drew KP the next weekend, and then he had to wait to the end of the month for payday. Then, with his money in his pocket, he took the shuttle bus in to Junction City. He was careful. He waited until it was dark, all the troops from Fort Riley off the streets, socked in for the night at the 3.2 bars and the private bottle clubs and the VFW hall.

It was only a few minutes before closing time that he entered the biggest of the three military supply and surplus stores to buy what he needed. He worried the clerk might ask him what he wanted the stuff for, but it was easy. He picked it out, paid his money, and took it back to Fort Riley on the shuttle, stashed it in his wall locker behind his issue fatigue uniforms.

Henry Peña bought a set of gabardines, because issue khakis never held creases any longer than it took to start sweating in the Kansas heat; all the good soldiers, sharp soldiers, owned a set of gabardines for summer wear. He bought a pair of custom jump boots because issue boots never took a good spit shine; he could spit shine the toes and heels of his new boots until they looked like they were dipped in glass. And custom jump boots had the double sole and heel paratroopers wore.

He bought the airborne patch for his garrison cap, the blue infantryman's cord, infantry collar brass, and a custom belt buckle, coated so it was not necessary to use Brasso to get a high gloss on it. Then he picked out the badges and the ribbons.

He got a Presidential Unit Citation for his right breast pocket, a Combat Infantryman's Badge, a parachutist's wings, and two rows of ribbons to go under them on his left breast: National Defense, Korean Service Ribbon with the two battle stars, Purple Heart, Bronze Star with V for valor, Good Conduct, Japanese Occupation, and the Syngman Rhee Citation. He bought two hashmarks for his left sleeve, two gold combat-time bars for his right, the ones they called chocolate bars, and staff sergeant chevrons. For his right shoulder, he bought the patch of the Fifth Regimental Combat Team, because he had seen a man with that who also wore the parachutist's wings.

Now he had the proofs he needed to make his lie work. He did his sewing late at night in the latrine, worrying someone would stumble in and catch him at it. But nobody did; a little luck was needed for a good lie to work.

He went to Manhattan, the Kansas State University campus, to find the right person to tell it to. He carried his new uniform in a dry cleaner's bag, rode a taxi in to Aggieville, the strip of 3.2 bars on the edge of the K-State campus. In a Phillips 66 gas station rest room, he changed into his new liar's uniform, carried his civies out with him in a grocery sack rolled and tucked under his arm. And then Henry Peña, looking like a staff sergeant who had served with the Fifth RCT in Korea, been wounded, decorated, a qualified paratrooper, walked in his new spit-shined custom jump boots to the nearest beer bar, where the KSU students gathered, to find somebody, the right person, to tell his lie to.

It took awhile. He sat in The Huddle for nearly an hour, on a stool at the bar, looking at himself in his new uniform, his stripes, badges, ribbons, infantryman's cord, drinking draft 3.2. But there weren't any women in The Huddle. There were only college boys, dressed in cutoff sweatshirts and T-shirts, shorts and tennis shoes without socks; they all sat at tables, drank pitchers of 3.2, laughing a lot. He overheard a couple of jokes told, but there was no one he could have talked to, so he sat alone at the bar, looked at himself in the mirror. When he ordered another draft, the bartender served him, took his money, made change without speaking. He put half a dollar in the jukebox, but did not recognize any of the songs he punched, and nobody at the tables seemed to hear the music he played.

When he ordered another draft, held his empty glass out to bring the bartender down from the other end of the bar, Henry Peña said to him, "Man, where is all the peoples?"

"End of summer school, Sarge," the bartender said as he drew on the tap.

Henry Peña did not understand what that meant, so he said, "Man, I mean how's come you don't got not even one womens in this place at night?"

"Oh," said the bartender, "if it's the bitches you're looking for, broads go mostly to Moxie's or Kampus Korner. You just move in out at Riley, Sarge?" he said. "Troops mostly go to J.C. for broads I'm saying. Your war suit there's as likely to scare off all the sorority gals, Sarge."

"Man," Henry Peña said, "don't tell me from how to get womens, see? I don't fight in the war in Korea and get shot up without I knew getting womens. You ever been to Japan, man, them womens in Japan?" he asked the bartender. The bartender shook his head no, but he leaned on his forearms on the bar, bent his head toward Henry Peña, ready to listen.

And Henry Peña almost began to tell about the women he had had in Japan, the fighting he had done in Korea, almost started to tell his lie, but he knew the bartender was not the right person, there in The Huddle with all the college boys drinking pitchers of 3.2, telling dumb jokes, dumb music playing on the jukebox, autographed photographs of KSU football players on the walls, pennants of all the schools in the Big Seven football conference. The place was not right, the bartender was not the right person—nothing would come of telling his lie here, nothing real happen. "Terrific stuff, man, the excellent gash in Japan," is all Henry Peña said to the bartender, and he paid for his last beer and left The Huddle.

He found Moxie's, and there were two women there, and even the bartender was an old woman; she reminded him of his mother back in Santa Fe. But the two women, college girls, were with their college-boy boyfriends, two couples at two tables way back in the dark corners of Moxie's 3.2 bar. One couple sat side by side at a small table, fooling around, tickling each other, hugging, kissing little kisses. The other couple had their heads together over a table, whispering, kissing little kisses when they stopped whispering.

The old woman tending bar said to him, "Hi there, Sergeant. What brings you out here from the fort with the frat rats?" Henry Peña drank one draft 3.2, then left.

Now he was afraid he would not get to tell his new, big lie, that it was going to turn out just like the one about his rich father who owned a rancho in Old Mexico, the one about his *Pachuko* tattoos. He found a package store, went in and bought a fifth of Paul Jones. "Nearest private club's way to other side of the campus, Sarge," the clerk, an old man wearing a hearing aid and an aloha shirt, said.

"I drink it on the damn street," Henry Peña told him; at least the new uniform kept the clerk from asking him for proof of his age—at least that much worked.

He took the Paul Jones in a paper sack, took it out onto the deserted streets of Aggieville, cracked the seal, drank as much as his throat and stomach would take of the burn, sat on the curb, looked at the vacant street, what he could see of the unlit buildings on the KSU campus, the open greensward, occasional darker shapes of trees, lines of shrubbery.

Henry Peña sat with his fifth of Paul Jones, wondered what was going to happen to him in his life. The whiskey made him sad. He could hear some jukebox music coming from one of the bars on the Aggieville strip, and he heard the cicadas grinding in the grass and trees, a sound he had never heard in Santa Fe. It sounded like the world laughing at him because all he was was a liar who could not tell any that worked. He felt the sticky weight of the humid air on his skin, the warm concrete under the seat of his gabardine trousers; the heat in Santa Fe was always dry, and the nights cooled there.

Henry Peña was very sad. He was in Kansas, and he was a bad liar, and if he could not even tell a good, big lie that worked, then he was never going to be anything, because a liar was all he had ever been, could be. The uniform cost him a lot of money, and all he had to show for it was a bottle of whiskey, and if he drank a lot of that he would get sick as hell. He threw the bag holding his civies into the gutter.

Then, for no reason, he got up from the curb and walked down the Aggieville strip, and at the corner he found himself standing in front of the Kampus Korner. And he went in, and there were women, college girls, lots of them, a lot of them with their college boys, but not all of them were— some sat at the bar, at tables, in twos and threes, even a few alone. And there, alone at a very small table, in the farthest corner from the door and the bar, drinking 3.2 beer by herself, as if she were the only person in the bar, Henry Peña found the right person to tell his lie to.

And the uniform worked. Some people stared at him when he went to the bar, and they moved aside to give him room, and he had two glasses of beer at the bar, and watched himself and everyone in the back bar mirror. And he saw how the woman, the college girl who sat all alone in the far corner, kept watching him. She kept watching him, the way a person watches someone or something he wants to touch, but does not dare. So when he got his third draft 3.2, Henry Peña went over to the college girl who sat alone at the very small table in the farthest corner of the Kampus Korner.

"Hey," Henry Peña said to her, "you looking all alone by yourself here. How abouts I sit down and we can talk or something, huh? I even got something special to drink here, we could share if you want," he said, and held up the fifth of Paul Jones in the paper sack. She looked up at him like she had not heard, or if she had, did not understand what he said. When she said nothing, he said, "Hey, you mind if I sit down here with you? It's crowded at the bar and my legs get tired if I stand too long." When she only looked at him, a surprised look on her face, as if the last thing she expected was someone speaking to her, wanting to sit with her, Henry Peña said, "See, I got shot in the legs with mortars and frostbite too, in Korea, so my legs hurt standing up so much, see?"

She said, "I guess you can if you want," and he took a free chair from the next table and sat down as close to her at the table as he could manage.

He expected her to say something then, but she looked away, down at the glass of flat beer she held with both hands. He almost got up and left, gave up on it, but the lie about his legs, wounds and frostbite from Korea, had gotten him the chair at her table, close to her, and so Henry Peña made up his mind to make it work.

"I'm Sergeant Henry Peña," he said, "You could tell me your name too so we could talk instead of just sit here, huh?"

"Cynthia," she said without looking up from her beer.

"Cynthia?" he said. "Hey, Cindy, right, that's a nice name. Cindy what?" He had to ask her to repeat her last name for him, because it was the kind of name he had never heard, nobody in Santa Fe or the army with a name like that.

"Von Eschen," she said, "Cynthia von Eschen."

"Cindy von Eschen. I'm Sergeant Henry Peña. Cindy von Eschen is a real nice name though. I like the name Cindy a lot."

"Nobody calls me Cindy," she said. "My folks always call me Cynthia, everybody at home, friends," she said.

"But I like Cindy better than Cynthia. Cindy sounds nicer. I know somebody once name Cindy in Santa Fe. Santa Fe's my hometown before I join up the army, see? Where you coming from, Cindy?"

He let her talk a while before he started into his lie. She told him her hometown, and that she was a KSU freshman, that she was not in a sorority, but she did not care that she was not rushed, sororities were all cliques, and she hated cliques. Henry Peña did not know what a clique was. But he asked her enough questions to keep her talking; she told him she was homesick for her family and her hometown, wished she had not come to Manhattan to go to college at KSU, that she would be going home next week for a visit before she came back for the fall semester, only she might transfer to the University of Wisconsin, except that was also a big frat and sorority school, full of cliques too. He kept her talking, and he got her to drink up her beer, let him buy her another. He asked her if she wanted a drink of his Paul Jones whiskey, and she said she had only tasted whiskey once in her life and did not like the taste of it.

"Hey, you got to try it, Cindy. It don't taste so bad, but then you get all warm and nice all over, you feel good as hell, you don't care about nothing the way nothing is except you feel great, see? You don't even feel homesick no more, you get some whiskey down you. Me, I get homesick ever for Santa Fe, I drink some whiskeys and don't worry about it none no more." He got her to tip up the fifth of Paul Jones, the neck sticking out of the paper sack. She choked on it, but got it down, and he promised her it would feel great if she would just wait a minute. "I learn to drink whiskeys when I was in the war fighting in Korea," he told her.

"Is that what all that means?" she said, pointing at the ribbons on his chest. "I know your stripes means you're a sergeant, but what's all that for?" Then Henry Peña really began to tell her his lie.

She listened and she asked questions at the right times, and he got her to drink up her beer, bought her another. He got her to admit the drink of whiskey had begun to make her feel good, and then he got her to take another small drink.

"See," he told her, "I never got to school or college away from home and all, like you, because I joined up the army to fight in the war in Korea. I was real young, join up soon as I'm seventeen, and I been in the army ever since, which is why I'm a sergeant, see, and how I got wounded and got all these medals here I'm wearing now."

"School's not so great," she said. "College stinks. KSU stinks. Wisconsin probably stinks just as much. Everyone's a snob or part of a clique. College is even more boring than high school."

She was not a good-looking woman. Henry Peña thought he liked women who were tall and had big chests; he liked long legs on a woman, big thighs, and he liked long blonde hair on a woman, or redheads, big dark eyes, big red lips. This Cindy funny–last name was pretty tall, but she was thin; she had real thin arms and legs, and almost no chest he could see looking down her blouse, and her hair was short and brown except she tied it in a little tail in the back; she had little eyes, and hardly any lips at all. He wondered if he would like kissing her. "How's come you squint, is it your eyes hurt?" he asked her.

"I got new contacts," she said.

But she smelled nice, like clean sheets when he put his head very close to hers to talk to her; she smelled clean, and she had clean white fingernails, and her clothes were clean, smelled clean. She was the right person to tell his lie to, and he was sure he could make something happen from it.

"See," Henry Peña said to her, "I was in Korea with the Fifth RCT. I was there for all the fighting. I got wounded in the legs, like I say before, and then I was a prisoner from the Chinese for over a year, too. This one here," he said, touching his Purple Heart ribbon, "is for when I get wounded."

"Really?" Cindy von Eschen said. "I was in high school when I used to read about Korea, or even junior high maybe. It's funny sitting here in Aggieville talking to someone who was there when I was in junior high. How did you get hurt?" she asked him.

"Drink your beer up, I get you another one. This 3.2 ain't no real beer like you get in Santa Fe or in Korea and Japan I had. Drink it all up, we have us a little taste more of my whiskey, don't you feel real good already from it?" Henry Peña said.

They finished their beers, and he bought two more at the bar, and they each tipped the fifth of Paul Jones up again. She admitted to him she could feel it; she said it made her hands and feet warm and light. "I'll probably get drunk for the first time," she said, and laughed. "I've never been drunk ever before in my life," she said.

"You learn to like it like I did when I'm in Japan and fighting the war in Korea. You get drunk, you don't think no more about all your trouble you got," he said. And then Henry Peña told her all about getting his wounds in Korea. It was the biggest lie he ever told.

It was the right place for it. The college boys and their college girls crowded the bar, at tables, talking loud, laughing, giving each other little hugs and little kisses, played their dumb music on the jukebox. What he said, only she heard. She put her head close to his to be able to hear; he smelled the good smell of her very white skin, her clean brown hair. She was not fine looking; she was almost ugly, but she was the right person to tell a lie to. She wanted to hear it, and she wanted to believe it, and as he told it it sounded more real than any other lie he had ever told, as real as who he really was, anything he had ever really done. When he glanced up at the Kampus Korner crowd, he felt himself a real staff sergeant with airborne badges and ribbons and combat decorations. When he looked into Cindy von Eschen's small squinting eyes he saw that he was a real staff sergeant, telling her about his war in Korea, as real to himself as he was to her.

What he said was easy. Things he had heard listening to soldiers who had been there came into his head to say, like they were his own memories. When he stopped talking to drink his beer, something always came to him to say.

"When I got wounded," he said, "it was winter. Terrible cold and all snow on the ground. You could freeze to death even if the Chinese guys don't shoot you," he said.

"We have the worst winters in the world in Wisconsin," she said.

"Sure, but this is terrible winter in Korea, fighting. Some people freeze to death, or their feet they have to cut off. We live in big trenches and tents and little holes we dig in the trenches. We got all barb wire to keep Chinese away, see? When they come at us at night, you hear them jiggle the wire. We shoot up flares and you can see them all coming through the wire. Then we shoot the hell out of them."

"How does it feel? When you shoot somebody."

"I like it," Henry Peña said. "See, it's like real exciting. You forget it all except to shoot the hell out of them because they trying to kill you too. Drink up your beer, Cindy."

"I'm afraid I'll get sick," she said.

"Never happen," he said, and he got her to taste the whiskey again. And he told her about the bugles the Chinese blew when they attacked, and about how he sighted his Browning Automatic Rifle on the Chinese in their padded coats, caught in the wire. "You know what they wear for shoes, Cindy? Regular sneaks, man. Honest, sneaks they wear for shoes in winter!" He told her about the mortars, how incoming sounded different than outgoing, about the one that hit close and cut up his legs with fragments.

"It must feel different to be you," she said. "I mean it must be something you could have had dreams about if you think about it a lot."

"I don't let nothing bother me," Henry Peña said, and told her then about how the Chinese overran his trench; he could not get up and run because he was hit in the legs, so they caught him there. "They shoot everybody what can't walk, so I make myself get up and walk off with them. I was bleeding like hell in the snow, real cold, see?" He told her about being a prisoner of war, how he nearly froze and starved to death before he was repatriated, all the bonus money he got, his rest and recuperation leave in Japan. And he kept her drinking her beers, got her to taste the whiskey again. He was going to tell her about the women in Japan, make it real for her, for himself.

"I have to go potty," she said, and got up, went to the ladies' rest room that said *Dolls* on the door. He waited for her, had some more whiskey, sat there in the Kampus Korner, Aggieville, Kansas, and he felt it was all very real—himself, Korea, his badges and stripes and ribbons, more real than the noisy college boys and their college girls, Fort Riley, the supply room where he worked shaking out and folding dirty sheets, Santa Fe, as real as Luis Roybal, who was a real paratrooper in Kentucky someplace.

When she came back to the table, he could see the drinking had gotten to her. Her face was even more pale, a light sweat on her forehead and cheeks and throat.

"Have you some more whiskey," he said. "It makes you feel better if it's bothering you and you just stay drinking it, you get better real soon."

"I better go," she said; when she stood up, she almost fell on the table.

"I can take you someplace," Henry Peña said, and walked her to the bar; her arm felt clammy as he helped her. He held her up while the bartender called a taxi for them.

The Kampus Korner bartender said, "Looks like you got you a problem with that little girlie, Sarge."

"Man," Henry Peña told him, "I know how to handle the womens, see?" Cindy von Eschen was able to walk out to the taxi when it came, but when Henry Peña tried talking to her, she only mumbled. The instant he got her in the taxi, she passed out. "Man," he said to the driver, "what's a room close to here?"

The taxi driver flipped on the dome light, twisted to lean back over the seat, looked at Henry Peña, Cindy von Eschen passed out, head lolling. "That's jailbait there, Sarge, looks like to me." The driver made a clucking sound with his tongue.

"Hey," Henry Peña said, "are you telling me about the womens, man? Don't tell me nothing about womens. I been at womens all over the world in Korea and Japan, see?" The driver shrugged, turned back to the wheel, hit the meter flag. "Just find me some room I can get for us, huh?"

They drove, and Henry Peña felt the driver's eyes watching him in the rearview mirror; Henry Peña held her up when Cindy von Eschen started to fall over, worried about the taxi meter clicking away as they drove the dark, empty streets of Manhattan, if he would have enough money for the fare, a room, a taxi back to Fort Riley. He held Cindy von Eschen up on the backseat; something real was happening out of his lie. He felt like telling the driver about the women of Korea and Japan, what he had heard from other soldiers about whores who worked in filthy cribs in places like Seoul and Pusan, scented Japanese whores who gave baths and massages and worked in rooms with round beds, tinted mirrors set in the ceilings, Tokyo, Eta Jima. What he had heard from other men came to him like sharp memories.

The motel the driver took them to was called the Blue Court, a big blue neon sign, small cabins ranged along a gravel drive, a blue lightbulb over each cabin door. "Wait while I get a room, huh?" he said to the driver.

"It's your party, Sarge," the driver said without turning to him.

The desk clerk was just a young kid, half-asleep at a card table, a television on with the sound turned off. "All night?" he asked Henry Peña as he got the key, peered out the window at the waiting taxi.

"What's the differences, man?"

"Twenty if you stay to check-out, otherwise fifteen if it's just a hot bed you need." The kid grinned at him. Henry Peña checked his wallet; he had more than forty dollars left. "Sweet dreams," the kid said, laughed, when Henry Peña gave him a twenty.

"Man," he said to the kid, "I ain't doing no dreaming. I'm for turning the bitch every which way except loose." He laughed with the kid.

When he paid off the taxi, pulled and lifted Cindy von Eschen out, stood her on her feet, teetering and mumbling about feeling sick, the driver said, "Ain't hardly no challenge if they're half-dead drunk, is it, Sarge."

"Man," he said, holding her up, cabin key in his hand, "I sober the bitch up first, see? I done this times before."

He half-dragged, half-carried her to the cabin, propped her against the door while he fumbled the key into the lock under the blue light. Her face and bare arms, her legs, were blue in the light, and he suddenly felt all the whiskey and 3.2 beer flip in his stomach, rush in his head. He looked at his blue hands working the key in the lock.

Cindy von Eschen almost fell into the room when the door opened. Just as he caught her by the waist, she vomited all over the doorsill.

"Goddamn, woman, you got to do that in the toilet," he said; the smell rose up to his nose, filled the small room even after he got her inside, door closed. He let her fall on the bed while he turned on the light. He felt sick, now, could not keep from staggering as he lurched to the tiny bathroom to throw up. He flushed the toilet, looked at himself in the mirror, his sweated face, loud breath heaving his chest and shoulders, his wrinkled uniform. "Okay," he said to himself in the bathroom mirror, "now you ready for it, Sergeant Henry Peña."

He stripped off his uniform, the badges and brass, chevrons, medals, hashmarks, threw them in a heap on the dirty floor. "Come on, baby, you," he said to Cindy von Eschen, but she lay face down on the bed, snoring, did not speak. "Hey," he said, rolled her over, "now for it," but her eyes were closed, arms limp. The smell of her vomit hit him again, and his vision blurred. "Bitch Cindy," he said, "I get you straight like six o'clock here!"

He took off her clothes, struggling with her flopping arms and legs, the bed shifting under them, barely able to make his fingers unbutton her buttons, unzip her zipper. "Damn," he said, his head whirling, "you skinny like a little boy, you ain't got no chest. Stink," he said, because the smell of her vomit was still on her, even with all her clothes off.

"I get you straight," he said as he pulled her off the bed, across the floor to the bathroom, her bare heels dragging. He did his best to get her into the bathtub without knocking her head against it. He stood over her a moment before he turned on the water; she looked like a little boy, asleep, curled up in the bottom of the bathtub.

He turned on the water, then had to find the knob that changed it to a shower. He stood up to watch the shower running hard, and did not know anything was wrong until he saw the steam all around him, filling the tiny bathroom. Then she began to scream.

He could hear her bare arms and legs smacking against the tub, screaming louder and louder. He stood there in the swirling steam, felt the searing heat of the water, hearing her screaming before he could think to try to find the faucet, turn it off. He groped in the cloud of scalding steam, yelled when the water hit his hands and arms.

Henry Peña could not find the faucet. He could only stand there, naked, hear her scream, and then he heard the pounding on the cabin door, and he tried to think what to do, what he could say, but nothing came to him, and he was still standing there when she stopped screaming, someone broke in the cabin door, grabbed him, threw him out of the tiny bathroom. He ended up on the dirty floor by the bed, wet, sick, unable to open his eyes; he felt around with his hands for the heap of his clothes, the uniform, but could not find them, and he could not think of any lie to tell that anyone would believe.

What does my story mean?

It means: all fictions are lies, however much truth goes into the making of them; a fiction writer is a liar, who, to make his fictions work, has to use his imagination and his skill with language to transform elements of the truth into a lie a reader can believe; if a fiction works, the lie is well told, then it becomes real, the truth again, because the reader is not who he was anymore when he believes something new.

It means everything is language, that anything that is real—the truth— is real only in the substance of the language that embodies it. And so the reason there will always be fictions is because fiction writers, like me, want very much to make real things, and to make real things last.

A successful fiction endures, but does not satisfy the fiction writer's need; there will always be something, someone, some words spoken, or not spoken, that must be made real, turned into a lie that somebody—if only the fiction writer himself—can believe.

Madness

. . . I shall not exist if you
do not imagine me . . .

—Vladimir Nabokov

LARRY GRAFF, MY BOYHOOD best friend, went crazy when he was nineteen; he has been incurably, hopelessly insane for more than forty years now.

Thousands of people—millions?—have had a like experience, a friend, parent, sibling, spouse, even a child lost this way, taken away by something as definitive as death itself, though so much less finite, so *unnatural*. Still, I seem to feel this—my friend, the closest friend I have had in all my life, gone beyond a border to a place where no one can find him, ever—makes me in some way . . . *special?*

I think this is because I was not there when it happened, because, try as I do, I can remember no warning sign, however subtle or incipient, that insanity awaited him.

We were, both of us, absolutely *normal* boys, teenagers, smugly sufficient unto ourselves all through those years of unself-conscious innocence. Energized by our exploding glands, blessed by the bliss of ignorance, mindlessly indifferent to anything and everything outside our delightfully narrow world, we so enjoyed our perfectly average youth! We were so healthy, so vigorous, so content to be exactly what we were, where and when! The beauty of our lives lay, I think now, in what we did not know was the unceasing *presentness* of existence, that we did not care for such minuscule crumbs of past time we were aware of, had no inkling, much less concern for, any possibility of futures—Larry and I were, in short, two beings totally devoted to, absorbed by, no more than pure *being*.

His madness, complete and final, coming at age nineteen, calls all that marvelous time of my life into question, leaves me now with only the nagging impotence of speculation, doubt, at times despair; I understand and appreciate the potential of old age's wisdom, but find it a poor recompense. Madness took my best friend from me, and, as I view it often, took from me also my own best memories. Larry Graff's insanity taints, as I see it, what

153

otherwise would be—*should be!*—a comfort to the remainder of existence left to me now.

My end, like an untreatable affliction, is necessary and, relatively, soon. I would like, during what is yet to come, to believe in something, if only what I once was—young, healthy, strong, confident! But the loss of my best friend to madness turns even that to an airy insubstantiality no more palpable than a half-recalled dream.

I imagine this accounts for my preoccupation with it, with him, accounts for my inability to simply forget him, forget my own past with him, and get on with whatever of life awaits me?

The years we were best friends—five, nearly six—are a kind of collage for me now; they have none of the stark vividness of his madness, are without definition or distinct delineation, a series of incidents unordered by clear chronology. We met when we were thirteen, entered junior high school, went out for the basketball team, became best friends.

When I graduated high school, turned eighteen, I enlisted in the army, spent two and a half years overseas; Larry Graff, a few months after I left for basic training, did the same. Within six months, he had gone mad, received a medical discharge, was placed on permanent disability, his life over.

The years of our friendship, my youth, surely the happiest days of my life—why do I not recall them more clearly? They are so . . . *summary!*

We played basketball. He was tall, talented; I was avid. We played basketball as though it were the sole substance of our lives, of life! He lettered on the junior- and senior-high varsities; we played pick-up games in church gymnasiums, at neighborhood social centers, school playgrounds, in municipal summer leagues played on asphalt courts, metal mesh nets on the rims; we erected a backboard on his parents' garage, played horse and one-on-one in the alley behind his house; we played in rain and when snowflakes floated around us.

Of course there was more than basketball!

We learned to smoke cigarettes and drink enough beer to make ourselves sick—Larry, tall for his age, was able to buy both at grocery stores. We got driver's licenses, borrowed our parents' cars, cruised city streets imagining we were looking for something we might find, drank our illicit beer, smoked, hummed and tapped time on the dashboard to the popular music on the car's radio. We discovered girls, double-dated, competed once for the attention of Natalie, whose last name I cannot now remember, but who liked neither of us. We went to a lot of movies, to one formal dance, even read a few of the same books not assigned by our teachers. I remember we got interested in cards, spent hours playing varieties of poker for sums we never paid up. We had odd jobs and part-time work to cover the costs of cigarettes, beer, gas for our parents' cars—I clerked in a drugstore, Larry drove a florist's van one summer, we were both pinsetters one winter.

We were so *ordinary!* I suppose we must have talked, about girls, sex, basketball, our parents, his brother and sister, money, our part-time jobs, about—I can only assume—what we meant to do with our lives after high school, a vista that seemed then to stretch out beyond eternity. But I do not remember a single conversation, hear no echo of any one sentence, not even a word, of what must have been millions!

We were so normal, so utterly *not-special,* so like our peers in every respect, those years are a kind of smear, but I am convinced it was a perfect time we enjoyed, perfect lives, and that I cannot catch hold of it more precisely is, at times, infuriating, enraging! It is Larry Graff's madness I remember in detail, cannot make myself forget.

We graduated high school, I turned eighteen, enlisted in the army—I am not sure what I had in mind, except that I wanted something new, knew I was not *college material* then, perhaps thought a uniform would make me attractive to girls? Someone, maybe my mother, another friend, wrote me while I was still in basic training, told me Larry had enlisted. I served my three years, came home from overseas, was, I think, greatly matured by the experience; the military was good for me. I came home with a determination to go to college, money saved to do it, a young man with serious purpose in life—a *career* of some sort, the hope of love and marriage and family set in place before me, the common vision, however indistinct. I had a *future.*

That was when I learned my best friend had lost his mind.

"Graff?" someone said when I asked about him. "He went off his rocker."

"No," I said. "Get off it!"

"I'm telling you. The army washed him out, Section 8 or whatever, he's in and out of the VA all the time, you see him hanging around, I'm telling you he's bughouse!"

"No," I said.

"You can see for yourself next time they give him a pass, they let him home for weeks sometimes until he flips and goes back in upstate, the VA. I wouldn't kid about this," whoever it was I asked said.

"No," I said. But it was enough to keep me from calling his parents, finding out for myself, as if not finding out would make it untrue, a lie, a bad joke. I remember how the news frightened me. I did not see him again until after I started college, that first winter, when there was a near-record blizzard.

Everyone knew the blizzard was coming; the forecast was on television, radio, emphatic weathermen citing Canadian cold air masses, moisture

wafting from the south—plows and truckloads of sand and rock salt readied, motorists urged to put their tire chains on, dire travel advisories, schools
sure to close. I left my last class of the day, trudged through the already bitter
wind for a cup of coffee at the greasy spoon on the edge of campus, seeking
warmth, my new college friends.

Larry was sitting alone at the table framed by the front window. He did
not *look* insane—I smiled and waved my gloved hand at him, only a little
surprised he looked at me as if he did not know me.

"Lar," I said as I sat with him, "I been looking for you, I heard you were
gone, what are you doing hanging out here?" He looked at me for what
seemed a long time before he spoke, as if he sought to place my face, name.

"Hello," he finally said. And, "I like to sit here and listen and look out
the window at people. They let you just sit as long as you want if you buy
coffees," he said.

As I spoke to him, told him I had been in school since September, what I
meant to study, that I could about live on my G.I. Bill checks, about my time
overseas, something like a little smile, a smirk, came into his expression,
slightly superior, mocking. The more I talked, the less I felt he heard me, the
more I felt the need to speak, keep him from telling me what he thought or
felt as we sat there in the crowded greasy spoon. I talked as long as I could
without saying what I wanted to know about him, what I was afraid to learn.

"So," I had to say at last, "I heard you had some sort of problems with
the army?" He smiled broadly, as though I revealed abysmal ignorance, had
embarrassed myself.

"I receive therapies," he said.

"For what?" I said without thinking, then said, "I mean, what kind of
therapy?"

"The very most modern techniques," he said, and laughed a short, loud
laugh; I was afraid people around us would turn and stare.

He did not look . . . *crazy*. But he looked changed. His hair was still
cut short, the near scalping they give you in basic training, but several
days' growth smudged his cheeks and jaw. He chain-smoked, first and
second fingers of his right hand stained yellow-brown, heaped ashtray on
the table. He wore his army fatigue jacket despite the overheated, smoke-
laden restaurant air, but beneath this wore the dark blue pajamas issued in
military hospitals. On his feet were sodden house slippers, and he shuddered
as if still chilled from his walk to the campus. His teeth were dingy, he licked
his lips frequently, darted his eyes from me to the window, watching the flow
of students bundled against the weather pass on the sidewalk. His smile,
usually a smirk, occasionally a full grin that came and went in response to
nothing we said, never left his face.

"So," I said. "How you making it?" He smiled a large smile, leaned across the table, his face close to mine; I smelled his bad breath, his unwashed odor.

"I'm recuperating," he said, watched me, laughed loudly again.

"Great," I said, and, "Right!" I think now it was panic led me to invite him to go snow shoveling at the city's ward yard the next morning. He did not look insane, there was no insanity in anything he said or did, but he was not the best friend of my youth, and I wanted him to be that. And I could think of no other way to get up, say good-bye, leave him there alone in the restaurant's front window, on display for the sidewalk's traffic. Outside, snow began to fall.

"Hey," I said. "I'm going down to the ward yard early tomorrow morning. I heard they hire casual labor to shovel out alleys and sewer drains and all, it's good money. You interested?"

"I'd dearly love to," he said, his face suddenly blank.

"Great!" I said, stood, put on my coat, hat, gloves. "I'll come by for you at six, we got to get in early if we want the work." I told myself, as I left and went out into the blowing snowfall, that his inexplicable leer was his agreement and understanding—he would be ready to go with me in the morning.

"I saw Larry Graff today," I told my mother when I got home.

"Did you really?" she said. "So is he the way you heard?"

"No," I told her. "He could use a bath and a shave," I said, "but he's no nuttier than I am."

"I'm surprised," my mother said, "he was such a neat, clean boy I always thought."

"I'm probably exaggerating," I told my mother, and told her we were going snow shoveling early in the morning; she said it was nice I was getting together with him again, we had been such friends when we were boys.

I have tried, over the years since, to decide the cause or causes of Larry Graff's madness, but no answer suffices. His family was unremarkable, very much like mine. His father was a quiet, small man, distant, like mine. When I was in their home, his father seemed always to be in the same overstuffed chair, feet on an ottoman, hidden behind the newspaper even though the television was always on—I cannot recall ever hearing him speak. He had an older brother, too many years older than Larry and me to pay us any attention beyond disdainful glances and contemptuous remarks as we passed in or out of their house. There was a younger sister; Larry and I treated her to the same coarse indifference.

Mrs. Graff was an unusually large woman—Larry's height came from her—who seemed to me very stern, speaking in a loud voice full of veiled commands. I see no sources of his disaster in this family, as quotidian as mine.

The morning of the snow shoveling was the coldest I remember from all the frozen, snow-covered winters of my life. It was pitch-dark as I plodded my way to Larry's through the deep drifts formed during the night by the sharp winds that still screeched, though it had stopped snowing. I felt like I was the only person alive, the city empty, only the sound of plows clanking distantly on main streets, streetlights like beacons to mark my path, the sky a blacker blackness above me, still dotted with the faint points of stars, all of it so cold, the frozen snow squeaking under my boots, my toes and fingers and nose numbed, eyes watering.

Larry Graff's house was as dark as its neighbors, looked abandoned, as if deserted by inhabitants who fled this total cold and dark and snow, left the city for a safer, happier climate. I banged on the front door until my fist tingled, then rang the bell again and again, furious he was not awake, dressed, waiting for me, something warming, coffee or cocoa, to offer me. I was too angry to simply walk away, go alone to the ward yard or home to warmth and light. The cutting wind's whistle was too loud for me to hear his mother approach—suddenly the door flew open, a hall light on behind her, and Mrs. Graff stared at me, her eyes enlarged behind her thick glasses.

"I came for Larry," I said, "we're supposed to go to the ward yard to shovel snow?" My voice did not sound familiar to me, my tongue foreign in my mouth. Mrs. Graff stared at me, wearing her bathrobe, long graying hair hanging down over her shoulders, witchlike. "Lar was supposed to be up ready," I said in a voice not my own.

"He doesn't tell anyone anything!" she spat at me, held the door open wider for me to enter, led me up the stairs of the dark house, past the second floor to the attic room that had always been his. I felt the skin of my face glow with the house's heat, but it was as if she and I were the only people inside. She stomped up the stairs, muttering to herself, slapping the railing at the landings, like some caretaker called from her bed to show the property to a rude potential buyer.

"Larry!" she shouted as she banged open his door, woke him. She snapped on the light; at first I saw only the mass of his tangled blankets, smelled a grimy scent. Then he stirred and sat up, blinking, as unknowing as someone brought from a trance. "Larry!" she shouted again and again, shook him, stood him up. I watched, began to sweat in my heavy sweater, coat, gloves, wool cap. I have never felt so embarrassed; I stood, watched her literally dress her son, berate him for oversleeping, not knowing where his scarf was, demanding he eat something before we went.

"We have to get there early, first-come, first-serve," I said.

"Where?" Larry said. "Tell me again where. I know, I just can't remember when I wake up right away."

"You're both so stupid!" Mrs. Graff said as we went down the stairs, her slippers stomping above and behind us. Our walk to the ward yard—a mile at most?—was the longest in my life.

"You don't have some alarm clock?" I said into, against the knifing wind.

"What?"

"We could be too late, they give out the jobs to whoever's first there," I said.

"I guess."

"Thanks a lot, Lar!" I said.

"For what?" he said. We made our way to the ward yard, hunched, leaning into the wind, skirting the big sloped drifts, through the dark from streetlight to streetlight, and were not too late to get shoveling jobs.

That day's work was brutal. We were signed up, issued shovels, trucked with a crew—wino derelicts, unemployed men twice our age, a few other students—to alley entrances where we shoveled away the berms formed by plows that opened the city's arterial streets, cleared sewer gratings to free them for the eventual melting runoff. My hands and feet turned to stone, face stiff, lips too cracked to want to talk; we exhaled in little clouds, the only speech a random cursing, grunting, abusive directions from the crew foreman. I had to monitor Larry all day.

I would look up from my work, find him standing still as a statue in some stage of shoveling—his blade sunk in a drift, or lifted, ready to throw a heap of snow, or standing, his dropped shovel at his feet, as if he had lost it, could not remember where, how. "Get a move on," I said to him, "he'll can your ass you keep goldbricking."

"What?" he said. Or, "Okay." Or, "I'm shoveling this snow." Or, "You notice it's only cold when you think it is?" Once I caught him standing over a sewer grating as we were ready to get into the truck, move to the next location; his shovel turned upside down, he pushed at the snow clinging between the grates, poking it down into the sewer below with the end of the shovel's shaft.

"The *hell* you doing!" I said. "Get on the damn truck!"

"Opening it up," he said. On the breaks we took in neighborhood taverns to warm up, the winos and unemployed drank beers and port wine shooters, but Larry sat at the bar without speaking unless I spoke—he seemed to like to look at himself in the back bar mirrors.

"How's come you're so quiet?" I asked.

"I'm thinking," he said without looking away from the mirror.

"What about?"

"Things," is the best he could tell me.

It was day's end when the foreman talked to me about him as we signed off at the ward yard office, turned in our shovels. "What's up with your pal there?" he whispered to me.

"Nothing," I said.

"You're welcome back if you want work tomorrow, just don't tag him along, he don't work worth squat."

Never again, never again, I told myself as I walked him back home through the cold, the early dark of winter already descending on us. I walked him to his front porch. "See you, Lar," I had to say before he seemed to understand he should go in. He walked to his door, went in without saying good-bye. *Never again,* I vowed.

"So did you make a pile of money?" my mother asked me when I got home.

"It takes two weeks to get your checks," I said. And I said, "I like to froze to death," and, "Graff's looney-tunes, I swear." She asked me what I meant, exactly, and I tried to tell her.

Even as I went to sleep that night, huddled under a quilt, I did not feel truly warm. I shivered into sleep, telling myself over and over that I would have nothing to do with an insane person, ever again. Over and over, I imagined myself grabbing him, as his mother had, shaking him into sense, hitting him with my fists until he stopped whatever he was doing, ceased being whatever he was, until he agreed to be himself, normal, sane. I would have cheerfully beaten him within an inch of his life, after that day, to make him the Larry Graff I knew once.

It is only as we approach the ends of our lives that we appreciate how swiftly they have passed, how little we have retained of our experience, how great have been the effects of coincidence, luck, and accident in creating the directions, the purposes, the meanings—if any—we have followed and served and embodied.

I graduated college, found work that was secure, challenging, and promised to be lucrative. I met a woman, fell in love, married. The last Christmas before the birth of our first son, we traveled home to spend the holiday with my mother; my distant father had died, a quick, easy death, an aneurysm stopping him as he slept, the previous spring. So it was a gloomy holiday, ritual without spirit, celebration without joy.

"You'll never believe who I saw the other day, just a week ago it was," my mother said.

"Who would that be?"

"Larry Graff," she said.

"You're kidding," I said, and, "I thought he was put away in the VA upstate."

"He may be," she said, "but it was either him or his twin I saw walking over by the college. I was stopped at a stoplight, so I had a good long look. He's got a beard, but I'll stake my life it was him. He dresses like a hobo."

"Who's this?" my wife asked.

"A ghost out of my dim and distant past," I told her. And I told her something of what there was to tell, and the next morning I telephoned him, arranged to meet. I do not think I understood why at the time. It had something to do with the loss of my father, his absence so present in the house, something to do with our failed effort to make a true Christmas from the decorated tree, gifts, the small talk of times gone forever—we hoped, my mother and I, we might salvage something lasting.

"You're going to *what?*" my wife said.

"Shoot some baskets," I said. "He says the hoop is still up in the alley behind his house. He invited me to come over and play some horse."

"It's freezing out," my mother said.

"What's *horse?*" my wife said.

"A game," I told her, "we played when we were kids."

"You play it outside? In this weather?" she said, looking at me as if I had taken leave of my faculties.

"Sometimes you don't show the sense God gave geese," my mother said, her voice kindly, indulgent, loving.

If anyone on Larry Graff's block looked out their rear windows, what must they have thought? Two grown men bounced a basketball on the alley's frozen snowpack surface, lofted inept shots at the bare iron rim mounted on the backboard warped by more than a decade's weathers, set above the Graffs' double garage doors. Two grown men moved awkwardly, slipping and sliding, in a bitter wind. The ball rang like metal on the snowpack, clanged off the rim, thumped against the warped backboard. Our breath huffed in clouds as we labored to speak in the cold air that threatened to paralyze our lungs, tongues, lips. Our faces and ears burned with cold, our gloved fingers felt like sticks, our feet and toes wooden in the boots that made us stumble.

"O," I said when Larry missed the shot he had to match. "That's O on you, right?"

"I think so," he said. Instead of passing me the ball, he simply dropped it, stood looking at nothing in the air as I came to him, picked it up.

"So I thought you sort of stayed in the hospital permanent," I said.

"I get to come here sometimes," he said.

"Good behavior?"

"They just let me sometimes."

"So you must be doing better?"

"Sometimes," he said.

I tucked the ball under my arm, stood close to look him in the eye. "Larry," I said. And, "Do you mind it if I talk frankly? Can you possibly tell me what's happened here? Do you mind talking about it with me? Hey, say the word, I'll shut up, but I can't see this and not want to understand, okay?"

It was as if he looked at me, directly into my eyes, but did not see me. The only expression on his face was that very faint smirk, as if he heard a fair to middling joke pitched at some level beyond my hearing. "Larry?" I said.

"Is it my shot again?" he said, reached for the ball. It was my turn, but this game of horse in the dead of a fading winter afternoon was so preposterous, so absurd, it could not matter. I gave him the ball, he bounced it once, threw it toward the rim—underhanded, the way my wife would have if she ever tried. The ball fell short, bounced off the garage door, rolled away down the alley. I huddled against the cold, shuddered, watched him plod after it.

I was surprised my mother recognized him on the street. He wore a navy watch cap from which his hair extended like brown rags. The beard she spoke of was not a *beard,* something cultivated, shaped; he simply had not shaved for many, many days, the growth more a thick brown smudge flecked with premature gray. His jacket was too light for winter, his shapeless trousers too thin, his boots unevenly laced. He walked with a slight hunch, head down, the way a man might shuffle to an unpleasant, unavoidable task.

He picked up the ball, but did not turn, bring it back or pass it to me. He stood holding it, back to me. I waited as long as I could stand to.

"Larry!" I said, went to him, spoke to his back when he still did not turn around. "Larry. You know I'm married now? Do you know my dad died last spring? Do you know if somebody came up the alley, sees us, they'll think we've lost it," I said, instantly ashamed for saying that. "Is your memory clear?" I asked the back of his jacket. "Can you recall the way I do how we used to play one-on-one out here until it got too dark to see the bucket? Tell me if you remember anything, Larry," I said. When he did not speak, I touched his shoulder, turned him to me. His smirk still showed on his lips, but he would not speak.

"I have to go, Larry," I said. "I'm freezing my wazoo off. My wife's waiting for me at my mom's."

"You have to go," he said.

"Go on inside," I told him. "Don't stand out here and get frostbit. Take your ball with you, don't leave it out here. I'll see you whenever, okay, Larry?" I said. And he turned to enter his yard, so I felt sure he would go inside, get out of this cold.

"You were one hell of a ballplayer, Larry," I said to his back. "You were always better than me on my best day," I said.

He stopped, did turn to me, almost smiling fully, said, "I like playing basketball," turned away, crossed his yard to his backdoor, and I trudged home through the deepening dusk of that winter's late afternoon, chilled to the bone.

"How is Larry doing?" my mother said.

"That's the oddest thing I've ever seen you do," my wife said.

"He's gone," I told my mother. "He should be kept in the VA where he can't hurt himself. Jesus, he's gone," I said.

"What gets in your head to do a stunt like this?" my wife asked me.

I told her, "I'm not sure I could give you a coherent answer to that one."

I would so very much like to understand what I call my *successes* in life to be the result of my effort, discipline, and dedication. I think I worked hard at my career, made the best choices at key moments, that I fully deserved the rewards that came to me—money, property, rock-solid security. I would like to believe my family, wife and two sons, was a creation I conceived and nurtured out of love and devotion and loyalty, the logical and necessary product, to put it in strictly technical terms, of my desire and need. I would be very content if I truly believed all this.

But if I am at all honest, and I mean to be *honest* if I can, the whole of my life, of what others would surely call my *successes,* came to me in a chain of happy accidents, a run of luck that defied the odds for more than twenty years. I made money because everyone made money. I advanced my career by what was probably no more than an instinct that led me to attach my future to the right mentor. Yes, I was diligent, but so are most people; fruits, as it were, fell on me simply because I happened to stand under the right tree at the right time. If I loved my wife and sons, I suspect it was because they were my wife and sons; yes, I was a good husband and father, but so are most men—or at least they think they are, or want to be, or are thought so by others.

So the years passed. We made holiday and vacation visits to see my mother, and when she died we attended her funeral and buried her beside my father, and I did not visit the city of my birth for many years. Years passed, and then I traveled there, on the pretext of business, alone. I do not remember the precise excuse I made to my wife to justify this journey. I cannot bring to mind the words, now, adequate to make tangible the reason or reasons urging me to go back.

Something, I know or feared, was missing, and without it what I thought of as the shape and direction of my life would not declare itself to me. I was a happy man, or should have been; if I was not, I wanted to know why.

And so I found myself sitting at a small table in an upscale tavern a few blocks away from my boyhood home, drinking away a late autumn afternoon, watching the street through a large window, as if it were a screen on which I hoped some vision answering my need would momentarily appear.

There was little traffic on the street, and few pedestrians. I watched them, scrutinized, but of course they were as unknown, as alien to me as fellow travelers in an airport, the hordes of fans in a sports arena, the extras backgrounding feature actors in a movie. I do not doubt I was just as anonymous to the two or three who looked in the tavern window and saw me, staring, a rude man of that age no longer young, not yet *old,* well dressed and idle, nothing better to do than drink away a perfectly good day.

Then, across the street, Larry Graff materialized suddenly, and as suddenly I knew our recognition was mutual, a kind of miracle that we knew one another after so much time. He might have been what we call a *homeless* now, his hair a dirty, tangled scruff, wearing a half-buttoned filthy shirt, tattered sweatpants, his pale sockless feet in shower clogs. He had never needed eyeglasses, but I recognized him instantly behind the round metal-rimmed spectacles he wore, the sort I am sure institutions issue their patients. I touched my newly prescribed horn-rims, then waved.

He literally charged across the street. I saw, or thought I saw, a fanatic glint in his eyes behind those institutional eyeglasses, and he came so fast, charged, arms swinging, I was frightened. He burst open the tavern door, wheeled to face my window table, strode up close, his face almost touching mine as he leaned over me. I reached out, offered him my hand, dropped the other in my lap beneath the table's edge, balled it into a hard fist, afraid he meant for some insane reason to attack me.

"Hi, Larry," I said, half-rose to give myself leverage, tensed, if I had to strike at him.

But he said only, "Hi," and smiled a great face-wide grin exposing the hole where a tooth was lost, and sat at my table. "How are you?" he said.

"It's been years," I said, "a coon's age," and he continued to grin madly at me.

We did not have anything like a conversation, no coherent exchange; whatever devil or disease infected him had become so powerful, so rampant,

I could only listen, baffled, horrified, terrified. I held on to my drink, certain the waitress would come, insist he leave, that we both leave, and I waited and hoped for some excuse to arise allowing me to get up and go, flee.

"Hear that?" Larry said, cocking his head.

"Hear what?"

"That's a woman. She shouts so loud I hear her miles away," he said, and went on to tell me of the many voices that spoke to him, sometimes all at once, making it hard for him to distinguish them. There was that woman, he said, who shrieked, and an old man who swore in a language Larry had to translate, and a man who could cause him pain with specific words Larry would not repeat for fear of hurting me, and an infant who cried incessantly, a man improbably named Brewster Fitz who read aloud from magic books, another woman who only asked questions only Larry could answer correctly.

"Tell me something they say," I said. "Anything."

"They hurt!" he said. And he winced, skewed his face in pain, his body jerking in his chair as if stuck randomly with needles. "Oh!" he said, "that was a really good one! That *really* hurt!"

"Talk to *me,* Larry," I said. "Are you out of the hospital permanent now? Tell me about your family. Are your folks still living? What's that brother of yours up to? Do you see any family now?" I said, and, "Where do you live now?" I could not reach him, could not break through the voices assaulting him with mine. I sat at the table with him, almost gagging on the sour reek rising off him like a mist, twitching sympathetically to his constant tics, his muted yelps, floundering after something rational in the garbled responses he made to the specters tormenting him.

"You know who I am!" I said. "Will you just listen to me? I have two boys, almost grown, you didn't know that, did you? I don't live here anymore," I said, "I live far away now. I own a big house, Larry. I make the big bucks now, would you believe it? Did you know my mom passed away?"

He did not seem to hear anything I said, and so I stopped, my own voice sounding as bizarre to me as his chorus must have to him, my words slurring into one another, a kind of hoarse moaning.

He continued his jerking and mumbling and grimacing. My drink went tepid in the glass, and when I understood he would not, could not stop, that I could not stop him, and that no waitress would come and tell us to leave, I stood up, unclenched my left hand's fist, tried to think of something to say, some good-bye that would not sound final.

"Aha!" he said, rocked in his chair, shook his head, teeth bared, "That's a hard one. That one was *so* hard!" I shook my head, blinked, as if I might make him disappear, and then I left, put money on the table and walked out the tavern door.

"God's mercy," I whispered to myself as I stood outside, and then I put my head down and marched away, past the tavern window without looking in, and I went back to my house in the city far away, to my wife and sons and my career that had proved so lucrative, as I had hoped, been sure it would. I was so certain I would never see him again.

I have given up wondering why I failed so miserably, so totally. I put all the right questions, but my answers all fell short. I could say the course of my disasters, personal and professional, describes a neat, almost mathematical downward curve, ever accelerating, but that is simplistic, fails to account for particulars. Nor does any specific instance over the several years after Larry and I met in that tavern suffice in itself. Events along the way are unfortunate, sad, pathetic, even traumatic, but the whole remains inexplicable, and I am not so arrogant as to call it tragic. It just happened.

A corporation acquired my corporation—it was not the first time, a commonplace of commerce—but this acquisition ended my lucrative career. I floundered for a time, did find another position, but that evaporated in a restructuring of some sort, and then I truly floundered, and then I was more or less unemployable, my age a handicap, and then it was clear I was what must be called a *failure*.

At about the same time, my sons left my house. One became a success, the other a failure, and then my failed son died as a result of his own stupidity, or perhaps of his failure. Of course I lost my fine large house, and—naturally, logically, it seems to me—my wife, who I loved and was sure loved me. She no longer loved me, so I lost her also.

This all happened very quickly, the process feeling like a fuzzy montage when I try to think about it. The end is clear enough. I was alone, and I had nothing, but I did not know why. And that is the hardest part; I think I would accept all this if I understood *why*, but I never get beyond that question, which is what makes it all so very hard to live with, even if there is not a lot of time left for living now.

It was very impractical, imprudent of me to travel home a last time, then upstate to the VA hospital to see Larry Graff. I could not afford the cost of the trip, yet I went, spent the money, took the time, a wholly irrational thing to do in my situation.

The VA hospital upstate is a large complex in a small town. It dominates the town with its multistory stone buildings, its broad green lawns that summer so at odds with the little town's cramped main street, its poor trailer parks and mean stores, the tacky motel where I took a room. There is a rattletrap shuttle for patients with day passes to visit the small town. The patients, in their blue pajamas, walk the main street, sit in the dingy taverns like an occupying army enjoying brief furloughs. I rode the shuttle with half a dozen of them, silent, vacant men of varied ages returning from their day passes. The driver told me which building to inquire at, which office to ask for permission to visit Larry Graff.

"He's permanent, I think," I said.

"Lots are, you can't tell from looking," the driver said, his voice loud, not caring what his other passengers heard.

I spoke with a receptionist, then with a clerk, then a program director, finally with a doctor who gave me permission to see Larry Graff. "You won't get much out of him," this doctor said after reviewing Larry's file. "And you're no relative of any stripe?" he asked.

"Just an old friend," I said. I asked if any of Larry's relatives visited him, but this doctor would not divulge that information. When I asked, he did say Larry would not ever again leave the institution grounds in any scenario the doctor could imagine. "So he's here for the duration?" I said, and this doctor said that was the most probable prognosis. Larry was routinely medicated, he told me, but it was nothing would affect his talking to me if he was in the mood. Larry's condition, he said, fluctuated more or less constantly.

A patient who did not speak a word to me escorted me to Larry's building, the complex like a huge resort, the guests in uniform blue sitting or strolling or only standing immobile. He led me to the building, to Larry's ward, to his bed area, where the best friend of my life sat on the edge of his bed. My escort pointed at him, turned and left us. There were only a few others on the ward, one fast asleep, another reading in bed, another at the far end watching a black-and-white television with no sound audible. They were all old men, as old as Larry, myself.

"Larry?" I said. He sat, his posture demure, hands folded in his lap, dressed in blue pajamas, slippers, a light bathrobe also blue. He did not look at me, eyes on his folded hands. "Larry, it's me," I said. His hair was cut close now, gone a stark, snowy white, a large bald spot glistening under the fluorescents. But he was clean shaven, and there was no odor about him, no smell except the vague antiseptic in the ward's air. "Larry, I've come to visit you. Can you hear me? Can you speak to me? Please say something to me, Larry!" I said.

But he only sat, hands in his lap, eyes fixed on them, statuelike. I did not stay very long. I kept asking him to speak, asked him how he liked living there, asked after his brother and sister. I tried to tell him a little about my life—my *failures*—even tried to explain it all as best I could, but I do not think he heard, do not think I made any sense, even to myself. "I *need* you to say something," I said, "anything!" And I realized I spoke too loud; the old man watching television without sound turned from the screen to look at me, the old man reading closed his book to watch—maybe I only imagined the old man sleeping stirred.

He—it—was a mystery without possible solution. So I left, knowing I would never see him again. What would be the point? He might as well have been dead already.

Now and again, despite my resolve, I still try, a little, to understand. I think about Larry Graff; I think about myself. Oh, I have tried to think of it all in the context of events beyond our lives—politics, wars, the economy, society, the world over the course of our lives. Of course that is useless, history no more than an uneven flow beginning before we existed, extending infinitely beyond our ends.

Larry may be dead, or may still live inside his insanity there in the upstate VA hospital. No matter. And when I am gone, sooner or later, what possible matter in that? I make every possible effort not to ponder this puzzle too much. Sometimes I succeed.

Return of the Boyceville Flash

What becomes of all the little boys
Who never say their prayers?
They're sleeping like a baby
On the Nickel over there.

—Tom Waits

PAFKO, SOBER LONG ENOUGH he'd stopped counting the days, wasn't sure what it was he was looking for when he checked out of his Chicago flop and thumbed up to Milwaukee. It was like he was in one of his dreams, doing and feeling like it was him in the dream, watching himself, but knowing it wasn't real because he knew he'd never really do what he was doing.

He just woke up when the flop rousted the residents, shaved standing under the spray in the gang shower like always, dressed in the Goodwill suit and shoes he must have bought to be ready for this, packed his personals in the airline bag he found in trash the day he worked day labor out at O'Hare, ate the flop breakfast, headed out on the el and the CTA bus to thumb the freeway north—as if something not him knew all the time where he was going even if he didn't have clue one why.

If it was like one of his dreams, then he woke up standing on the corner at Farwell and North, checking out what looked the same, what was changed, as confused as waking up from a bout on the skid, entirely blacked out. Like the times he came to on Greyhounds going places he'd never been, sleeping on tables in joints he could have swore he never entered, curled up cold and wet in a park once, still holding the jug put him to sleep, thinking at once about where the jug to start the day could be had.

He knew where he was, suddenly thought of Marino, who had the hook for a hand intimidated people to come across in the days when Pafko and Marino buddied, worked the two sides of any downtown street, scoring a dollar a block average each hustling the panhandle on shoppers—what in God's name, Pafko wondered, would have become of Marino after they split that time on the row in Minneapolis arguing over the one jug just enough to wake up one of them, not both?

Pafko shook his head, blinked his watery eyes. He knew where he was. There was Hooligan's, like always, where he'd cashed G.I. Bill checks, college days, where it was kicks to see the regulars start off on port wine with beer chasers at six in the A.M., world's largest bar and workingman's friend, supposed to be—except now there was neon advertising the east side's best pub food, and the brick was sandblasted clean. What the hell happened to Hooligan's?

And there was the Oriental, where he worked part-time, high school, set pins in the alleys downstairs, and there was the eastside branch library where he read his eyes out under the fluorescents when he was a kid. And there was Oriental Drugs where they hung out those high school days he ran with the Red Arrow Park boys—what must have become of the Red Arrow guys? Pafko wondered.

But there was a lot of new places, a travel agency, a Greek restaurant, *Olympia* and *Gyros* signs, employment agency—check it out for day labor, Pafko thought, maybe something clean with the Goodwill suit and shoes— Honda dealer where Heiser Ford used to be, office supply, a big restaurant, new, German, across from the Oriental, a lot of big glass windows bouncing the midmorning sun like needles into Pafko's eyes.

He pivoted away from the intersection to look up Farwell, check for Bette and Dad's, Champ's, the Murray Elbow Room where they'd give you the first shot in a water glass so your morning shakes didn't spill it. And there was Champ's, but Bette and Dad's and the Elbow Room gone, and Champ's bigger than he remembered, with a big sign, *Champ's,* all lighted up in the bright sunlight, and he knew he was going in, but like a dream Pafko he dreamed, without knowing what he was doing or why.

And there *he* was, Pafko, checking himself in one of the big glass windows on North Avenue, seeing if he looked okay. He thought he looked okay. *I look okay. Pretty much,* he figured. Naturally he needed a haircut, and the Goodwill suit was loose, which hid his sprung gut, and out of style, like the suits he wore when he sold all-risk auto insurance to beat the band, fast and fat days. The Goodwill shoes needed shined.

But it was his face, Pafko, and he looked pretty okay if he stood straight, took his hand out of his pocket, squared his shoulders. *Sober,* Pafko thought. With change and a few small bills in his pants he felt against his leg, and a hundred inside the sock inside each of his scuffed shoes. He should have popped for a topcoat—even if wasn't cold, it would have looked better. If anybody should ask, he'd come up with a story for the airline bag carrying his personals.

So he walked up to Champ's heavy glass and brushed metal doors, went in as if that's where he was headed from the minute he left the Chicago flop.

Pafko was blind for a second, Champ's cave-dark after the sharp daylight. It was like waking up on the skid again. His pupils eased open to show him Champ's. It wasn't at all like it was. It was *big!* The bar was as long as he remembered Hooligan's, tables with tablecloths with glass candleholders, candles burning, winking like stars in night sky, or streetlights when you squinted, half-gone, to clear your vision, and big booths, leather upholstery, brass nail-heads, some Muzak music or maybe FM sounding like it came out of the walls with the faint recessed lighting, Tiffany lamps over the tables and booths, big green plants in planters, and everywhere Packers and Brewers and Bucks pennants, and framed photographs and what looked like cartoon drawings and newspaper headlines, all framed and hung on the long wall in this huge Champ's he didn't recognize. Monster TV screens turned on showing sports shows with no sound on.

A waitress in a get-up showing leg and cleavage, good-smelling perfume like a cloud around her, came up to him with an oversize menu in her hands, frozen smile on her face, too-red lips pulled back over too-white teeth, a certified stunner. She said, "Can I get you a table?"

"Bar," Pafko said. His croak of a voice always surprised him. He stepped around her and walked to the long bar of the enormous Champ's that wasn't what it was any more.

If he'd ever sat at a posher bar, it was so long ago—a dozen, fifteen years?—Pafko couldn't remember it. He set the airline bag of personals down beside a stool. It was such a long bar, the stool he took a padded captain's chair that swiveled without making any noise, a carpeted shelf for his feet in the Goodwill shoes, a padded leatherette rail for his forearms and elbows, the bar top like black slate reflecting no light. And the back bar. Bottles with chrome spouts rising on tinted glass tiers, like organ pipes, filled with every color. The booze glowed softly, seemed to pulse—red, blue, green, orange, gold, yellow, vodkas and gins pure clear as spring water, every shade of brown and tan—labels Pafko couldn't quite read in the dimness, like languages he couldn't read, never heard. Over his head, glassware in all possible shapes hung by their stems from dark wooden racks. To his right, the handles of half a dozen beer taps rose like ceramic statues.

He wanted to say something, knew his dry mouth wouldn't speak, tried to swallow, but there was nothing in his cracked, hot throat to go down. He found his reflection in a space of mirror over the register that looked like a computer rig, knew it was his face looking back at him, as strange to him as if it was someone he dreamed or met somewhere on the skid.

He forced himself to look away, find the waitress with all the leg and cleavage, find customers to check out—there was a man, business suit, head down over a drink, so far down the bar he was almost a shadow in shadows. Swiveling his stool-chair, he found a couple in a booth beyond the tables, man and woman, dressed-up looking, leaning toward each other so far their heads nearly touched, whispering or silent, or if they spoke their voices lost in the Muzak music oozing out of the long wall.

Pafko swung himself back around, and in that moment the bartender—gleaming white shirt, black colonel's tie, red vest silver-buttoned, frilly garters on his sleeves to keep his cuffs dry, was there facing him, like he'd popped up out of a secret trapdoor. "Pick your poison," the bartender said, laying a napkin that said *Champ's* in big letters on the bar.

Pafko thought it was Old Man Champion, but bigger, fatter than he remembered him, which was impossible—Old Man Champion had to be dead, long ago . . . if this was Old Man Champion he had to be maybe ninety years old now. But it *was* Old Man Champion, the big head of meringue-white hair, bushy eyebrows, walrus mustache, waiting for him to order up, tapping the bar top with his sausage fingers, a heavy gold ring with a big stone on one pinky.

"Mr. Champion?" Pafko said to what could be a ghost or the real, impossible Old Man Champion. He was surprised he could speak through his dry, hard lips.

"Make it *Champ*. We're just folks, unless you're here with a summons for me," the possible ghost said, smiled, cocked his head like a big fat old owl. Then Pafko knew it was Jimmy Champion grown old as Pafko, fatter than his old man had been, almost the carbon of his old man.

"Jimmy," Pafko said, and, "I'm guessing you don't recognize me. It's been some years," he said. He took a deep breath, pulled himself up straight in his stool-chair, squared his shoulders, shot a look at the space of back bar mirror to see if he looked okay. *Mostly okay.* Jimmy Champion! Jimmy Champion squinted at him.

"Pafko," Pafko said. "Thaddeus. Teddy." When Jimmy Champion said nothing, he said, "Pafko." There was just a second that felt longer to him, while he waited and hoped and prayed all at once that Jimmy Champion would remember him from way back then.

"You scared me," Pafko said, and, "I thought you were your old man, you're the exact carbon almost exactly," he said. And then Jimmy Champion recognized him, remembered.

"Pafko!" he said, smiled big, put out his big fat hand with the pinky ring, took Pafko's, squeezed hard, laughed a big laugh the carbon of his old man's. He said, "Pafko for the Christ's sakes!" And he said, "How in the holy hell long's it been? Am I hallucinating or you're actually sitting there after how many goddamn years, a coon's age!"

"A whole lot. I can't exactly recall, time flies so fast," Pafko said.

Jimmy Champion slapped the bar, the smack sound so loud the business suit far down the bar startled, looked up from his drink at them like somebody goosed him. "I will be dipped in shit, this calls for libations!" he said. "I am pleased to have the first of the day in your honor," he said. "Name it, I got it or can get it, auld lang syne," he said.

For just a second, Pafko, grinning like his face would split, for just the smallest second, like a window slid open to light up a dark, empty room, only that long, Pafko thought to ask for a double-on-a-double with a chaser maybe. But the window slid shut—he wasn't positive why—he knew who he was, so said, "Maybe a diet soda, or even a coffee black. It's early in the day for me at my age now."

"Oh, never too early, Teddy," Jimmy Champion said. He poured himself a stiff Wild Turkey over an ice cube in a rock glass, called the waitress with leg and cleavage who smelled so good to bring a black coffee. "I know this character since who laid the Chunk," he said to her when she brought the coffee. "You believe this character took me for my old man, God rest his soul, left us, what, sixteen years ago if it's a day?" he asked her. And he laughed the carbon big laugh of his deceased old man, said, "Bumps!" as he raised his glass, tossed off a good half of his Wild Turkey.

Pafko raised the steaming cup to him. "Back at you," he said, sipped, tried to find some taste, flavor in it that would do, and then they talked.

"So what brings you to our fair city after all this time?" Jimmy Champion said.

"Sort of business or pleasure, some of both," Pafko said. He didn't know where the words came from, didn't have a clue to the answer to the question. He said, "I flew in on kind of a whim's what it was," and suddenly thought of the guy who picked him up in a Toyota on the interstate—the guy was about Pafko's age, a talker, the smell of peppermint, some kind of cologne, or maybe a lozenge he sucked to cover his breath. Pafko figured he was maybe half in the bag, a talker, was tempted to ask him if he kept a pint in the glove compartment or under the driver's seat. But didn't for fear it was true, the guy'd offer him a pull.

"And you're still the big insurance mogul I suppose," Jimmy Champion said. When he poured himself another Wild Turkey, held the bottle out to Pafko, Pafko shook his head.

"It fed the bulldog and then some," Pafko said. Jimmy Champion had to go down the bar, serve two more suits who bellied up, talking loud. Pafko swiveled his stool-chair, saw Champ's was steadily filling with suits, a few women, all dressed for offices, talkers and laughers, some carrying briefcases, styled hair, a lot of rings and big gold wristwatches, some gold chains. They ordered up from the bar, and now there were two more waitresses with the leg and cleavage gal, and they came and went from the rail with trays of drinks—martinis and wine coolers and wine, foaming beers in tall pilsner glasses. And Jimmy Champion was joined by another bartender, kid with a matching red vest, sleeve garters, and now the Muzak music stopped or was covered by the voice babble, and there was sound from the monster TV screens' show now. Pafko's coffee was tepid on his tongue, tasted metallic.

He was in Champ's, but it wasn't Champ's. Where was *Champ's* from back then? Two decades? He closed his eyes, concentrated, brought up Champs—no tables, just booths and the bar, scarred with cigarette burns, an electric shuffleboard, bumper pool, cigarette machine that worked with a plunger you pulled, Old Man Champion ready to shake the dice cup for a round anytime. The regulars.

The regulars. The old Greek coot, Tsoris, smoking a pipe smelled so bad Pafko kidded he'd take it away, throw it in the commode in the men's. Knees Gazapian, always off on how his bad knees kept him from a career in pro football, which everyone knew was bullshit, and Wheezy O'Brien with *Let Me Tickle You* stitched on the back of his windbreaker, big metal taps on his heels so you heard him a block away. The Neery brothers, all five in their construction-job work clothes. Old-timers and young bucks like Pafko, living it up, the good times after they outgrew running with their gangs— Red Arrow Park, the Dago Regiment, Polack Eagles, Fighting Irish, all that behind them because they were *men* then, living it up in Champ's together, charged up on all the energy was going to explode them into futures they couldn't see but knew were waiting, all of them!

"You about ready there?" Jimmy Champion said, pointed at his coffee cup, nodded toward the tiers of bottles on the back bar. Pafko wondered if he saw him sitting with his eyes closed—did he look okay? Now he stared back at Jimmy Champion, Champ's full of people, suits and dressy women, talking, drinking, eating, laughing, silverware clanking on plates, the long bar's stool-chairs almost all occupied. Were people keeping their distance from him at the bar? Maybe he didn't look okay?

"Not just yet," Pafko said, and, "Maybe a diet soda?" And he said, "You do a land office lunch trade, Jimmy," when Jimmy Champion looked funny at him before he filled a glass with Diet Coke from a hissing nozzle on the end of a thin hose.

"Can't complain," Jimmy Champion said. Pafko checked his eyes—oh yes, Jimmy Champion had *his* buzz. Pafko knew the look in the eyes, the sure sound of it in a voice.

"It's all changed," Pafko said. "So big."

"Years ago," Jimmy Champion said. "I bought out the whole building after my old man passed."

"Bette and Dad's?" Pafko asked. "The Elbow Room?"

"They went when the leases ran out. We tore out the walls, did it all over. We're three times the size," he said.

"I don't recognize anybody," Pafko said.

"You wouldn't hardly. You been gone too long, Teddy. The whole east side's changed. We're Yuppieville. Strictly upscale high-rent."

"Really," Pafko said.

"I shit you not," Jimmy Champion said. "You got to go with the flows. The jigs crowded out west and north from the ghetto, so people moved east if they didn't go to the burbs to hell and gone. A lot of refurbishment construction and all since your time, Teddy."

"That's sort of sad," Pafko said.

"You don't catch me complaining," Jimmy said. He said, "Far be it from me to brag on myself, but I'd be embarrassed to tell you my gross." And he said, "So you won't join me in a libation now?" Pafko looked straight at him, into his slightly buzzed eyes, shook his head, picked up his soda, and Jimmy Champion went off down the bar to help his assistant with the drink orders coming and going from the rail with the waitresses. Instead of closing his eyes, Pafko looked at his reflection in the mirror space.

Champ's lunch trade thinned out. He heard the clatter of glassware dumped in the bar sinks, sunlight coming on, shutting off as suits and their dressy women left for their offices or wherever, costumed waitresses passing money and credit cards over the bar to Jimmy Champion, the digital register flashing red numbers in the corner of Pafko's eye. Old Man Champion had a big bronze register that rang loud when the drawer shot open, raised numbers behind a window, made a steely grating noise when the drawer snapped shut.

What became of everybody? Knees Gazapian, Wheezy O'Brien, the Neery boys, the codger Tsoris, The Polacks, Chinski and Kenny Lewandowski who legally changed his name to Lane so he wouldn't be Polack to anybody didn't know him from when. The Dago Regiment, Frank and Angelo Valenti, Tony Vitucci, and the tough little wop Pafko fought in his only real fight ever for Red Arrow Park, Tommy Cincotta. *Where? What?*

"Got one with your name on it," Jimmy Champion said, there in front of him with the Wild Turkey bottle in his big fat fist.

"Give me a pass on that for a little yet," Pafko said, and, "I need to visit your men's, coffee and soda on an empty stomach." He got down out of his stool-chair, moved in the direction Jimmy Champion pointed with the Wild Turkey bottle. Was Jimmy Champion giving him a fish-eye?

Champ's men's room was back in the far darkest end of the room, around a corner where the long wall broke into the kitchen doors. He passed the leg and cleavage waitress, who gave him a funny look too. I probably don't look so good, Pafko thought.

He couldn't remember the last time he'd used a men's as nice, clean, as Champ's. It glistened, smelled sweetly of air freshener, white hand towels on rollers, fake marble sinks, a big mirror with a bluish cast in it. He checked himself out—he didn't look so good. Washing and drying his hands—pink liquid soap smelling like flowers—he had a little spell of the shakes, almost ducked into one of the commode stalls to wait it out, but the shakes went away for some reason, so he splashed his face, dried, combed his hair with his fingers because if he had a comb it was back at the bar in his airline bag of personals.

Jimmy Champion was waiting for him. "So," he said when Pafko was seated in his stool-chair.

"So," Pafko said. When Jimmy didn't speak, he said, "This is your down time now, I figure." Champ's was empty, the TV sound off, Muzak music back up.

"Until Attitude Adjustment Hour," Jimmy said, "which comes pretty early for us here. We offer a Double Bubble from three o'clock right on to seven brings them, and then it's dinner shift and late-nighters to who laid the Chunk."

"So," Pafko said again.

"So," is all Jimmy said. Pafko searched for something to talk about.

"I meant to ask, Jimmy," he said at last, "if you're married and all. I didn't recall you marrying before I left town."

"Thrice," Jimmy Champion said, holding up three fingers, half-smiling under his walrus mustache. "Four if you'd count my current arrangement, but we didn't formalize it. You'll meet her if you hang around, she comes in during the dinner hours, we always eat supper together," he said.

"You got kids? Children?" Pafko said.

"Also three, by two separate mothers," he said. "You?" Jimmy Champion asked. Pafko had a second afraid the shakes were coming back, but they didn't. "I remember it you were married pretty young, the big tall looker we called Legs, some of us," Jimmy said.

"Just the once," he said, trying to remember any of it. "And only two kids, they're grown. I have to tell you I'm very out of touch for some time in that department, Jimmy."

"Happens in the best of families," Jimmy said, and he said, "Speaking of which, you still have people in Milwaukee?"

"Again very out of touch," Pafko said. Then he asked for another diet soda to keep from having to talk or think about his former wife and two children, about his sister who for all he knew still lived in the neighborhood, her family, any living or dead relatives.

"So where you been in your life, Pafko?" Jimmy Champion said. "I mean, I recall your going to the college for a while, and then the story was you made big bucks hustling high-risk insurance to jigs or whoever?"

"I had my own company, actually incorporated," Pafko said, but could not remember its name.

"Then you took off somewheres?"

"I sold out for a good position in Kansas City." Pafko remembered Kansas City for just an instant. "That soured, pretty much everything soured, so I went a lot of places after that." He remembered Chicago, Oklahoma City, Chicago again, Minneapolis. He remembered on the skid with Marino. Chicago again—then he went blank until he was in Chicago, a fourth time at least, day labor and drying out for no reason he could figure, the flop he left that morning without knowing why, thumbing north.

"If you don't mind me inquiring," Jimmy Champion said, "are you all right? I mean, you're trembling there." Pafko put both hands on his soda glass.

"I don't know," he said. "I think I was probably feeling nostalgia or something for the old days before—"

"Before what?" Jimmy said, but Pafko talked through it.

"—I was just living my life without thinking about it, if you get me. For instance I'm trying to remember people from when we were all young bucks, you and me and everybody, Jimmy."

"To be frank, you're sounding on the strange side, Pafko," Jimmy said.

"For instance," he said, "what became of all the guys from the gangs we ran with those days?"

"*Gangs?*" Jimmy Champion said. "If you think you guys were *gangs,* you got another think coming! Read a newspaper. See the TV. Now we got *gangs,* jigs, they sell dope and shoot the shit out of each other over the business."

"Red Arrow Park," Pafko said. "The Dago Regiment, Polack Eagles." Jimmy laughed.

"And maybe you forget I didn't have time for that horsing around, my old man had me at work here all the time."

"I do just now remember that," he said. "But can you tell me what became of those guys? Knees Gazapian, the Valenti brothers, Polack Kenny Lane?"

"Sweet jumping Jesus!" Jimmy Champion said. He said, "Gazapian was the big jock, last I ever knew he was coaching football at some high school or junior high in the burbs. I think he was the only one besides you went off to the college to get higher educated. Valenti—Angelo, not Vince," he said, "got a bar over on Brady, has rock and roll bands in to play weekends."

"Chinski?"

"*Him* I remember, the horny sucker, anything hot and hollow, from the cat's ass to a stovepipe! Search me on where in hell's half-acre that one got to," Jimmy said.

"Can you remember them? Can you remember us?" Pafko said.

"You need something to steady yourself there, Pafko," he said. And, "Why would I have occasion to think about ancient history, for the Christ's sakes?"

He waited for an answer while Pafko tried to come up with one, until Pafko said, "I don't know." Jimmy laughed a laugh that was more a snort, turned and walked away down the bar, leaving him alone gripping his soda glass with both hands. It could have been a spell of shakes coming on, but wasn't.

Pafko sat alone at Champ's bar for what seemed like a long time, but couldn't be sure. He had no sense of time, what a minute or an hour felt like, no sense of how many years, exactly, he'd been gone from this city, not counting the times he and Marino passed through on the skid. He closed his eyes, concentrated. *Why? What?* he asked himself.

No clue about how long he sat alone at Champ's bar, Pafko flinched when Jimmy Champion spoke, standing in front of him. He said, "You talking to yourself there, are you, Pafko?"

"Jimmy," Pafko said. He said, "I think my thoughts wander sometimes."

"Get you something to drink?" Jimmy said.

"For the moment, no," he said. And he said, "Something just came to mind here. Jimmy, you remember how we all had nicknames back then? It just came to me, everybody I can remember had a name we gave them, right?"

"So?" Jimmy Champion said.

"Like," Pafko said, "Knees was Knees Gazapian because he hurt his knees playing football, Wheezy O'Brien because of the asthma, Kenny Lane Polack for changing his name, even my wife I married, you referred to her as Legs for how tall she was," he said.

"Why are you talking so loud?" Jimmy said.

Pafko said, "We all had personal names, you remember?"

"I remember," Jimmy said, "for what it's worth," and, "You guys, you and your pals, called me Widesides because of overweight I couldn't help."

"*Widesides!*" Pafko said. "I remember that! We called you Jimmy Widesides!"

"I came by my bulk by hereditary, from the old man. That was hurtful to me when I was a kid, Pafko. I thought I'd forgot all that crap until just this minute," he said.

"We didn't mean hurt by it," Pafko said. "Everybody had a name for something personal is what it was, see? Remember mine, Jimmy? I can remember my nickname clear as anything, but see, that's almost all I can remember!"

"You're shouting, Pafko. Simmer down," Jimmy Champion said. Pafko swiveled, saw the leg and cleavage gal, the assistant bartender, an old guy wearing cook's whites had all come out of the kitchen, staring at him.

"What was my nickname, Jimmy? Can you remember it?" he said quickly, trying to lower his voice. But he wasn't sure how loud he was. He felt like a shaking spell was coming, wanted whatever he needed to be said before shakes hit him. He looked to Jimmy for an answer, but Jimmy said nothing, shook his head like there was a mess he had to clean up, made a clucking sound with his tongue.

"The Boyceville Flash," Pafko said.

"The which?" Jimmy said.

"The Boyceville Flash. After *Andy* Pafko, played outfield for the Braves when they won the Series? Because he was originally from Boyceville. Upstate, remember? Andy Pafko. He was with the Cubs before they traded him here. Remember?" He heard the waitress laugh.

"I suggest you take yourself out of here, Pafko," Jimmy Champion said. He said, "You don't fit quite so good here, Happy Hour's soon, my lot out back's going to fill with Broncos and Beemers, so you better take a hike, okay? I'm sorry, Pafko." Pafko very carefully got down out of his stool-chair, careful not to slip, fall.

"Tell me, Jimmy," he said, groping at his feet for his airline bag of personals, "can you remember me? Could you possibly tell me anything about who I was, what sort of a person I was, Jimmy?"

"I begin to think you're pure stone cracked," Jimmy Champion said. Pafko heard the waitress and the assistant bartender and the cook laughing back somewhere by the kitchen doors.

"It's possible," Pafko said, "or even possibly my brain's wet for all I know, I sometimes don't remember the least thing, don't know the time of day, but I could be satisfied with anything you might tell me about anything, Jimmy."

"Don't," Jimmy Champion said, "make me to come out from behind this bar and escort you physically, Pafko."

Pafko tried to stand straight, held his personals bag with both hands to keep off shakes. He looked at Jimmy Champion, who folded his big arms across his fat chest, at the tiers of bottles rising behind him, glowing, like an organ in a church.

He knew if he just concentrated, ordered up, put money on the bar, he'd be okay. Everything would come easy and clear as always if he just ordered up, asked for Champ's Double Bubble. "You hearing me?" Jimmy Champion said.

Pafko nodded. Before he turned and walked out the door of Champ's, he said, "You were Jimmy Widesides. I was The Boyceville Flash. I'm certain." Going out the door, he heard some words: *bizarre, fucking seedy nutso.*

Outside, eyes squinted and tearing in the hard sunlight, he stood still until he was sure of his balance. He hefted the airline bag, breathed deep, concentrated, remembered the change and small bills in his pants pocket, the hundred pressed against the sole of each foot inside his Goodwill shoes.

Then Pafko started walking. He lacked a clue as to where, any clue as to any point in being where he was. If nothing else, Jimmy Champion—*Widesides Jimmy!*—would make a bar story out of him, tell it to his eastside Yuppie trade, make a joke out of Pafko who was The Boyceville Flash, however long ago that was.

Saint Philomena, Pray for Us

Yea, though I walk through
the valley of the shadow of
death . . .

—Psalm 23

MORE THAN FORTY YEARS ago, the sudden death of Kevin O'Leary, my student, made me remember Saint Philomena, patron of dentists.

When I was sixteen, my mother remembered I had not seen a dentist since I lost some baby teeth. "Why should I go to a dentist, I brush," I said.

"I have an appointment for you at Marquette," she said.

"Marquette? The college?"

"The university dental clinic," she said, "you get your work done by students studying to be dentists."

"Why can't I go to a regular dentist? Besides, it's Catholic and we're not Catholics."

"And I'm also not made of money," my mother said.

So I began a regimen of treatment—prophylaxis, X-rays, a dozen serious cavities drilled and filled, one difficult extraction, two gold crowns—lasting nearly a year, a cycle of boredom and pain, the whole of it marked in my memory by the image of Saint Philomena. I think of it, now, as a year spent in exile, my innocent, unruly, resistant then-self banished intermittently to dwell among hostile and exotic aliens, the Jesuits who walked the campus in their black suits and dog collars, the dental students and instructors in white smocks—instructors identified by a red shoulder-tab—the motley community of destitute and semidestitute patients I joined.

But where I truly lived in these periodic exiles was in the casual torture of pick, chisel, drill, extractor, the brief respite of only occasional novocaine.

Ascending a staircase, past the mural-size portrait of Saint Philomena on its landing, to the waiting room, I checked in at a window like a bank teller's, showed my card, took a seat on one of the long wooden benches as inhospitable as church pews. I avoided all eye contact. We were a shabby crew of unfortunates: Negroes, harried mothers and their crying or screeching children, some thin unshaven men clearly skid row winos.

Name called by a bored clerk, I rose, entered the clinic, a hall the size of a basketball court, row on row of dental chairs, the whir and whine and buzz of a hundred drills, a pervasive smell vaguely medicinal, faintly metallic, white smocks everywhere, walking briskly, bent over patients, gathered at the counter where materials were dispensed.

I found my assigned chair—two rows in, seven down—and greeted my assigned student. "Hi," I said, or, "Hey," or, "How you doing?" He never spoke to me; I suspect he did not like juveniles, wonder if he *liked* anybody. His name was Styron. *Styron* said the plastic badge over his smock's breast pocket. He nodded, gestured me into his chair, and after a cursory look at my X-rays and chart, set to work, set to the infliction of pain.

The pain—*pain!*—has dissolved over time into an amorphous mass, a kind of cloud over my otherwise quotidian teenagehood, one instance almost inseparable from another. The probing of Styron's needle-pointed pick, releasing mouthsful of warm, sweetish blood on my tongue, elides into the burn of the slow-speed drill he seldom lifted to allow it to cool, merges with the explosive jolt of nerve response stiffening my spine, rendering my muscles rigid, freezing the grip of my fingers on the chair's armrests, melds with the crack and crunch of his chisel deep in the shell of a tooth, transmogrifies into my throat's spasms, gagged on my saliva, is absorbed into the shock of chill water rinse bestowed without warning, the flood of cold air Styron squeezed from a rubber bulb to clear his view.

Perhaps the most intense was a sensitivity test. "We need a sensitivity test on that before you go bothering with an amalgam," the red-tabbed instructor told Styron. Styron wet a paper napkin, wrapped it around a metal baton, handed it to me to hold; from the baton, a thin cord ran to a black box with a dial set in its face; from the box ran another cord, ending in a wire he placed at the bottom of the cavity just drilled. He flipped a switch, the current ran through my nerve—the tooth was live, could be saved!—and I jerked in my chair like an executed criminal.

The only interruptions of these two- and three-hour sessions were instructors' inspections of each stage of the work, Styron's trips to get mercury and silver to blend fillings, returning with a receipt for my mother's money fished from my jeans pocket, and the random breaks he took, rare occasions for speaking to me. "I got to step out a sec," he said, left, returned to resume, breath rank with his just-finished cigarette.

Such talking as he did was confined to his friend and fellow-student working the next chair; I never learned his name. "So how many inlays you done now?" Styron might ask him. Five, or ten, a dozen, his friend might reply. "Just shows what a fucking prick you are," Styron would say, or, "You must be as lucky as you're ugly, huh?" or, "Beats the living shit out of me." They spoke frequently of their various instructors, Styron calling them pricks, turds, bastards, sons of bitches, ass-faces.

This year's regimen, I am convinced, left me the physical coward I have been throughout the rest of my life.

The day's appointment done, I walked out of the clinic, through the waiting room, always nearly full with the destitute and near-destitute, all awaiting *their* pain and boredom, down the flight of stairs, past the portrait of Saint Philomena.

She was depicted, in full color, on her knees, hands folded in prayer, a yellow halo like a dinner plate surrounding her head, her large eyes turned upward in ecstatic search of the deliverance she presumably had no doubt of. Her bloody mouth, lips collapsed inward, was stark against her dead-white skin. Arrayed about her on the ground were all her teeth, torn from her jaws with pincers wielded by Moors before they martyred her by fire. This was in north Africa, in the fifth century A.D.

Coming up those stairs to my appointments with Styron, this picture terrified me with its promise of torment, but, descending, I could confront her with something like smugness; I had not died, nor was I likely to—at least not under Styron's indifferently harsh hand.

My family was nominally Protestant, most tenuously Lutheran. Approaching Christmas, my mother topped our tree with an angel, arrayed a hand-painted crèche at its base among the wrapped gifts. On Christmas Eve, she took me to midnight services. "Do I have to?" I complained.

"It won't hurt you," she said, "and it might even do you some good."

I asked my father, also compelled to go, "Do you believe in religion?"

"It's alright to believe so long as you don't get all fanatic about it," he said. He wore a Masonic ring, but I never knew him to attend any lodge. He loved to laugh at Oral Roberts, then a Pentecostal working out of tents in Oklahoma, calling on viewers to place their hands on their television sets to receive his healing. "Get a load of this!" he shouted. I laughed with him; my mother tried to smile. I once watched him behave with great rudeness to a Jehovah's Witness who came to our door with her small son, offering *Awake!* and *The Watchtower* for only a quarter.

When my mother insisted I enroll in a confirmation class, I appealed to him. He shook his head in sympathetic disgust, said, "Grin and bear it if it makes her happy, okay?" When I dropped out of the class, conducted by an icy-dour pastor with rimless spectacles who required the memorization of impossibly numerous scriptures quoted in Luther's small catechism, however, he stood with me against my mother's disappointed anger. "She'll get over it," he advised me.

When I once asked him to explain Freemasonry to me, he told me about Hiram Abiff and the building of the temple, said, "It's sort of like a religion. You follow it, it kind of takes the place of a religion. You can make a lot of contacts," he said.

Whenever I brought my mother to the edge of her patience, to the verge of tears, she exclaimed, "Jesus H. Wept!"

When my father died, I was surprised to find he had asked for a Masonic funeral in his will; I remember the strangers wearing their stylized carpentry aprons who presided at the ceremony, but cannot recall anything they said.

When my mother died, a Lutheran minister who never met her delivered a eulogy derived from things I told him of her life.

I have not set foot inside any church for nearly half a century. I have only recently begun to think so often about Saint Philomena.

Educated entirely at tax-supported institutions of higher learning, I was hired to teach at Saint Bernardine College, run by Franciscan friars. I was only mildly apprehensive. The dean who offered me the position, Father Brian, sprawled in his swivel chair; I remember feeling a momentary fear he might expose a thigh or worse as he shifted, crossed and uncrossed his bare legs, adjusting his robe, beads at his waist clicking. He did ask if I feared being proselytized, assured me nothing of the sort would happen—the truth, for nothing of the sort did. I told him I had no such fear, no feeling one way or the other concerning his religion; I lied.

I enjoyed teaching at Saint Bernardine's. My students, all male, mostly of Irish, Italian, and Polish descent, ninety-seven percent Catholic, were eager, diligent, and docile, dedicated to their education as a certain vehicle upward from their blue-collar origins. I exulted in the breaks in my schedule their mandatory retreats and feast days dotting the semester's calendar gave me.

My first class informed me it was custom to begin and end each session with prayer. I told them, I hope without sneering, that, while I could not, would not participate, I would appoint a class chaplain to conduct the exercise, would stand by, look out the window at the manifest of each season expressed in the beautiful campus grounds.

I soon grew used to the crucifix in each classroom, learned to ignore the initials—*JMJ,* for Jesus, Mary, and Joseph—they jotted in the corners of writing assignments submitted to me. The opening and closing prayers became a kind of bracket to each meeting. "Saint Francis," my designated chaplain would lead, or, "Saint Dismas," or, "Saint Bernardine"—the choice was the student chaplain's—"pray for us, now and in the hour of our deaths," they choof before the amen and genuflection.

I admired some of my Franciscan colleagues. Father Capistran pursued serious secular philosophy, had a bishop's dispensation to read books on the Index. I disliked some. Father Amadeus was a rabid anti-Communist, his doctorate in history from Franco's Madrid, organizer of the Cardinal Mindzenty Club chapter. Father Giles had been Goering's confessor at Nurenberg. Father Cyprian confessed John F. Kennedy aboard PT-109. Father Peter confessed the wife of the state governor's director of taxation, so could retail reliable insider political gossip.

Several of my colleagues, I later learned, reverted to their given names, a few resigned their vocations, and at least one married in the aftermath of John XXIII's Vatican II.

In my third and final year on the faculty of Saint Bernardine College, I appointed Kevin O'Leary chaplain of one of my freshman composition classes.

What can I trace to my childhood? Bits and pieces:

My friend Ronnie Makowski's parents invited me to eat supper with them. In their dining room hung a cheap depiction of the Sacred Heart. His parents talked, Ronnie talked; I ate my meat loaf and mashed potatoes in silence, fascinated by the garish reds and golds, the heavy metal frame above Mr. Makowski's head. Sometime after Palm Sunday, a yellowing frond was tucked behind the frame to stiffen and wither. I of course did not dare ask what all this was, what it might mean. Asked perfunctory questions, I replied politely, as I had been taught by my parents—to question another's religion, I understood, was as rude as staring at a blind man and his dog, or at a cripple's limp or crutches.

We—my nominally Protestant friends and I—called Catholics *mackerel snappers* for the fish they ate on Fridays. Ash Wednesdays, they came to school with smeared foreheads they were forbidden to wash. Questioned, they joked, said they were angels with dirty faces.

Swimming at our neighborhood's municipal pool with my friend Ronnie Makowski, I saw the scapular he wore on a thick string around his neck. "What's that?" I said.

"A scapular," he said. When we played basketball, Ronnie Makowski crossed himself before shooting free throws. This was fashionable for some years, but long ago disappeared from the game.

When the husband of our seventh-grade teacher, Mrs. Lillian Leet, died suddenly, Ronnie Makowski brought her a prayer card when she returned to our classroom after the funeral and a short period of mourning.

On his birthday, Ronnie Makowski treated me to a movie matinee; I do not remember what movie we saw. He reached in his pocket for his money, withdrew it, his rosary caught on his fingers, clattered to the pavement in front of the ticket window. He picked it up, rolled it into a ball, stuffed it back in his pocket. Instead of asking him what it was, I thanked him again for treating me to the movie.

These bits and pieces come from scattered days, all before I saw the portrait of Saint Philomena.

Ronnie Makowski became a first-rate athlete. Marquette University gave him a football scholarship. Preparing for his first varsity season, he worked out in the university gym to get in playing shape. He was doing sit-ups, I read in the *Journal* sports section, when he suffered a heart attack, was found dead, stretched out on his back on the floor mat. The person who found him, the newspaper reported, thought at first he was asleep.

This happened three years after my dental work was complete, when Ronnie and I were no longer friends, when I had forgotten all about Saint Philomena and the pain inflicted by the student named Styron.

What is more contemptible than contemporary religion?

My father hooted at a sweaty Oral Roberts, then a Pentecostal holding revivals in circus tents, claiming to heal through television sets. I watched Oral Roberts, turned Methodist for respectability, emcee slick variety specials complete with Hollywood guest stars, hair-sprayed, attired in designer suits, claiming to have spoken to a giant apparition of Jesus, but could not transcend my disgust to laughter.

Cable channels bring us smarmy frauds—Bakker, Swaggert, the Crystal Cathedral, a host of blatant swindlers and pitchmen and women—*ad nauseam*. On prime time, the networks coddle the likes of Billy Graham, Jerry Falwell, and the reactionary pope from Poland.

What could be more contemptible?

I find some solace in their inevitable humiliations. Their sham universities and theme parks declare bankruptcy, they are compromised in sleazy motels, they are strangled in lawsuits. Or they simply fade, are forgotten, like aged rock musicians. Who remembers Bishop Sheen? Who mourns Ezra Taft Benson?

Ichabod! Jeremiah would cry—if there were a Jeremiah among us today. The Glory hath departed us.

And beneath contempt, unworthy of laughter, are the faceless ranks of the mock-pious, the dressed-in-Sunday-best crowding fast-food restaurants and sports bars after services scheduled to conclude in time for lunch. *Drunkard's Mass,* I heard my boyhood friend Ronnie Makowski call the late worship permitting Saturday's revelers to sleep off their hangovers.

Oh yes, there are those who feed the starving, shelter the battered, comfort the despised, march shoulder to shoulder with the outraged dispossessed. But this is politics, of no interest to me.

In the end, there is precious little to laugh at, scarce sufficient cause for righteous anger.

Kevin O'Leary.

Kevin O'Leary, class chaplain, led the prayer to open the semester's last meeting before final exam week. I do not remember which saint he called upon to be with him and his classmates, then and in the hour of their deaths.

I did not think it was a good class. I was ready for the semester to end, anticipating summer, so struggled, I think, to be enthusiastic, to inspire my students to enthusiasm. And they were tired of the semester, anticipated the coming summer. I do not remember why we should have been discussing poetry at this last class meeting. The poet was Emily Dickinson, the poem her "Because I could not stop for Death." My students sat, lethargic, indifferent, bored as I all but shouted the lines at them. I do not know why I should have cared so much to generate some response to this poem. There were only a few minutes left when I snapped my text shut and scolded them.

I said: "You think this has nothing to do with you. You think this is this quirky old maid nattering away at you, you could care less, right? Well, she's talking to you, and you should listen. You hear what she's saying? She's telling you Death is coming for all of us, and you can't stop it, and you don't know when it's coming, or how it's coming, but it's coming. Not you though, right? All you can think about is summer vacation, getting out of here, going home, what you're going to be doing tomorrow and the next day, this summer, you're all bound up in your own little lives, aren't you!"

My students did me the courtesy of pretending attention; I understood very clearly I was having no effect at all.

"You just *assume*," I told them, "you'll wake up every morning, the way you assume the sun's coming up, right? So you care less about Miss Emily's little poem here, right? Well," I said, "you shouldn't." And when there was no flicker of response to this, I looked at my watch, saw we were only a minute from the bell, said, "Shut us down one last time, Kevin."

Kevin O'Leary stood, led the closing prayer while I stared out the window at the greening, blossoming late spring of Saint Bernardine's campus, tired, momentarily disappointed in my students and myself, glad the semester was over.

Which saint did Kevin O'Leary call upon to be with him and his classmates, then and in the hour of their deaths? I cannot recall.

They come to me in a rush, a torrent, an illogical, incoherent flow:
Scapulars and prayer cards, rosaries and ashes smeared on foreheads; bleeding hearts and crucifixes and holy candles and holy water, counterfeit relics; the eyes of statues weep; the hands and feet of celebrated priests and nuns ooze blood at Easter and Christmas; trees and windows and clouds and even vegetable roots exhibit the likeness of Jesus or Mary; plastic Christophers are mounted on dashboards; *love offerings* shamelessly hawked in exchange for tithes; Reverend Ike's prayer cloths guarantee prosperity; crosses worn in the ears, dangled in cleavages; incense and gongs, Buddhas in all sizes; Muslims unroll their rugs in response to prayer calls broadcast from skyscraper minarets; the earlocks of skull-capped Jews flop to and fro as they rock in prayer against the Jerusalem wall; aboriginals gather at their totemic bamboo control towers and miniature airstrips to coax airplanes out of the sky; Mexican penitents crawl their knees bloody, scourge their backs with thorns; Shinto monks clap hands to summon the spirits of their ancestors; stone ruins of Aztec sacrificial alters; Indians chew peyote; naked Dukhobors assemble to watch their homes burn; snake-handlers and strychnine drinkers; speakers in tongues and recipients of Inner Light epiphanies; bearded Amish in their buggies, Mennonites rebuild houses destroyed by acts of God; hex signs on barns; hot cross buns baked on Good Friday; Nostradamus's riddles; Masonic aprons; horoscopes and polished lucky stones, rabbits' feet and horseshoes . . .
I once drank wonderful coffee, fresh-ground in the refectory, with the faculty of a small Benedictine college in Louisiana; the view from the picture window was the cemetery where they would all eventually join the brothers gone before them.
Saint Philomena.

Late on the night of the first day of final exam week at Saint Bernardine College, Kevin O'Leary, having spent all day and evening cramming, left his dormitory alone and walked off campus to the state highway. He walked down the highway toward a quick-trip store, open twenty-four hours, to buy . . . what? A soft drink? Snack food? Cigarettes?
He wore a dark T-shirt, dark slacks, sandals. He walked on the right-hand side of the pavement, just on the gravel road shoulder.
What might he have been thinking about as he walked toward the quick-trip? I can only imagine. He might have thought how balmy the night air felt. If he looked up, he saw no stars, for they were masked by cloud

cover. He may have thought about what he went to buy at the quick-trip—soda, snacks, cigarettes? Perhaps he thought about his final examinations, maybe even of questions about poetry he knew he would find on my final examination.

Nothing is certain. He may have been humming, singing, talking to himself, may have walked hands-in-pockets, jingling coins, may have strode, arms swinging, or strolled, even shuffled lazily. Pure speculation.

If he hummed or sang or spoke, he possibly did not hear the automobile that struck him, killed him instantly, from behind. Did he not see its headlight beams cast on the pavement and gravel ahead of him? Did he walk with his head down, lost in thought? Could his eyes have been closed just in that instant? Why did he walk so close to the road?

Kevin O'Leary was struck, killed, thrown into the deep ditch running alongside the state highway; he was hit so hard his feet flew from his loose sandals, found on the shoulder, marking his last steps.

That is all. There was of course a somber memorial gathering on the campus of Saint Bernardine College, but final examinations were held on schedule. We opened my class's exam with the usual prayer, and an extra prayer for the repose of the soul of Kevin O'Leary; for this I appointed a new class chaplain, because, of course, I could not lead any prayer, could not pray. That is all.

Kevin O'Leary. Ronnie Makowski. My mother and father. The priests and ex-priests of Saint Bernardine College. The Benedictine brothers of that small Louisiana college. Styron. I believe I could compose a very long list. If there were ever to be such a list, I wonder who would add my name to it? That is a vain, foolish thought!

What I truly wonder—and it is *not* foolish or vain!—is if there will be anything I can hold in my hand, or any words I can speak, any name I can call out to, when my hour is upon me?

Acknowledgments

THESE STORIES, since revised, appeared originally in the following:

"When Times Sit In," *Perspective,* vol. 13, no. 1, autumn 1962; reprinted in *Such Waltzing Was Not Easy,* 1975.

"Haskell Hooked on the Northern Cheyenne," *North American Review,* vol. 251, no. 6, November 1966; reprinted in *The Entombed Man of Thule,* 1972.

"Wouldn't I?" *South Dakota Review,* vol. 8, nos. 1–2, spring/summer 1970; reprinted in *The Entombed Man of Thule,* 1972.

"Getting Serious," *The Sewanee Review,* vol. 85, no. 4, fall 1977; reprinted in *Prize Stories 1979: The O. Henry Awards,* 1979; reprinted in *Getting Serious,* 1980; reprinted in *Into the Silence,* 1988.

"Hog's Heart," *The Antioch Review,* vol. 37, no. 1, winter 1979; reprinted in *Getting Serious,* 1980; reprinted in *Best American Short Stories 1980,* 1981.

"Ah Art! Oh Life!" *The Bennington Review,* no. 8, September 1980; reprinted in *A World Quite Round,* 1986.

"The Good Man of Stillwater, Oklahoma," *Mid-American Review,* vol. 1, no. 2, fall 1981; reprinted in *Men Who Would Be Good,* 1991.

"Whiskey, Whiskey, Gin, Gin, Gin," *Quarterly West,* no. 17, winter 1983; reprinted in *The Pushcart Prize X,* 1985; reprinted in *Men Who Would Be Good,* 1991; reprinted in *Re-Publish: A Magazine of the Literary Arts,* 1994.

"The Parts of Speech," *The Kenyon Review,* vol. 6, no. 3 (new series), 1984; reprinted in *A World Quite Round,* 1986.

"Return of the Boyceville Flash," *Quarterly West,* no. 43, autumn/winter 1996.

"Saint Philomena, Pray for Us" first appeared in *Transactions* of the Wisconsin Academy of Sciences, Arts and Letters, vol. 85, 1997; reprinted with permission.

About the Author

GORDON WEAVER is the author of four novels and seven previous story collections, most recently *The Way We Know in Dreams* (University of Missouri Press). He is currently Adjunct Professor of English at the University of Wisconsin–Milwaukee. Recognition of his work includes two National Endowment for the Arts Fellowships, the O. Henry First Prize, the St. Lawrence Award for Fiction, and numerous other prizes and citations. His stories have appeared in a wide variety of literary and commercial magazines, including *Pushcart Prize, Best American Short Stories, Prize Stories: The O. Henry Awards,* and other anthologies.